A
STUBBORN
CASE

A NOVEL BY

Charles Frankel

A  STUBBORN CASE

W · W · Norton & Company · Inc ·
New York

COPYRIGHT © 1972 BY W. W. NORTON & COMPANY, INC.

First Edition

Library of Congress Cataloging in Publication Data
Frankel, Charles, 1917–
    A stubborn case.
    I. Title.
PZ4.F8285St [PS3556.R335]   813'.5'4   72-3426
ISBN 0-393-08472-8

PRINTED IN THE UNITED STATES OF AMERICA

1 2 3 4 5 6 7 8 9 0

To V.

A
STUBBORN
CASE

1

I'm not the type that's sensitive to the supernatural; I don't have the talent of a lot of people I know for that sort of thing. I don't mean they believe in God. They may or may not. But they believe in the supernatural, they feel it's a good thing. They like to think that whatever it is you're looking at, you're looking at something else. They get messages; they see portents, signs, shadows, invisible presences. I don't say they're wrong; I'm merely confessing a limitation of my own. I like to think that things are what they are. If there's anything that's far more deeply interfused, I want it to keep its distance from me, and it usually does.

So you will understand why I had some difficulty adjusting to the events I'm about to describe. They took place in front of me, I was involved in them, but I never quite felt that I belonged. The feeling I had as the story unfolded, the feeling that stayed with me till the end, was that the material world wasn't solid. It kept fading in and out; something else was butting in. It's a disconcerting feeling.

It began come over me while I was still in the airport at Montevideo waiting for the plane. It hadn't been easy to get to the airport; I hadn't been out of the hospital more than two or three days. By the time I'd got through passport control I was pretty tired and my leg was throbbing. I could feel the pins in my thighbone. And then, of course, the usual happened: once I was penned in the waiting room beyond the customs gate, the message came over the loudspeaker that the plane would be delayed. So I sat around and read the Montevideo paper—it had a little story about me, down in a corner of an inside page: "Señor John Burgess, the American who was kidnapped by terrorists last year, and wounded in the course of effecting his rescue, will leave for the United States this morning"—and then I pulled myself over to the bar and had a coffee, and then a brandy, and then another brandy.

You could tell who were the Latinos in the room. They were there, in the room, just where they seemed to be, their eyes looking it over, their minds taking it in. The rest of the people were someplace else, looking at some interior landscape, moving on a stage they'd brought with them. They were the usual clutch of returning travelers—a couple of businessmen, half a dozen young people in hair and jeans, a sunburned blonde, a pair of middle-aged people, man and wife, I suppose. The feeling they gave me was that everybody was sending out a message, and everybody was getting a message back—his own. The businessmen were letting the world know, they were letting themselves know, that they weren't grubby types who spent their lives looking over profit-and-loss statements, but champagne-and-sun tennis players on tour. And the young characters were cultural alternatives, and the blonde was a *femme fatale* two men had just fought a duel over. Not many words were being spoken, but the North American part of that airport was full of statements: I am not what I seem, I *am* what I seem, seeming is believing—as you see, it was confusing. It was like having double vision.

The signal finally came to board, and I followed the crowd slowly. My damn leg dragged behind me. When I tried to move it, it felt like a stone, and when I put my weight on it, it felt like a rag. The brandies I'd had didn't help, either. I got to the ramp leading up to the plane, and for a moment I didn't think I'd make it. I had to stop at each step and pull my leg up behind me with my hand. They'd saved a seat for me up front, and I flopped down into it. I spent the first fifteen minutes of the flight trying to stop sweating.

When I looked up, there was the stewardess smiling over me.

"Hi," she said for openers. She looked fresh off the cheerleaders' line at UCLA. Her message was: My, we're going to have fun. Outdoor fun. And I know what's on your mind, but it's not on mine.

"Hello," I said.

"Would you like something to drink?"

"Brandy."

She brought me two. When she came back again, carrying some olives, I was into the second.

"Anything else I can do?" she wanted to know.

"No," I said.

"I'm glad you didn't ask me what else can I do," she said. The oval of her face tipped to the side a bit. "What did you do? Walk into a door?" she asked.

For a second I didn't follow. "Oh, you mean this?" I said, pointing to my leg.

9

"Didn't watch where you were going, huh?" she said, and flashed marvelous white teeth at me. She had her name on a tag pinned to her dress. "Trilby," it said.

"Is that your name?" I asked. "Trilby?"

"It's what people call me."

"How come?" I asked.

"No kidding," she said, "how'd you get the leg? Not watching where you were going?"

I took some more brandy. "That's right, Trilby," I said.

"You'll never learn," she said. She smiled, a new smile, with a new message: We're getting to know each other, aren't we?

"Can you bring me a drink of water?" I asked.

"Sure," she said. "I'll bring you something to eat too."

The man on the other side of the aisle, one of the tennis players, was drinking a Martini. He looked as though he were fifty yards away.

"How you doing?" he shouted.

"I don't know," I shouted back, thinking that somewhere people must be using the gift of language to better purpose.

"That's the way it is," he called.

"I guess so," I returned.

"I know what you mean," he screamed. It was as though we were trying to talk to each other through a pillow.

Trilby came hurrying back. "You'd better not shout," she said.

"We're all shouting," I said. "We have to shout. It's hard to hear."

"Nobody's shouting," she said, "only you. Have something to eat."

"I'm the only one shouting?" I asked.

"That's right," she said. She didn't look like a cheerleader anymore. More like a dental assistant I remembered, when I came out from under gas once. Reassuring, helpful, cheerful, my friend. Not that she knew me from Little Eva, but my

10

friend. It was an expression that settled me down, and I ate some beets.

It was a long flight, and Trilby didn't have much to do. She sat down next to me after I woke from a nap. I was soberer.

"Going home?" she asked, and didn't wait for an answer. "Where do you live, New York?"

I told her where I lived.

"There's nothing but a college there," she added.

"That's right."

She looked puzzled. "What are you, some kind of student?" I mean, well you know."

"I'm a professor."

"You're kidding," she said. "Well, what do you know? What are you going to do with all those kids?"

"Teach them, I guess."

"I bet. Didn't they have a lot of trouble at that place last year?"

"I wasn't there. I guess they had some. Not too much as things go these days."

"You've got to be kidding."

"They broke some windows, threw some stones at cops, closed the place up for a week. But I mean, no bombs, no bank robberies."

She giggled. "Well, you'd better get in shape. What are you going to do? Hit 'em with that?" She pointed to my cane.

I shrugged. "I'll make out."

"Have you had it for long?" she asked.

I picked up the cane. "No, I bought it last week," I said.

This time it was the cheerleader's look, but a little impatient. "No, I don't mean the cane," she said. "I mean the—you know." She lifted her little finger and waggled it at my leg. "Did you have an accident?"

It didn't seem like a story I should try to tell her, but the words came out of me anyway. "I was machine-gunned," I said.

The wink. "I'll bet."

"Okay," I said, "I'll think of something else." I was glad she'd given me an escape route. "Do you think maybe you could bring me another drink?" I asked.

She looked at her watch, and then inspected me. "Sure," she said, "you're entitled."

She came back with two brandies and left me alone to drink them. I was half through the second when I noticed that she'd sat down across the aisle, next to Don Budge. She winked playfully.

"What are you a professor of?"

I heard my own voice answer, "English." I could feel it making the effort to speak quietly.

"Coming back from vacation?"

I heard my answers coming obediently. "No, not a vacation. I was working."

"I bet."

"You bet." A pretty pert answer. I was beginning to get the hang of talking to Trilby. I decided to try to pay closer attention.

"You mean you were teaching English in Uruguay?"

"Not exactly. I was teaching people how to teach English in Uruguay."

"No kidding."

"You bet."

"And you said the wrong thing, and that's how you got that?" She waggled her little finger delicately in the direction of my leg again.

"You might say that's how it was," I heard myself saying.

"That's how it was how?" she said.

"That's how it was they shot me."

"You're putting me on."

"So help me, they shot me. No kidding. You bet."

"Who shot you?"

"Policemen."

"What were you running away from them for?"

"I wasn't running away from them. I was running to them. For help."

"No kidding." Her voice was still pretty far away, and for a moment I didn't hear anything at all. I began to be aware of the drone of the plane. Then, inches away, there was Trilby's face.

"Why were you running to the police for help?" she asked.

"I wouldn't be sure," my disembodied voice said.

"I bet," she said. "Well, fasten your seat belt."

When the plane landed at Kennedy, I stayed in my seat to let the other passengers out first. Don Budge was standing in the aisle next to me, waiting for them to open the door. He nodded at me. I thought he was saying good-bye, but then realized he was saying hello too. He stuck out his hand and took mine.

"What's your name?" he asked.

"Burgess," I said.

"No," he said. "Your name. What people call you."

"You mean like Trilby?"

"Yeah, like Trilby."

"John," I said.

"So long, John."

I was home, back in the U.S. of A., on a first-name basis with my countrymen.

As I dragged myself through the door, all Trilby said was, "Take it easy now."

2

I'd forgotten what Kennedy Airport looked like, but it fit my mood. It wasn't an airport, it was a world's fair; they were obviously going to take it down next year and try something else. When the porter who was leading me through the crowd slowed down so that I could keep up with him and said that he bet my leg hurt, I could have hugged him. It wasn't the sympathy, which I didn't feel the need of. It was just that he was actually talking to me, not to himself. I was really there for him. Besides, he was dressed like a porter, and he was a porter. I found that refreshing.

He got me out to the street, and found me a cab. The driver made me feel better too. He was young, cheerful-looking, and dressed like a taxi driver. But it turned out, on the ride into the city, that he wasn't really a taxi driver but a Columbia student. Well, not really a student but an ex-student. Well, not really a student or an ex-student, but a student on leave of absence. He was going to school of course, that is he guessed so, maybe. The dean's office had suggested he take a year off and think. "Think about what?" I asked. "Like just think," he said.

We got stalled in traffic, and while we sat there he found out that I'd just come from Uruguay. He told me that there was an excellent workers' movement down there, and that led him to other things. It turned out he'd been involved—was still involved—in activist activities. Those were his words. He was one conspirator you couldn't accuse of being close-mouthed.

"You remember '68 at Columbia? Mark Rudd? I was the power behind him. Unfortunately, as the movement developed he took an incorrect position."

"What would be a correct position?" I asked.

"The students must reach out to other revolutionary elements, link up with the workers."

"I've been away. Are the workers revolutionary these days?"

"In China they are."

"I see what you mean."

"It depends what you mean by revolutionary. There are different stages. The workers here, in an advanced capitalist country, are in a pre-revolutionary stage. Actually, not really. They're in like the last stage before the pre-revolutionary stage."

We hiccuped to a stop again. There was a radio talk show coming from the next car—a cheerful voice was discussing a new fat-free diet. The traffic picked up.

"We're publishing a newspaper," the driver said, "exposing the theoretical errors of the Ruddites."

I asked him why he was thinking of going back to school if

his target was to link up with the workers. Anyway, did Columbia really want him back?

It was our most cheerful moment in a cheerful drive. He laughed and said they'd suspended him before and let him back in, and this time he wasn't even suspended, not exactly if you know what I mean, so why shouldn't they let him in again. As a matter of fact, he'd just seen one of the deans, a good guy, a little, you know, like bureaucratic maybe, but a progressive, you know? They'd had a fantastic talk. And anyway Columbia didn't have a choice. They had to let him back in: the objective historical situation, that was the reason. Of course, the student movement was split, some elements had been co-opted, other elements had been weakened by adventurism, but there were inner contradictions in the Board of Trustees, and the power balance . . .

"You mean your getting back is a matter for the Board of Trustees?"

"Sure, they have to figure whether a direct challenge to the revolutionary movement is worth it in the present stage. Sooner or later, of course, they're going to have to do it. They're aware of what the revolutionary movement means. It poses a direct threat to their interests. They protect their real estate through Columbia. We have the whole story in our newspaper."

We drove by Shea Stadium. It was lit up and the flags were flying. The first people were just coming out. It must have been the ninth inning of the ball game.

"Do you ever talk to other drivers about your ideas?" I asked.

He grinned the same happy grin. "They still lack a clear understanding of the situation," he said. I could hear the syntax of the soap-boxers on Union Square in the Thirties. The One remains, the many change and pass, I thought. Where

had he learned the lingo? No matter. The invisible church en-
dures.

He let me off at Grand Central, and while he was making
change I asked him what it was he studied when he studied.
"Oh, like mathematics," he said, "you know."

They'd reserved a private room for me on the train. It was
only a three-hour ride, and I'd thought it would be better not
to spend a night in New York, but to get right home. I realized, as I tried to settle back on the narrow seat, that I'd made
a mistake. The plane had been late, I hadn't had a minute to
catch my breath and nothing to eat since the middle of the
afternoon. I sat there, spent and vacant, looking out through
the dirty windowpane. My eyes felt hot and dry, and the
throbbing in my leg filled the whole room. I felt stupid for
ever having gone to Uruguay and stupid for having come
back.

They'd come for me in the middle of the night and I hadn't
been surprised. There wasn't any reason they should want me
more than anybody else, but they'd been in my mind, and so
when I opened my eyes and saw them standing there I knew
who they were.

"You want me to come with you?" I asked.

Anna, the old woman who'd taken care of the house, was in
the corner of the room weeping quietly, not for me, not for
them, but for the world. They had masks on, but their eyes
were gentle, and I could see they were glad I understood
them. I packed some things, and went off with them. They'd
blindfolded my eyes, and we'd driven for an hour or so on
roads that kept getting worse. Then we'd come to a farmhouse,
they'd taken off the blindfold and showed me to my room.
In about half an hour one of them came back. He'd taken his

mask off, and he was carrying some bread, cheese, and wine. He laid the food out gravely on the table, and invited me to sit down.

"I am very sorry to do this to you, Mr. Burgess," he said. "And by the way, for our purposes, why not call me Castillo? There is nothing worse than being held prisoner by people without names."

He poured himself some wine. He didn't offer me any. He merely left it there for me to take if I wanted it. He wasn't going to press. My reactions were up to me.

"I suppose there's no point in my asking why you're holding me?" I knew the answer, but I didn't know how not to ask. I felt as though I were going through some ancient, well-established form: when kidnapped, the guidebook says, always ask your kidnappers why.

"There's every reason you should want to know," Castillo said. "First of all, it is always much better to kidnap a man who is simpatico. The whole business is difficult enough without taking on a man whose company you will find disagreeable. And then, you have the right kind of friends. I don't mean simply powerful friends, people with influence or with access to money. I mean people we can reach, people who, now that John Burgess is gone, will ask who we are and why we have done this terrible thing, and will understand a little. It is a way of reaching those who will listen and take notice— if you will permit me, it is a way of teaching Uruguayan to people who are going to teach Uruguayan to the gringos. Do have some wine."

They gave me the run of the house, and on the third or fourth day Castillo brought me some books, and stayed and ate in the room with me. After about a week he came in carrying some clothes like his own, and told me to put them on. "You are beginning to look pale," he said. "I am going to take you out for a walk, and I want you to look like the rest of us. Of course you must promise to make no trouble."

After that we went walking three or four times a week. First Castillo brought some of his people along; after a while the two of us went out alone. I had the chance once or twice, when a car came by on the road, to do something to get the driver's attention. I never did. What was the reason? A sense of Castillo's courtesy? The dislike of bringing him down? Sympathy for him? Or quite simply, not wanting to act out of not knowing what would happen? I didn't know. Probably Castillo didn't know either. But he noticed, and he seemed amused, and in some vague way flattered.

"Have you thought that if our demands aren't met we might kill you?" he asked me one day as we were out walking.

"I've thought it possible," I said.

"But you've made no trouble."

I shrugged.

"Do you think if you make no trouble, we shall deal with you better?"

"Perhaps. I don't know. Perhaps I feel simply that if I fought against all this it would make it unbearable for me to take. If I let the game play itself out, if I make no demands on it, well it's like being sick and lying back and accepting it. If I let the game play itself out, it's easier. It's not in my hands."

"The roll of the ball on the roulette wheel, is that it?"

"Something like that."

"And you've no responsibility for what happens, even to you?"

"My wife died five years ago, suddenly, like that. Cancer. It happened. This has happened."

"But you didn't choose cancer. And you did choose to be in Uruguay. So it isn't entirely an accident you're here."

I didn't feel like talking about it any more. I didn't have much to say. But Castillo, after a few moments, picked up the conversation.

"Your wife. From the way you spoke, you loved her?"

"Yes."

"I am sorry she died." We walked a while in silence. "I don't think you were wrong to come to Uruguay," he said. "To teach English here, that is a good thing. Spanish all alone —that is what the priests and the novelists would like."

There's such a thing as too much understanding, particularly when the man who's showing all the understanding happens to be your kidnapper. I was irritated. "If English is such a good thing," I said, "why have you taken me from my work? Or do you think Russian or Chinese are even better?"

He caught the inflection of my voice, and looked at me gravely. "I know nothing about Chinese," he said. "And in any case it's too difficult, and too remote. And Russian too, probably. Besides, like Spanish, it appears to be a language for priests and novelists: Torquemadas, Don Quixotes, Zhivagos, murderers and the murdered, the chickens and the men who pronounce a benediction and then ring their necks. No, I like English; it makes the truth seem prosaic, not worth fighting over."

"You forget the Puritans," I said. "And don't you ever listen to American propaganda?"

He shrugged. "You have your priests too."

"Castillo," I said, "let me go. You're bad for me. What are you in the kidnapping business for? Are you trying to tell me it has nothing to do with your ideas?"

"Very little," he said. "Of course, a man must have ideas, and I have some. But I've told you what I'm in the kidnapping business for. If you don't have money, you can't advertise. You have to think of other ways to get attention. I want people to pay attention—people like you. I want them to pay atten·

tion today, not tomorrow. Tomorrow one thousand chickens will be dead, their necks wrung, when they could have lived, and two thousand chickens will be born that should not have been born. You can let the ball roll, Mr. Burgess, and drop into the hole it does, and not try to tip the wheel. I can't. It has fallen for too long into the wrong hole. I want to tip the wheel differently."

"There are lots of ways to tip the wheel."

"Not so many. Not so many for people like me. You know, of course, that I'm not a Uruguayan. I was born in Mexico."

"I suspected it from your accent."

"Do you want to know about my father, Mr. Burgess? He fought for ten years in the revolution. Once soldiers on the other side caught him. They were very nice to him. They cut off only one of his hands, and only his left hand, before they threw him in prison. And then the people in the prison revolted, and burned it, and my father got away, and went on fighting with one hand. And when the revolution was over he came home, and he became mayor of his village. Then his friends came, the people with whom he had been in the field, and some of them were high officials of the party of the revolution. They had been chickens but now they were big birds with long beaks. And they had fat wives, and their wives had priests. Naturally, big birds like that must eat more than ordinary chickens. It is only natural. So they redivided the land their way, and when a villager protested they wrung his neck, and when my father protested they were kind to him because he was an old comrade, and merely sent him to prison again. They let him out five years later, and he no longer protested. He sat in the dust in front of our house and said nothing. If someone gave him a cigarette he smoked it. If they offered him wine he drank it. But he asked for nothing, he expected nothing. Should I be like that, Mr. Burgess?"

I kept quiet.

"My grandfather—my father's father—was luckier," Castillo said. "He was saved those last years of sitting in the dust. The bandits used to come—I say bandits, they were government men, they weren't government men, it made no difference—and take part of his crops for taxes. Each year they came more often and took more, and one day he said no. So they took him and buried him in the ground up to his neck, and then rode their horses over him until his head wasn't there any more. I come from a long line, Mr. Burgess, and the odds are very bad for people like me. But somebody must pay attention."

About a week later, before dawn, the great searchlights suddenly flashed on, all around the house, and the voice came over the loudspeaker ordering everyone to come out of the house except me. I was to stay in place until it was safe. Castillo and two of his men burst into my room. Downstairs there was a shot and one of the floodlights burst and went out. The machine guns opened up on the other side, and then they stopped. The loudspeaker began again.

"We have our way out," Castillo had said. "But we won't take you. We are going to let you go." For a moment he seemed almost to smile. "If your friends will let us."

One of his men took me and pushed me against the wall and took out his automatic. Castillo slapped him, and told me to get down on the floor. He had waved a handkerchief in front of the window, there were shots, then silence, then the voice asking if they were surrendering. Castillo shouted an oath, there were more shots, and then the handkerchief waved again. This time the voice over the loudspeaker asked what he wanted. We are not surrendering, he had shouted, but we will send Burgess out.

Somebody shot out another floodlight, the machine guns started again, and then there was silence. Castillo sent one of

his men downstairs—the man who had had his gun on me—
and I could hear him talking with the others. There was a
tunnel in the cellar; while I went out the front door, they
would go out their way.

The voice came over the loudspeaker: "You don't surrender?"

"We fight or, if you leave us alone, we don't fight," Castillo
shouted back. "It's your choice. But we give you Burgess. He's
in the way."

There was silence for some time, and then the shout came
back: "Let Burgess out the front door."

They had pulled me downstairs and opened the door and
pushed me out. I couldn't see in the floodlights. I started forward, then looked back to see where Castillo was, and then
turned and ran, stumbling, toward the lights. I felt an axe
hit my leg, first the weight of it and then the hot knife-edge.
As I fell I heard the machine guns, in front of me, where the
police were. I lay there, and all I remembered now was that
I felt vaguely embarrassed to have fallen down.

It was a year before I was out of the hospital. They couldn't
send me home—I was too close to dying—and they operated
four times. I let the ball roll on the wheel. They put a rod
down the center of my thigh bone, pinned it in place, and did
what they could to repair the muscle and nerve damage. Once
I began to sit up, the authorities paid some calls on me. Their
men had been nervous, they hadn't been sure who was running toward them, the authorities hoped I'd understand. I
didn't argue.

And now the train was bringing me back home—I hardly
felt that I'd decided to be on it—and the leg was throbbing,
and I didn't much care. In a way I felt liberated. The leg let
me off; it let me out. I could go my own way. Not that I was
going anywhere. But the pressure was off.

The train came into the station around two in the morning. My sister Martha was there to meet me. I'd settled in with her after her divorce, and it had worked out for both of us. She was getting older, she didn't move in the world much, and keeping house for her brother kept her occupied. For me it meant no strain, no tension, no family decisions. I had two sons, both grown up, one living in Hawaii, the other in Switzerland. I was a dog that belonged to himself.

Martha had been down to Uruguay to see me in the hospital. She embraced me, and her voice broke a little when she said, "John, you're walking, you're walking." She thought I looked much better. But it was dark. I don't know that she really had a good look.

3

At breakfast the next morning, Martha told me that there was to be a faculty meeting at three o'clock, apparently an important one. The committee that had been working on interim rules was making its report, and the faculty was to vote on the rules.

I found Martha's message a little puzzling. What were interim rules?

"Oh, of course," she said, "we get so used to all this new language that I forget it's new. The interim rules are rules that will be in effect until permanent rules are adopted."

"What are the rules for?" I asked.

"They're rules governing the conduct of students and teachers."

"I thought the university had such rules."

"It did but their legitimacy was denied last spring. And so the administration has agreed to have new rules drawn up and to have them adopted in a constitutional convention."

"And this is it?"

"You've been away too long, John. This is just to adopt rules that will tide the university over until the convention. And did I tell you, by the way, that Donald Rhodes called yesterday, and said there was a special departmental meeting at noon. Something to do with an ultimatum, by letter, from the new graduate students. He knew you'd just be back, and said it was all right if you didn't come, but he thought he should let you know."

"Classes are still a couple of weeks away. Since when did everybody get to work so early?"

"Since this year, John. They're expecting trouble. They're trying to be ready."

I grumbled, said I was tired, which I was, and went off to lie down. Around eleven, my curiosity got the better of me. I decided to go to the departmental meeting, and asked Martha to drive me to the campus. She dropped me off at the main gate, and I started to wrench myself down the path to the department offices in Rollins. It was a hot September day, and the campus hardly seemed threatening. More bedraggled than I'd remembered it perhaps; the lawns looked trampled, there were foot-paths across them where there hadn't been before, and the few students around looked limp. But everything seemed more or less in place, right up to Dietrich Wisniewski, whom I saw coming down the path toward me. He had his eyes on the ground, and I had to put my cane in his way to keep him from walking right past me.

"Hello, Dieter," I said. "How are you?"

"I am as I am," he said, nodded perfunctorily, and walked on. Half a dozen steps down the path he stopped, and I could feel him beginning to turn over the fact that I wasn't a familiar presence on the landscape. He turned and looked at me cautiously. "So it's you," he said. "So you're back." He sounded aggrieved, as though life had been complicated enough.

"Yes, I'm back," I said. "How are you, Dieter?"

"I am as I should be," he said. "Is there any reason you do not think so?"

"No, not at all," I said.

But there was, as a matter of fact. He didn't look like the man I'd last seen three years before. The two of us lived more or less on the fringes of the English Department. He did comparative philology; my specialty was varieties of English speech. I'd first met him after the war, when he'd come to the campus from central Europe. He'd gone to Vienna from Warsaw during the Thirties, and had got out of Vienna and gone to Prague after the Nazis had taken over Austria. Then, when Prague fell, he'd returned to Warsaw. How he'd survived during the war no one quite knew. There were stories that he'd been in the underground, that he'd crossed back and forth across the Russian lines, that he'd ended up being hunted by the Communists as well as the Nazis. Wisniewski didn't talk about it much: he'd survived, that was all. If he'd been a hero, it had left him debilitated. He'd come to us, a gaunt little man with a nervous hitch in his walk, who sidled up to you eager to ingratiate himself, and giving off an aura of slyness, intrigue, anxiety. But through the years he'd gradually relaxed. As his reputation as a scholar grew, he'd filled out physically, expanded in spirit, taken a large American wife addicted to horseback riding, even developed a certain standing as a campus wit. But now, as he stood there in front of me, the old uncertain look, half-defiant, half-furtive, was in his eye again.

"The campus," he said, "do you find it changed?"

"I haven't been back twelve hours, Dieter," I said. "I haven't been on the campus two minutes."

"Why did you come back?"

"Why not?"

His jaw stiffened. "I ask you why, you ask me why not. You don't answer my question." He moved two careful steps toward me. "I shall ask you another question. Where are you going?"

"To the department meeting. Aren't you?"

A conspiratorial look came into Dieter's eye, and he moved closer. "I no longer go to department meetings," he said. "Do you approve? Do you agree with my position?" He was looking at me as though the wrong word from me would put him to flight. "I no longer recognize the legitimacy of the department," he said.

"You're talking riddles, Dieter."

He pulled back from me. "I do not trust my colleagues," he said. "Last spring the hoodlums ran loose. They broke into my class. I asked my colleagues to support me. They said there was nothing they could do. I have seen it all before. The thugs come, and the others, the professors, the polite men, make excuses for them."

"This is all new to me, Dieter," I said. "Is it possible there wasn't anything the department could do?"

He'd moved farther away. "So you are one of them," he said. "Go to the meeting." But he didn't turn and leave. I felt he was waiting for me to say something, anything, that would tell him he wasn't wholly cut off.

"Dieter, come with me," I said.

He hesitated. "I don't think I should," he murmured.

It was a question as much as an answer, but I didn't know what the whole fracas was about, and I didn't press him. Who was I to give another man advice? I hadn't even managed to keep myself from getting shot. So I simply shrugged and left the question dangling. He looked at me sadly out of the corner of his eye, and turned uncertainly and left.

I resumed my walk toward Rollins, sitting down a couple of times to get my breath. At one bench alongside the path a boy in jeans and an undershirt sat down next to me. His bare shoulders were frail and white. The hair on his head fell over his eyes and down his face in uncombed, wiry curls. He smiled at me sweetly. I noticed that he didn't have shoes on but was wearing socks. There was something companionable in the way he was sitting next to me and I spoke to him.

"I hope you don't mind my asking," I said. "I like walking barefoot myself—at least I did before this happened to my leg—although I find shoes are a comfort on hot dirty streets or rocky roads. But what's the sock bit?"

He smiled at me sweetly again. His eyes were hidden behind dark glasses. "I've found there are three kinds of people," he said. "Those that don't notice at all. They don't count. Then there are those who notice but who are afraid to ask. They're loathsome. Then there are the people who ask. They're my kind."

"It's a simple test," I said.

"It's not the only one. But it cuts through all the social nonsense. Besides, I'm different from you. I don't like shoes and I don't like to walk barefoot."

"And that leaves socks."

"Right."

"What do you do about winter?"

"I don't think about winter. Everything in its own time."

I got up to go. "Are you a student here?" I asked. "I'm a professor."

He pointed to my leg. "Are you Mr. Burgess?"

I nodded.

"I heard about you," he said. He walked back along the path with me, setting his pace to mine. "You're sort of like Professor Higgins, aren't you?" he asked. "You know, in Shaw."

"Well, I'm more or less in the same field."

"Fascinating, absolutely fascinating. But it's all wrong. What difference does it make how people talk?"

"I don't know. But it's fascinating, absolutely fascinating. Like why people wear socks and no shoes."

He laughed, a sudden, pleased, shy laugh, and held the door open for me as I walked into Rollins.

"Ta ta, ciao, you know, good-bye," he said. I said good-bye and worked my way down the hall to the department meeting room.

Most of them were already there, sitting around the table looking preoccupied. I'd been thinking how to turn off questions about Uruguay and my leg, but I could have saved myself the trouble. No one looked up when I came in, and no one said hello when I took a seat. As far as I could tell, there wasn't anything personal about it. Some people asked you why you were going around in socks and no shoes and some people didn't. Some people said hello, how are you? when you'd been away, and some people didn't. My colleagues didn't. They weren't there to say hello. Or maybe they weren't there, but someplace else. Mind over matter. Just because you see somebody in a room, that doesn't prove that's where he is. I'd learned that at the Montevideo airport.

Donald Rhodes started the meeting. He'd become chairman while I was gone. He was wearing his hair longer, I noticed, and smiling harder. He had to smile quite a bit and raise his voice before he could get the conversation to stop. He never more than half succeeded. All through the meeting there was a buzz of separate conversation at the table. It was like trying to listen to a radio program that wasn't properly tuned in.

"We've got this problem," said Rhodes, smiling some more.

Ralph Singer spoke up. "I'm sure it is a problem," he said. He had been a quiet man, self-enclosed, almost gloomy. One knew what he thought about the romantic poets, and not much else. Now there was a note in his voice that I didn't recall, something more assertive and premeditated.

"Well, I think it is a problem," said Rhodes. "After all . . ."

"What *is* the problem?" Godderer was talking. He was the department jester. Chaucer and cackles.

"A good question." I didn't get who said it. It may have been one of the younger men I didn't know.

At this point I felt a friendly hand on my shoulder and looked up. It was Joe LaRosa, who'd just come in. He greeted me silently, almost consolingly, and went around the table to a vacant chair. I felt a little better, as though something agreeably familiar had been returned to the scene.

Rhodes was forgetting to smile. The buzz of talk in the room was irritating him. "Very well," he said, "I shall try to give you the facts without adornment. As you know, we admitted twenty new graduate students last spring. During the summer we received separate letters from three of this group, asking for the names and addresses of the other new people who'd been admitted. Naturally, we told them."

"Naughty, naughty," Godderer said.

"Why shouldn't you have told them?" Singer asked.

"I saw no reason not to tell them," Rhodes said. He was working at his smile again.

"It's their right," one of the young men said.

Off at the end of the table Joseph LaRosa spoke up. He seemed terribly weary. "Let's do try to get the story before we discuss it," he said.

"It may prejudice us," said Godderer.

Singer threw his pencil down impatiently.

"Naughty, naughty," said Godderer.

"Naughty, naughty," said Rhodes, "all of you. May I go on? I sent them the names, and last week I received this letter. It was signed by all but three of the entering students. Shall I read it?"

"Read it."

Rhodes read: "As new members of the Department of English, we hereby state our unwillingness to submit to the program for first-year students described in the official catalogue. We do not assert that this program is a bad one, although many of us think it is. The reason for our position is more fundamental. The program has been adopted without consultation with us. We are being subjected to a program of education over which we have had no control. Accordingly, this program, so far as we are concerned, is null and void. To meet the problem this creates, we propose, in a spirit of co-operation, that no classes be held during the first month of the term, and that the time be devoted to a discussion of the nature and purposes of graduate education in the Department of English."

Rhodes looked up. The smile came. It did its job: If you liked the letter you could say that he approved it; if you didn't like the letter, you could say he was amused by it. "That's the letter," he said, "except for the seventeen names."

"Who signed it?" William Shanley asked. He was the senior man in the department, a year or two away from retirement.

"That's irrelevant," said Singer. His voice was clipped. "They are seventeen students in good standing, and they had the right to send us that letter."

"I hardly meant to deny that," said Shanley. He started to say something more, thought better of it, and faded out.

"The question," asked Singer, "is whether we're prepared to do what they ask." I'd never heard him sound so definite.

LaRosa spoke, the gloom in his voice edged by a faint tone of amusement. "You say do what they ask, Ralph. But I don't think they asked us anything. They told us."

"We needn't quibble," said Singer. "They've presented us with a principle, and the question is whether we agree with it."

"They've presented us with an ultimatum," said LaRosa, "and the question is whether we take it."

"No, no," said Rhodes. "We can't call it an ultimatum. There's no profit in calling it that."

"What would you call it?" LaRosa asked. "An expression of eagerness to study English?" He wasn't really arguing. It was as though he were just talking for the record.

"It's an invitation to us to think," said Singer fiercely. He seemed to remember himself, and his manner softened. He brushed back his shock of white hair and smiled. Eyes, ears, nose, mouth, they all smiled: Peace on earth, good will to men, and didn't we all see the truth? Of course we did. Anybody could see it. "Gentlemen," he said, "we have all been teaching, some of us for many years, and we have never asked, 'Why?' We ought to thank these young people."

"Of course," said Godderer. "These students must be thanked. In verse:

> Seventeen graduate students came into the land
> Attacking their teachers for being so bland. . . .

Not so good, is it? Well, it's a beginning."

Underneath the table, my bad leg was turning cold. I wondered how long the meeting was going to go on. I looked around at my colleagues. Except for those who had talked, their faces were passive, impassive.

"I think the immediate thing on our agenda is to call in the three students who are waiting outside to talk to us." Singer was speaking again.

"Are there three students outside?" Shanley asked. "Who

elected them?" He didn't sound as though he was objecting. He was puzzled.

"Come, come," said Singer. "Seventeen students signed the letter. We can speak to three of them."

One of the younger men spoke up, the same chap who had mentioned students' rights earlier, and the debate swirled on. We would talk to the students, we wouldn't; we would limit the discussion to what was in the letter; no, we would ignore the letter and just talk. Rhodes smiled, Godderer rolled his eyes, LaRosa sat silent, the sun shown steadily from Singer's face.

It took some time, but the problem was ironed out. We would see the students, but it was in no way official, and we wouldn't discuss the letter, but we would discuss the issues it raised. That motion passed, three votes in favor, two against, one abstention (my own), and the rest present but not voting, and not abstaining either.

My bad leg ached, my good leg was turning cold. I knew I shouldn't but I wanted a drink. I can take ten minutes more, I thought. If it's not over by then, I go. I can say it's my leg.

The three students came in, two young men and a young woman. The young woman was tall, slender, blonde, with a doubting look in her eye. Not the cheerleader type. Not at all. Rhodes introduced her as Miss Bell. Norman Wade, sitting next to me, suddenly proved that he hadn't forgotten how to talk in the three years I'd been gone. He leaned over to me and whispered solemnly, "She's from the Alexander Graham Bell family." Miss Bell sat down in the empty chair between Godderer and Singer, fluffed her long hair back off her shoulders, took out some knitting, and set to work.

The young men were less well-defined; maybe they were suffering from stage fright. And Rhodes made it worse by neglecting to introduce them—they weren't female, they didn't

34

have family names worth mentioning, I wouldn't know. Anyway, they had to introduce themselves, which they did with apologetic smiles, not so much telling us their names as coughing them. Sledge and Hedge was what I heard, and I decided that under the circumstances that was exact enough. Sledge was dark and had a Fu Manchu mustache. Hedge was blond and wore glasses and boots, circa 1910 Moscow. He was carrying a small leather peak-cap to match. They sat down, more hesitantly than Miss Bell, one on each side of Rhodes.

"Well, what have you got to say to us?" said Rhodes cheerily, after he'd explained to them, with some difficulty, the terms under which we were meeting/not meeting with them.

"Since we are at an impasse," Hedge said, "I don't know what there is to talk about."

"Shall we have ten minutes of silence?" said Godderer. Cackle.

"Professor Godderer means," said Rhodes hastily, "that if you don't know what there is to talk about, then why did you ask to see us?"

"Well," said Hedge, the lines of thought forming on his brow as he struggled with the puzzle, "that's the point."

"He means," said Sledge helpfully, "that it's up to you to say something."

Miss Bell's knitting needles clicked.

It took some time to decide who should put the ball in play first. I looked at my watch. I still had three minutes to go. Then Shanley's voice broke in on my consciousness.

"If you don't mind," he was saying diffidently, "you must have read the catalogue before you applied. You knew what was expected of you. If it wasn't what you wanted, there were other places to apply. And once you accepted our offer of admission, doesn't that imply that you accept the program for which you applied?"

Miss Bell kept right on knitting, but her eyes came up and sent a message across the table to Shanley: Disbelief, yet expectations confirmed: impossible to believe a man could say that sort of thing, impossible to imagine he was capable of saying anything else. She was way ahead of her ancestor; she didn't need sound-waves to communicate.

Meanwhile Hedge was pondering Shanley's question. He fell back on the same answer he'd used before, but this time put it in the negative. "That's not the point," he said.

"I had always thought," said Shanley gently, "that there was a most comfortable division of labor between teachers and students. Teachers set the requirements for the degree. Students decided whether they would fulfill them."

"That's the point," said Hedge.

"I'm delighted you think so," said Shanley. "Because then there's no problem and we're not at an impasse. You decide whether you'll follow the program in the catalogue or not. It's entirely up to you. Obviously, we can't and shouldn't try to force your choice."

"And if we decide not to follow the program?" said Sledge. "No, I mean, like we've already decided not to follow it. It's abolished as far as we're concerned. So then what?"

"I'd have no idea," said Shanley. His voice was kind. "It's your life, you know. It's all up to you. There's no law requiring you to have a Ph.D. from this university."

"That's not the point," said Hedge.

"We're making a threat," said Singer, breaking in. "I'm sure we can all do better than that, Professor Shanley."

Shanley looked up in surprise. "A threat?" he asked softly. He receded.

Sledge took over. "We don't want to approach this in a spirit of confrontation," he said. "We want to work with the faculty. I came here knowing that this university was being

36

restructured. That's why I came—to be part of the restructuring, to be a member of a great university, a member in full standing, working equally with everyone else to remodel it. I wish to be part of such an experience. I thought it could be thrilling, exciting."

He was getting carried away. I could feel LaRosa squirming, though he was three seats away from me. He gave up trying to control himself, and spoke. "I have so many questions to ask," he said, "that I feel like a child." His voice was thick with weariness. "And I fear the answers you're going to give to them. Nevertheless, might I ask whether, when you decided to be a graduate student in English here, a member in full standing of this, as you put it, great university, did an interest in studying English figure at all among your reasons?"

"Well like of course. I mean, you know, that goes without saying. But it was the feeling that we could have a community here . . ."

"Don't let's be pedantic, Joe," said Singer.

"No, as you said, I must be grateful to these young people," said LaRosa. "They have made me ask, and it's high time, why I'm teaching. And I've pondered that question and I thought until a moment ago that I had an answer: it was love of English literature. But now I'm confused."

"Temper, temper," said Godderer.

LaRosa turned back to the students. "And might I ask why you should have wished to come, to quote you again, to be part of a community that was so obviously a failure? A community with faults so evident that someone who hasn't even been here one day can know that he has something useful to contribute to its reform?"

"We have a right to participate in decisions affecting our lives," Sledge said.

"That's not an answer to my question," LaRosa said. He

was very quiet, and he was getting very angry. "Let me put it this way. This university is two hundred years old; as members of it you are hardly one day old. Do you suppose that no matter what you do in your ignorant meddling with it, you can't hurt it? And when you've left, do you suppose that I want to pick up the pieces?"

"This isn't constructive at all," said one of the young professors.

"If we are going to have an honest talk," said LaRosa, "telling it like it is, which is, I'm told, the purpose of confrontations such as this, why not answer the questions I've asked?" He was enjoying his anger. The adrenalin was washing the weariness out of him.

"I think we shall get nowhere discussing such matters," said Singer.

"I'm afraid not," said Rhodes. He smiled, and that wasn't enough, and he tried to laugh. It came out a little choked.

"I think," said Singer, "that I would put the issue this way."

Miss Bell interrupted him. "Before you do, Mr. Singer, may I say something?" The needles clicked, and she didn't look up from her knitting.

"Yes, of course," said Singer.

"By all means," said Rhodes.

"I think there is a question," said Miss Bell, eyes on her knitting, "whether everybody in this room is properly here. We can only meet if that's the case."

Rhodes looked around the room puzzled. "I see no one here who's not a member of the department."

"That may be," said Miss Bell. "But it may also be that there's a representative of a government agency in this department. The CIA, to be exact."

I'd just been on the point of leaving. I sat down again.

"Oh my God," I heard LaRosa mutter.

"What in the world are you talking about, my dear young lady?" Godderer burst out.

The knitting needles paused for half a second and then went on their way. "I am talking about what should be obvious. One of the people in this room has just come back from Uruguay, where he was the head of an institute supported by outside funds, and where he was involved in the struggle between the people and government repression."

It was absurd. I began to laugh, and then I saw no one else around the table was amused. The half-dozen younger members of the department, the new ones whom I didn't know, were looking at me curiously, one of them with a kind of fierce pleasure in his eyes. Godderer looked intrigued. Singer's eyes were on me, calmly, interrogatively, as though a straight statement had been made, and he was waiting for me to answer it. And Rhodes? Rhodes had decided to smile.

"That is an absolutely shameful statement, Miss Bell," La-Rosa said.

She shrugged, and stopped her knitting. "Would it not be more honest," she said, looking across the table at him, "to ask if it was true?"

My God, I thought, the girl's crazy. Or she's testing the group, playing a game, putting us on. She's crazy or she's a bitch. Stay out of it. And then it dawned on me that I was, after all, giving this advice to the wrong man. I was the subject of the accusation. It was my turn to say something.

"Have you thought about the fact, Miss Bell, that I was shot, and by the police?" I had wanted to keep my voice light, and I half made it.

She had gone back to her knitting. Her voice was almost indifferent: she'd known I would ask that question, and she knew the answer. "They could have killed you. They would have if they'd wanted to. Wounding you made your story seem plausible. It won sympathy for you, took the heat off. Nobody asked about your institute, or why the revolutionaries picked on you."

"But they did ask. The reporters all asked." It was a mistake to answer her, to get pulled into an argument. I tapered off.

"No one asked you seriously. And it was months after the event. The cover was back in place, people no longer cared."

"Miss Bell, I can't help but ask, do you *know* all this?" Rhodes was speaking. "If you're speculating . . ." He was pursuing the matter. I couldn't believe it, but he was.

"I've made my statement," she said.

"But what possible proof do you have?" Rhodes asked.

"Proof?" said LaRosa. "Are you mad, Rhodes?"

"It seems to me," Singer said, "that it's John Burgess who should be speaking." He looked at me with an air of candor, asking me to be candid too. "If it's false, he can deny it."

"Do you think it can possibly be true?" I asked. I looked around the room.

Except for LaRosa and Shanley, they were silent. Godderer, at the other end of the table, was looking at me quizzically.

"You mean that some of you think it's true?" I asked.

Silence again. Then Singer spoke. "We would like to think it's false, but we have a right to hear you say so."

"I'm not going to deny it," I said. "You'll have to get to the bottom of the mystery without my help."

"But this creates a problem, John," said Rhodes, and he wasn't smiling any more. He looked miserable. "You've heard: your right to be at this meeting has been contested. If you take the position you have— if you won't deny the story, and nothing could be simpler, I'm sure—we can't go on with this meeting."

I stood up. "That's one problem I can solve for you," I said. "I'd been intending to leave anyway." I couldn't move to the door very fast, but I did my best.

4

It was too long a walk to go home, and I didn't think a CIA agent, once he'd been exposed, could just walk into the Faculty Club and say, "Hello, I'm back, and can I pick up my old membership?" So I hitched myself back to the main gate of the campus and went across the street looking for a bar I remembered. It was still there. I had a Scotch, ordered a sandwich, thought about the meeting—not the accusation so much as the spirit of objectivity, the wide-open openmindedness, with which my colleagues had greeted it—and told the waiter to hold up the sandwich and bring me another Scotch. I finally got around to letting him bring me the sandwich, and I was looking at it and wondering what to do with it, it looked so small and weak, when somebody sat down next to me. It was LaRosa.

"I decided that you were either going home or coming here," he said, "and you weren't home. So I'm here. How's that? Got a job for me in the CIA?"

"It's not been like this before, has it?" I asked.

"Well, there was a new note of ingenuity this morning, but the answer is yes."

"It was easier to know where I was when I was kidnapped."

"Did you know?"

"Not really. But better than here. I knew the names and numbers of the players. No, not that either. Oh, forget it." I bit into my sandwich, and felt better. It was an honest sandwich: it tasted as bad as it looked.

"Cheer up," LaRosa said. "There's worse to come."

"How do you stand it?"

"I don't. Eat your sandwich. It's time to go to that faculty meeting."

"The hell with the sandwich. The hell with the meeting. Have a drink."

"No. I don't want to go to that meeting any more than you. But we're both going. I need allies."

"I'm not an ally. I'm neutral. But thanks for standing up for me just the same."

"That's all right. You'll have the chance to do the same for me one of these days."

"What's got into Singer?" I asked. "He used to be a quiet type."

"Hadn't you heard? Last spring he discovered the difference between right and wrong. Now the emptiness in his life is gone. He's young again, a new man."

"That's no way to talk about a colleague."

"That's right. No way at all."

"But how did he come to this discovery?"

"It wasn't really a discovery, more a rediscovery. He'd known

43

the difference between right and wrong when he was twenty, but he'd forgotten. Last spring's events reminded him."

"Have a drink."

"No. Get up and come to the meeting."

We got up and went to the meeting.

There's something to be said for restructuring: I'd never seen the whole faculty—eight hundred of them—in one room before. There was a little commotion outside. Half a dozen students were picketing, demanding that students be permitted to attend the meeting too. Gloomily reflecting that people never knew when they were well off, I entered the auditorium. LaRosa and I found seats in the back.

Richard Nevis was on the platform, his gray locks carefully combed to look careless. He'd been called in as president only the year before I'd left, and I'd never got to know him very well. Greaves, his predecessor, had been president for twenty-five years; he'd been a professor of Greek at the university before that. When he retired, the trustees apparently decided that the university had had enough of a good thing, that it had a reputation for being stodgy (which it did), and that they should try something else. To quote young Leon Trotsky, the taxi driver from Columbia who'd indoctrinated me the night before, there were inner contradictions on our Board of Trustees: stodgy they were, but stodgy they wished not to be. They found the answer to this dilemma in Nevis. He'd come from a small experimental college, a kind of broken-backed Antioch, and he was undeniably with it: sensitivity sessions, the new films, post-linear communication, the multi-media art forms. And he was a smiler besides, not an equivocal smiler like Donald Rhodes, an affirmative smiler: the world was on the move and it behooved us professors to keep up with it. He opened the first faculty meeting he chaired by saying, "Fellow students . . ."

He opened this meeting by saying, "Fellow citizens of this

community." Then he told us how much we had learned from the experiences of the preceding spring—I wished he told us *what* we'd learned, because I felt the need to be filled in, but he kept his own counsel on that matter—and expressed his belief that we were ready now, if we would let him use the expression, and even if we wouldn't, and a look of modest daring came over his face, we were ready now, he repeated, "to take a great leap forward." We were going to consider a new set of rules for the governance of our community. To be sure, he disliked the term "rules." He would prefer some other term that didn't have so authoritarian a ring, but he couldn't think of what it would be: no doubt there would be suggestions in the course of the meeting, perhaps from the members of the Department of English, for after all—he stopped to look mischievous—we had to get something useful out of them. He was a great kidder. Then he turned the meeting over to Elliot Wright, the dean of the faculty. "This is a faculty meeting," Nevis said, "and I feel it should be chaired by one of your own. As you know, I have always felt that I do not represent the faculty alone, that I speak for the students as well . . ."

Wright took over the meeting. He'd been around the university a long time, had written three books in economics that had won him a major reputation despite the fact that they were in intelligible English, and students had always talked about him, at any rate in my hearing, with special respect. A year after Nevis had taken over the presidency, the dean who'd served under Greaves quit. Nevis had asked the faculty to nominate a successor: there never was any question who it would be. Wright grumbled a bit but took the job. I think he felt that he'd written his books and it was time to try something else. I'd never really seen him, however, on the job. I left the campus a week after his appointment.

He didn't waste any time when he took over the meeting.

He himself had been chairman of the committee that had put together the interim rules, the report had been sent out in the mail, and the faculty had had a chance to study the proposals. (Not me, I hadn't, I mentally interjected; but I had a bad leg.) Did he hear a motion to adopt the report? Wright asked. If there was such a motion, we could move directly to the discussion of whether to adopt the report, amend it, or reject it entirely.

"Point of order, Mr. Chairman." A fellow was standing up in the first row, looking surprisingly angry in view of the fact that nothing had happened so far. I seemed to remember that his name was Sinclair, and that he was a sociologist. "Is it proper that the chairman of the committee which prepared this report should also chair this meeting?"

"I'd be quite happy not to be in the chair," said Wright. "How shall we proceed? Shall we elect a chairman pro tem . . . ?"

Cries of "No, no . . ."

"Or shall I name a chairman . . . ?"

Cries of "No, no . . ."

A man in the third row stood up. "Mr. Chairman, can we go to Roberts' Rules of Order for guidance on this matter?"

A shout: "Roberts' Rules have no legitimacy until we've adopted them."

Dietrich Wisniewski stood up. His hands were shaking. "If I am properly informed, this faculty, last spring, permitted to be made the decision that we have no rules for adopting anything. I have it on the highest authority. From professors of philosophy we are told we are in a state of ultimate doubt. From professors of politics, we are in a state of nature. From the president of the university, we are in a state of grace. I congratulate you all." He sat down and looked around him, a despairing smile on his face, to see if anyone had heard him.

Elliot Wright said drily, "Well, it's not last spring, it's now, and we'd better get out of the state we're in. I suspect that even the philosophers here will agree that one can't conduct an inquiry without making at least some provisional assumptions. We're here now to discuss rules which will themselves be only provisional. Might I suggest that we avoid a long discussion about adopting provisional rules for discussing provisional rules? I am prepared to step down as chairman, and I would recommend that the associate dean take my place. That's what normally happens when the dean is unable to chair a meeting."

Nevis came forward on the platform and stood in front of the microphone. "May I?" he said to Wright.

"With pleasure," said Wright.

"Gentlemen," Nevis said, "as you know, I have always believed in the advantage of unstructured situations. We have such a situation now. We should regard it not as an obstacle but an opportunity. With good will we can make it work for us. I recommend—not as president, you understand, I'm not wearing that hat at the moment—that we accept Dean Wright's proposal. If at the end of the meeting, when we've achieved a result, or perhaps I should say *if* we've achieved a result"—pause, rueful smile—"and someone then wishes to raise questions about the procedure we've adopted, we can review the whole matter."

LaRosa stood up next to me. His voice was almost indifferent, as it had been in the morning. "I'm not sure, Mr. President, that I understand. Do you mean that we shall have a meeting, and presumably, at the end, take a vote, and that then somebody can challenge the whole proceeding?"

"Professor LaRosa," Nevis said smoothly, "you forget that that can always happen. All decisions are subject to review. They should be." LaRosa sat down, and I heard his sigh.

Wright left the stage and took a seat in the auditorium, and a young chap named Knapp, the associate dean, whom I'd never seen before, took his place. Nevis was still at the microphone.

"May I say, gentlemen," he said, "while I still have the microphone—and now, if I may, I speak as president, as spokesman for students—that they are watching us even if they're not here, that they are expecting constructive results to come out of this meeting, that they have a right to such results. I'm sure I need not have said this, that you all recognize this point, but since no students are here I felt I must make it."

He was unduly pessimistic about his isolation. At this point, there were some cries outside, a hoarse shout, and a violent jolt against the main door to the auditorium. A mass chant broke out: "Let the people in!"

Knapp, apparently, was a veteran of this sort of situation. He spoke coolly: "I had meant to inform the faculty, but apparently I am a few moments late, that a group of students have demanded the right to participate in this meeting, and have said that they would break in if the meeting wasn't opened to them." He had to raise his voice at the end. The chant was getting louder.

"Why shouldn't they be let in? Who is keeping them out?" Sinclair wanted to know.

Nevis stood up. "There are, though I don't like to say so, guards at the door. The dean and I thought that it was up to the faculty to decide whether these students should be admitted."

"Exactly who are they?" Roberts' Rules of Order, in the third row, wanted to know.

"They are," said Knapp, "members of the April 30 Movement, which was formed last spring out of part of a splinter of the SDS. As their name suggests, they are the vanguard of the proletariat, whose day is May First."

"Shame!" shouted a short fat man in the row just in front of me. He rose up, his eyes brilliant with outrage, his nostrils quivering as though there were a bad smell in the room. I'd never seen a man so entirely lifted by pure indignation out of his chair, and it solved his height problems: when he stood up, he stood tall. With a visible effort he controlled himself, sniffing hard, shaking his shoulders, rubbing the ridges over his eyes. Then he lowered his head to his chest as though he were listening to a congregation of voices inside him and deciding which one to call on. As if to help, the noise outside subsided. Silence reigned in the room, in the whole wide world.

I'd had some disorienting experiences over the course of the last twenty-four hours, and this was too much. "I'm getting out of here," I muttered to LaRosa.

"Now, now," he whispered, "stay and face reality."

"It's not here," I said. "This place is under a spell, I swear it."

"You can't get out anyway," LaRosa said. "The doors are locked to keep the students out. So you're locked in." He could be smug.

The shame-sayer began to speak. His voice spread out over the auditorium, pure and melodious. "May I ask Dean Knapp on what basis he makes these allegations?"

The dramatic pause had been so long that Knapp had forgotten what he'd said. "Allegations?" he asked.

The organ tones began to come up fuller. "I mean the innuendos, the distasteful descriptions, regarding the students outside. I would remind you that they are *our* students, and we are responsible for them, responsible, if I may say so in these secular surroundings, for their souls." The voice changed.

49

It snapped; it was sharp and businesslike. "Unfounded and prejudicial allegations should have no place among us. On what evidence has Dean Knapp permitted himself to make the statement that these students are members of the April 30 Movement?"

Knapp was a crisis-manager, I give him that. He answered, his eyes round behind his glasses, "Well, I confess it was a complicated process of inference. We have received two letters from a group of students identifying themselves as members of this organization. In these letters they stated their intention to invade this meeting if they weren't invited to it. Subsequently, I had a meeting with this group of students. They reiterated this intention. And just a half-hour before I came here they called me on the telephone to tell me their plan again. Walking to this meeting, I saw them conducting an outdoor rally and heard them repeat their intentions to be here. From these scattered bits of evidence I have leaped to the conclusion that the noises outside are being made by members of the April 30 Movement."

A lot of people in the room thought that was funny, including me. We went so far as to laugh. We regretted it. The organ-tones came up majestically. That man had a remarkable voice. "Is it the policy of this administration," he boomed out mournfully, "to identify students antagonistically before they have had even a chance to speak? Are we to assume that they are on trial for their political opinions? Has the order gone out, may I ask, that we must accept the administration's official— and, if I may say so, uninformed—characterization of their political opinions?"

On the platform, Nevis, so help me, was looking pleased.

The organ hit some wistful, regretful notes. "We are here to discuss mere rules. These students, in contrast, have come to ask about principles. We on our side care only that their external behavior conform to certain standards, so that they won't make trouble, so that we can carry on business as usual. But they care about the inner condition, the sickness, of this university. Are we content to sit here quibbling over peripheral matters when they have come to remind us of the heart of the matter?"

Outside a chant had picked up again: "Tricky Dick Nevis: rise up and leave us."

"I ask," said the spokesman for the heart of the matter, "that our students be admitted without further debate, and that the prejudicial remarks of the chairman be stricken from the record."

"That's all right," said Knapp. "There is no record." I was beginning to like that young man.

"It is on the record!" the organ crashed. "It is on the record of our consciences!"

"Who in the name of Peter, Paul, and Mary is that?" I asked LaRosa, who'd sunk deep in his chair trying to get out of the line of fire.

"Exactly who you'd think. That's our shepherd of souls. He's the Protestant counselor."

"I'm going to stand up," I said. "I'm going to demand to be let out of here." But I was too late. Dietrich Wisniewski was on his feet, intoning in a wooden voice, "Mr. Chairman, Mr. Chairman . . ."

Knapp recognized him. "I believe," Wisniewski said, "that the previous speaker is not a member of this faculty, and has no right to make a motion . . ."

"We have no rules," Sinclair, up front, shouted. "You said so yourself. Sit down."

"Let him stand," the organ pronounced imperiously. "Let him stand before us taking the position that a matter of principle be dealt with by a parliamentary maneuver."

51

Outside the chant had gone back to the plaintive cry of the homeless *moujik:* "Let the people in!"

"Are we going to let the students in or not?" a young man in the back shouted.

"We are not," someone answered.

A man with bags under his eyes stood up and signaled to the chairman. Knapp nodded in resignation and gave him the floor.

"We're about to hear the truth," LaRosa said to me, and hunched down farther in his seat. "He's the village psychiatrist." Dr. Bledsoe was his name. Dr. Bledsoe informed us that the reason we wouldn't let the students in was that we were worried about our manhood, but that he was confident of his own manhood, so he had no fear about letting them in. He took more words to say this than I've used to repeat it, but that was the message. At the conclusion of this expert testimony quite a number of manly voices were raised, seeking the floor.

Nevis stood up, Wright came back to the stage, Knapp looked more owlish than ever, and the meeting developed kaleidoscopic effects. A moment later—or was it ten minutes or an eternity?—I heard a new voice, friendly, reasonable, addressing the throbbing throng.

"Can we not deal with this matter sensibly, and in the interests of all?" He was about forty, a neat, compact man, speaking as he might speak in his own living room to three or four old friends. "There are students outside, locked out. We are inside, locked in. I recommend that two or three members of this faculty go out and speak with them, and find out under what conditions they would agree to send in one or two spokesmen."

"They have already told me," Knapp said, "that they have

no spokesmen, that that is undemocratic. They have all reserved the individual right to speak."

The new man smiled confidently. "I'm sure that a few of us who know them can work this out," he said. The torture is stopping, I thought. Somebody is making sense.

"That's Joseph Lawton," LaRosa said to me. "He was very active as a mediator last spring. He's an anthropologist."

The meeting seemed finally to have been pulled together, though we weren't discussing what we'd come together to discuss. But somebody stood up and proposed that a committee, chaired by Lawton, go out and talk to the students, and come back and report. Someone else said, No, give the committee the power to decide whether to let the students in. And someone else said, Send them out to talk while we debate here what their mission is. And that's what was done. As I say, the meeting was getting pulled together. In about five minutes Lawton returned, the large smile on his face signaling total satisfaction. "We have agreed," he said to the group, "that there will be three student speakers, and that the other students will simply take their seats in the auditorium."

"I protest." It was Dieter again, but this time he wasn't alone.

"I think it is the only way to deal with the problem," said Lawton. "Otherwise nothing that comes out of this meeting will be accepted as legitimate by the student body."

Nevis came forward. "I cannot say how relieved I am that this group will not lock its doors against students. We are always ready to talk to them.

"We have business of our own!" somebody shouted.

"We can have no business more important than this," said Nevis. His voice turned reflective. "We all realize that they're getting upset over a purely symbolic issue. But it is important to them. I hope we're mature enough not to insist that it is important to us. I would prefer not to make an issue of this. I think that Dr. Lawton has done us all a service." He turned and looked at Elliot Wright. "Do you have an opinion, Dean Wright?"

Wright looked at him and shrugged his shoulders, "No," he said.

So they brought the students in, and as they did Dieter Wisniewski stood up and walked out through them. The group seemed evenly divided between males and females.

"The first speaker," Knapp was saying, "is Miss Gloria Gottshalk, who is a student in . . ."

Hoarse cries from the students in the back interrupted him: "No identification . . . We agreed . . ."

"Well," said Knapp agreeably, "Miss no identification."

The young lady stepped forward. She was a neat, trim little thing. Deep brown eyes, a soft mouth. "Tricky Dick," she began, nodding to Nevis, "Dean Wrong," she continued, flicking an eye toward Wright, and "Faculty Finks," she concluded, turning to the Demos: "The people have had enough of your bullshit discussions of bullshit rules. We want to know why you continue to follow oppressive real-estate policies in this city; why you repress workers, blacks, and other minority groups; why you do research for the war machine; why . . ."

I'm not sure, but I may have blacked out for a moment. It had been a swirling twenty-four hours. What I do remember is being on my feet, forgetting I had a bad leg, and trying to climb over LaRosa to the aisle to get out. "The door's open," I said, "it's our chance." Of course, my leg collapsed, I fell all over LaRosa, and after I picked myself up, or rather after he did, I felt somewhat chastened. But I got out of there just the same. I wasn't the only one. There must have been a couple of dozen people going through the door.

I went back to the bar, and had a double Scotch and said what the hell, and had a beer to go with it. I wanted something that would remove my giddy feeling, make me feel closer to the ground. But it only helped a little. For one thing, the waiter was wrong. He had a bandanna around his throat and a mustache like Captain Blood's, and it wasn't restful to have him in the vicinity. So I sent him off to call me a taxi, and took my beer over to the bar where I wouldn't be sitting in a dark corner.

And there were Hedge and Sledge. I edged up to them, if you can edge up when you're using a cane that goes scratch-tap like a warning signal, and said, in what I like to think is my genial manner, "I didn't get your names quite right this morning. Would you mind giving them to me?"

They were eager to please. Hedge said his name was Hodges. Sledge said his name was Slater. I took a notebook from my pocket and wrote all that down. "What beer do you drink?" I asked them, friendly as a bird. Colt 45, they said. I wrote that down in my book too.

"Say," Sledge/Slater said, "we're sorry about this morning, Professor Burgess. We knew Dorothy Bell might say that, but we didn't really think she would. She gets like ideas, you know. We didn't know what to do."

"Think nothing of it," I said. "It's the risks of the game. Everybody around here has a second line of work, students, professors, everybody. So why not me? Take you, for instance: you're restructuralists."

"That wasn't really our point," Hedge/Hodges said.

"Deny they're restructuralists," I muttered, and wrote it down in my book.

"Okay we deserve it," said Sledge/Slater, "but like you're kidding, aren't you?"

"Now that's a good question," I said. "But how would I

55

know? Do you know if you were kidding this morning? How would anybody know who's kidding and who isn't around here? It's a problem in metaphysics. What we need is an index of measurement, an objective test to show who's kidding and who isn't and how much. It'd be a service to humanity." Then Captain Blood announced my taxi, and I flipped my little black book at them confidentially and left.

The taxi driver was sent by God. He drove me home on a straight path, and didn't say a word. He had a little trouble figuring the arithmetic at the end, but I forgave him that. I walked into the house. Martha was in the living room reading a magazine, and I collapsed into an easy chair across from her.

"Is the meeting over?" she asked.

"I don't know," I said. "I'm not even sure it ever began."

"Didn't you go?"

"I think I must have. But Martha, the day has had a certain amount of confusion in it. This morning I met a young man who wasn't wearing shoes, but he was wearing socks. And I met Dieter Wisniewski, who talked to me as though this were central Europe. Then at the department meeting somebody from the Alexander Graham Bell family identified me as a CIA agent. And at the meeting this afternoon, which I strongly believe I attended, a Miss God's Hawk addressed the faculty."

"Who?" Martha asked.

"I'm giving it to you straight, Martha. Hear me out."

But I found I didn't have anything more to say. I sat there, a kind of blankness in my mind, and simply said, "Well, it's been a day."

Martha said, "You've had worse. Think of it as a period of adjustment. Would you like some coffee?"

I said I would, and I drank the coffee obediently. And in a little while the telephone rang. It was LaRosa.

"Did you get home?" he wanted to know.

"No, I never made it," I said.

"John, don't be so damned cantankerous. I was worried about you."

"All right, thanks, but there's nothing to worry about. What happened after I left? Did they ever get around to voting on the interim rules?"

LaRosa's voice came over the phone with the same fatalistic note in it I'd heard during the morning. "Well, let me try to put it as exactly as I can. After the three student speeches had finished—they took an hour—the motherfucking faculty . . ."

"That's what the faculty is?"

"That's what it was called, and nobody got up and denied it."

"Proceed."

"As I was saying, the Oedipal faculty debated the rules for a half hour or so, and concluded that they were (a) too precise and (b) too vague, so they should have more study."

"So we haven't got any rules?"

"Well yes but then again no. The interim rules weren't formally adopted. However, it was the sense of the faculty—we voted it—that these rules were informally adopted as general guidelines, but only for the interim, until satisfactory interim rules were voted. Oh, and I forgot; nothing that we did do today is official . . ."

"I thought it wasn't official, it was just informal."

"That's right. But it stands only if the students take parallel action when they're back on the campus."

"Do they have procedures for taking such action?"

"No, of course not."

"Then we don't have any rules."

"We don't need any rules. As Pritchard said . . ."

"Who's he?"

"The Protestant counselor. As he said, we have principles, and principles are more important than rules. Nevis backed him up, so it must be true."

"What about this morning, Joe? The ultimatum, the impasse . . ."

"Oh that. We appointed a committee. Shanley, Singer, and Rhodes. They'll meet with the students, if the students are willing to have a committee. If not, we'll see . . ."

"Thanks for calling, Joe."

"Not at all. And, John, take it easy, will you?"

It was good advice. Martha was in the kitchen working on dinner, and I poured myself a drink. My mouth felt full of cotton and my sinuses were clogging up on me. Martha came back in the room and looked at me curiously.

"Were you doing a lot of drinking in Uruguay?" she asked.

I overlooked it. I was going to overlook everything, I decided. The pebble on the hill, the ball on the wheel, that was me. I'd roll with the punch. Nobody was punching anyway. There was nobody there.

Like Trilby says, you're kidding, you must be kidding, you bet.

5

When I woke up the next morning, the ache in my leg had moved from dull to sharp, and something was pressing on the back of my eyeballs. I went downstairs and Martha looked at me and told me to go on back up. I'd been doing too much, going too fast. Meek and, I don't mind saying so, relieved, I went back to bed.

Nevis's office called around nine-thirty. I heard Martha answer it and tell them that I was a bit under the weather, and was staying in bed. There was a long pause, she said what she had said all over again, and then there was another pause and Martha came into the room. "The president is very eager to see you this morning," she said. "I'm very eager to stay where I am," I answered. She obviously approved my answer and went back and told them. "Yes, of course, as soon as he's out," I heard her say, and she signed off.

I drowsed off, had lunch in bed, and read a Simenon detective story in the afternoon. I enjoyed it. A crime had been committed, there was no doubt about that, and you had to find the criminal, because there was no doubt about that either, there was a criminal. Godderer called in the afternoon to invite me to a weekend party, and I answered through Martha that we'd have to put it off till later. There were other calls too: Rhodes, Elliot Wright, they hoped I'd come in to talk to them, and, of all people, Pritchard the organ-grinder. Same message to all: Professor Burgess was recuperating after his long trip, and as soon as he was feeling better he'd do what he could to satisfy his fans.

"My brother's more popular than I thought," Martha said to me as I was sipping some broth in the evening. I had a slight fever, but I was feeling better. Also, I was halfway through another Simenon. Wonderful stuff. First the crime and then the punishment. No academic shenanigans, like first the punishment and then look for the crime, there must have been one, the punishment proves it. The man stayed on the up and up with you. I smiled peacefully at Martha, and went to sleep.

Joe LaRosa and my old friend Moses Epstein, the geneticist, came over the next day after dinner and spent the evening with me. Joe seemed less tired than usual, and Moses was as ebullient as ever. He looked me over dispassionately and said, "For you, John, you don't look bad." I remarked that I hadn't seen him at the faculty meeting. "I ration myself," he said. "Two hours a month. Any more and it becomes an addiction."

By the end of the evening there was no doubt about it that I was glad to have come back. LaRosa and Epstein got into a discussion of the Victorians—Ruskin, Carlyle, Dickens, Matthew Arnold, Tennyson—and their reaction to evolution and the coming of industrialism and democracy. Epstein had read these men, and, what's more surprising, since he's a professor of English, LaRosa is fairly sophisticated about biology, and has studied economic history and even some Victorian law. He wants to know not only what Victorian writers thought but what they might have thought if they hadn't been so militantly ignorant about the things that were shocking them. I wish that more literary men took a cue from him. But of course there aren't so many scientists who are as conversable as Epstein. At any rate, I spent an enjoyable evening listening to my friends.

After a while we got around to our graduate student days, how we'd lived, girls we'd known, teachers we'd had. And that led us to those moments when an idea had dawned on us, luminous, with a being of its own.

"The best idea I ever had in my life," Moses said, "walked up and winked at me one night in a Chinese restaurant when I was out with a girl. On the way home she told me that I'd suddenly stopped talking, and had just sat there, looking solemn and foolish. It took me a month before she'd go out with me again, and she brought along a book in case another accident happened."

"I wonder if accidents like that happen to students nowadays," Joe mused.

"Why not?" said Moses. "They're human, they're students. Of course, a lot of them are hacks. But a lot of us were hacks too—still are for that matter. What do you want? An idea for every man? Like a guaranteed annual wage?"

"I don't know," Joe said, still on his own train of thought, "it's just that students today seem to have so many other things on their minds."

"So did we, Grandpop," Moses said. "Are you forgetting? There was a war in Spain, and Hitler, and that waffling, timid, fake reformer Roosevelt—everything you'd want to make a young man think that life was meaningful. Not to mention girls. Who had his mind on his work all the time?"

"We also worried whether we'd ever have jobs," I put in.

"It was more than just jobs," LaRosa said. "I remember my feeling: it was something like fear—fear that I didn't have it in me, that I'd have nothing of my own to contribute to a subject that enthralled me. When you're a student you don't know what you can do. It's a tough time of life."

"Yeah, yeah," said Moses, "absolute misery."

"All right, not exactly," said Joe.

"Of course not," Moses said. "Girls, friends, Spain, ideas in Chinese restaurants, a little music maybe or a game of tennis. With all that the anxiety's manageable."

"No," LaRosa said, "you leave out the *Weltschmerz*."

"So put it in," Moses said. "That's fun too."

"You're making my case," said Joe. "Universities are impossible places. You bring together people going through a critical period of their lives, full of their own preoccupations, and put them in the same room with a man who's spent thirty years concentrating on a highly specialized subject . . ."

"And is going through a critical period of his life, and is full of his own preoccupations," Moses said, interrupting. "There's no reason to be lugubrious about it. It's just the way things are. What's all the fuss? There's a lot of noise, a little inconvenience maybe, but not much more. I go on with my work. My good students show up. That's enough, what more do you want?"

I slept pretty well that night, and the next morning, when I woke up, my cold was nearly gone, and I felt it was time to go out and enjoy the sunny world.

Martha reminded me of Nevis's call, so I telephoned his office and they said to come right over. They seemed so eager, that I was a little puzzled. Martha put me in the car, talked her way past the guard at the campus gate, and drove me to the front door of the administration building. I took the elevator to Nevis's office on the top floor. The waiting room reminded me a little of your friendly neighborhood art gallery. There were a lot of paintings around, one or two pieces of sculpture, two or three mobiles hanging from the ceiling. Some of the things were good, some indifferent, some frightening. But the message rang through loud and clear: there was room in this gallery for one and all. Nothing from last year though, please.

Nevis came to the door and invited me in. The gray locks were still carelessly in place, and he certainly was glad to see me. He said so, smiling and laughing and nodding his head knowingly at me. "Yes indeed, yes indeed, we've been waiting for you to come back, John. I can't tell you how much." He overdid it a little, because this was the first conversation, one-to-one, I'd ever had with him in my life. But I sat back and enjoyed the thought of the university, from the president on down, holding its breath while waiting for Burgess the charming, Burgess the wise, to come home again.

"What did you think of the faculty meeting the other day?" Nevis asked me. "You managed to get there?"

I said I had. Managing to stay had been a little harder.

He just about broke up. "I tell you, we've needed you, John. Somebody caustic. Does us all good. But seriously, I liked the spirit there. I think we made some real progress."

I didn't want to risk being caustic again, so I said I hoped so. Then I subsided. He was studying me affectionately. We sat there in silence and every once in a while he would nod his head in approval of what he saw. Or perhaps he was listening to something and agreeing. I don't know. I sat there, getting appraised, and trying to keep my chin pointed bravely at him. I caught a look at the two of us in the mirror on the wall behind him. There we were: him with the back of his head poised gracefully, as beautiful and pensive a back-of-the-head as anyone would want to see, and me, looking back at him with a kind of half-guilty, half-defiant, grin on my face. I hadn't known it was there, and I took it off. I don't suppose we'd been silent for more than fifteen seconds or so, but it seemed like a lot more, so I said, "Well, I'm certainly glad that you're glad I'm back," and took my cane in hand to push myself up from my seat.

"Well, there was one other thing I did want to speak to you about," Nevis said.

"Oh?" I settled back again.

"The story has moved around the campus quite a bit now— it's too foolish even to discuss, but these are in some ways difficult days, hopeful but difficult—as I say, the story has gotten around that you were an agent of the CIA in Uruguay. It's too bad you couldn't have come in two days ago. We might have nipped it in the bud then. Stories like that move very fast, and grow and grow. Still, I think we can manage it."

"I don't follow," I said.

"You're not a member of the CIA, are you?"

"Of course not."

"And you weren't associated with it in Uruguay?"

"No."

"I don't blame you for feeling as you do about the story," he said. "But wouldn't it be a good thing to make a public statement denying it?"

"And if some nut says I'm Jack the Ripper, do I make a public statement denying that too?"

"This is different. The CIA is a sensitive subject on this campus."

"Well, I'm glad to know what is and isn't a sensitive subject here, but the answer is no. I've told you the story isn't true. If anybody asks you, you can say I told you, and that's the end of it."

"It would be much better coming directly from you, John."

His voice was liquid with friendliness toward me, but I noticed that his Adam's apple was beginning to live a life of its own. It was moving up and down in his throat.

"Mr. Nevis," I said, "suppose the story had got around that I was a member of the Communist Party—a secret member, a courier, something like that—and you'd called me in to ask about it . . ."

He was indignant. "But I'd never do anything like that," he said. "Why would I?"

"Well, you've got me in here to ask about the CIA."

"But that's different, as different as night and day."

"All right, but let's play with the hypothesis. If you asked me if I was a member of the Communist Party, I'd tell you no. Would you then go on and ask me to make a public statement of my innocence?"

"I find the whole analogy hard to understand," he said. "And to be perfectly frank, I think you're being a bit defensive about the whole thing." Smile number three, the disarming one, came my way, slightly marred by the fact that that independent-minded Adam's apple of his wasn't feeling good about the situation at all.

"Defensive is just what I don't intend to be," I said. "The whole thing isn't worth thinking about."

"John, I'm surprised. It's simply beyond me why you're reluctant to make a public denial of these allegations."

"Because my father told me when I was a boy in Indiana that it was a mistake to get in a pissing match with a skunk."

He tried laughing some more, but I had my impatient face on, and this time his attack of the gasps didn't last long. "I wonder if there's anything in the world that's harder to lead than a university," he said.

I took it he didn't expect me to help him out with the answer to that one, and I sat there silently.

He picked up the phone on the desk. "Why don't we do it this way? I can call the student newspaper; the editors are back on the campus. I can say that you happen to be here in my office, that the CIA story came up, and that you of course denied it, and that you're right here to tell your story." He pressed the buzzer to get his secretary to put in the call.

"It's your party," I said. "Go ahead. But leave me out of it."

He told his secretary never mind. "I'm sorry you're so unco-operative," he said.

"Mr. Nevis," I said, "when I came in here, you said you were certainly glad I'm back, and I said I was glad you were glad. Now I'm sad that you're sad. I'm perfectly serious. I work here and I hope I can make your job easier. But I can't do what you've asked. Ask me to do something else and I'll do my very best to be helpful."

I pulled myself up from my chair, reached out and shook his hand, and turned to make my way to the door. Calm and resolute, that's the approach, I said to myself as I began my move out of the room, not angry with anybody, just a simple quiet man who knows his mind. With my hand on the knob, I turned back to Nevis. "I can only repeat what I said," I said. "Ask me to do something I can do, and I'll do it."

"What you can do," Nevis said from his desk, "is make a public denial of an ugly story which, so far as anyone can know, could very possibly be true."

I don't say I'm particularly proud of my answer. The fact is I don't take credit for it at all. It was Nevis's work; he was a stimulating man. I suppose that ever since I'd seen *High Noon* the idea of playing Gary Cooper had been festering in my unconscious. Up it came to the surface: I was Gary Cooper, cool, soft-spoken, but steely-eyed. "Well, now we have a perfect way to handle the whole thing," I said. "Why don't you say that the story about me might be true? Say it out loud, on the library steps. Then we can meet in the quadrangle, just the two of us, ten paces, the crowd keeping clear, and I'll ask you to repeat it. We'll settle it like men. How's that? You can't say I'm not willing to play ball." I repeat, I take no credit for that speech, thank God. I give it all to Nevis. The man was a great teacher. He helped people discover hidden sides of their personalities.

Unfortunately, he didn't seem pleased at what he'd done. "You're being quite outrageous," he said. "I've asked you to do something that couldn't be simpler."

"I would advise you to do something simple, Mr. Nevis," I said. Gary Cooper was gone; Dr. Freud, helpful, professional, therapeutic, was on tap. "Decide whether you're running a university, a revival meeting, a public confessional, or what. You really have to make up your mind." Then I closed the door, firmly but kindly, and started out through the waiting room, step, click, scratch, step, click, scratch.

"You forgot your hat," a woman's voice said behind me. I turned around, and stepped-clicked-scratched back to get it. The woman was holding it, and as she held it out to me, she kept her face averted. As I took it, she turned her face to me, and I saw she was trying not to laugh.

"Here's your hat," she said, "and there's the door." Then she did laugh. It was the last straw. Cooper surged to the surface, Dr. Freud tried pushing his head out from under the waves, and then I laughed too.

"I'm Irene Howell," the woman said, "the president's administrative assistant." She had an interesting face. Everything was there: eyes, nose, mouth, and a quite arresting jaw-line where it turned up toward her ears.

"I'm John Burgess," I said, "one of the president's advisers."

"You'd better go while the going's good," she said. In her presence, the going didn't seem so good, but I went.

6

In my office I was looking with despair at the dust on my books when Donald Rhodes followed his smile into the room. He'd been hoping to see me. Had I had a talk with Nevis? I told him I had. Wasn't I being a little stubborn? he wanted to know. Not a little, very, I said.

"But it's such a small thing, John . . ."

"Then why all the fuss?"

"John," he said, "let's sit down and talk it over."

"All right," I said, "but I could be dusting my books."

"In my office," he said. He smiled. Smile, John, the smile said. I could feel Cooper beginning to ride tall in the saddle again. Hastily, I smiled back at Rhodes and Gary went away. "On my turf," Rhodes said, "if you know what I mean. I want you to see the problem as it looks from the chairman's office."

I went along. Rhodes sat down, I sat down, Rhodes stood

up and paced. "John, this is a political situation," he said. "I don't know if you realize that."

"Well, I've been looking for a word to describe it," I said. "Enlighten me."

He enlightened me, and I might as well pass the illumination along. The situation was political, and that meant that different people wanted different things, and a man in a position of responsibility, for example the chairman of a Department of English, had to be pragmatic. It wasn't easy, having responsibilities while people who didn't have them sniped at you. But he hoped that the idea was getting across to the department, although it certainly wasn't an easy idea to communicate. Take Wisniewski: he was simply out of touch. Worse perhaps, though one hated to say so, he might very well be unbalanced. One had to live with facts even if they were unpleasant, or, at any rate, with speculations. As for Shanley, he was of course a nice man, I didn't need Rhodes to tell me that, and he'd made great contributions in his time, nobody, and least of all the chairman of this department, would wish to deny it, but he was simply out of touch. Not where it's at, if I'd permit him to use that expression despite the overtones it might have. And LaRosa, a first-rate scholar of course, that went without saying, and a friend of mine, an old, dear friend of Rhodes himself for that matter, but that was the trouble—not the friendship, of course, the scholar side. He was remote, hung up on abstract principles. Or one could describe his error more sympathetically: the trouble was that LaRosa insisted on approaching the problem as though it were a rational one. But of course it wasn't, it was a political problem, and, to repeat, one had to be pragmatic. LaRosa was, well, it had to be said, and I would understand that the chairman, with his problems, was confiding in me, LaRosa was a bit unbending.

And so we rocked along. Rhodes was trying to look at the matter objectively. He wasn't going to make any value judgments. This wasn't a moment for that kind of self-indulgence. To tell the truth, he had to admit it, he knew what was troubling LaRosa, and perhaps even me. He himself didn't feel very affirmative about what was happening, he had to admit he didn't really like the new culture, but he'd learned that wasn't the issue. Or rather—that is, if I was still following him—that *was* the issue. It was a new culture like. In all probability, didn't I think so too, we were living through a cultural revolution, moving through a cultural watershed if you like, and we had to adjust if we were to survive. Speaking for himself, he accepted what was coming, and the new dispensation would probably be no worse than the old. It was politics, and he was, if he might so put it, a Buddhist about it.

"I thought you were a pragmatist," I said.

"It comes to the same thing," he said.

"And as a good Buddhist, I ought to stand up in public meeting and confess, is that it?"

"John, why be perverse? If you are in fact innocent, why not say so?"

"How shall I say it? I'm innocent, I am, I am, I swear I am?"

"John, an issue has been raised. The least we can do is show we're responsive. It would clear the air if you treated what has been said with enough respect to deny it formally and to give some evidence that you're telling the truth. The students have a legitimate reason to be worried if the CIA is on the campus. Try to see your own story in that context."

The memory of my horse opera performance that morning kept me from getting up and practicing that walk to the door again. "What story?" I asked Rhodes. "I have no story. A blank isn't a story. There's nothing to tell." I smiled. This was a new Burgess, a better Burgess: cool, affirmative, helpful, sympathetic. Home three days, and I was a changed man, half a dozen changed men.

I looked up from counting this cast of characters and caught the end of what Rhodes was saying. "You can surely give some evidence that there's nothing to tell, John."

"Of course. And I can also give evidence that I've never committed murder. Not once. You can check back." I looked up at Rhodes, and heard the old familiar churlish tone return to my voice. It picked up my spirits. "Who is this Dorothy Bell? Is she crazy? Does she know what she's doing? You don't mean to say that there's a plan in all this, or that ordinary sensible students will believe her, do you?"

Rhodes looked at me almost protectively. "Those are irrelevant questions, John. When you're back here a bit longer you'll realize it makes no difference whether people have a plan or not. A seed is planted, it grows, it explodes. And as for who's crazy and who isn't, well . . ."

"Well, what?"

"That's a relative question." He shrugged, he smiled, benign wisdom flowed from his eyes. "Lunacy is a matter that depends on the attitudes of the audience. You're crazy only if the world says you're crazy. I can assure you, John, that the audience to whom Dorothy Bell's remarks about you are addressed isn't going to think she's crazy. Daring—yes, perhaps, but, crazy, no. Few of them, to be sure, are going to be convinced that what she's said is true. But most of them are going to think it's in the bound of possibility. The fact is, they think that pretty much anything is possible."

He'd talked himself out of the chairman's seat. For a moment he was talking to me personally, and I was grateful. "These are young people, Donald," I said, "still unformed, certainly likely to want to go along with the group. Don't you think it would help if we—I mean the teachers, the people who are forty or fifty years old—made our own notions of what is crazy and sane very plain? Not everything needs to be possible, at least not here on a university campus. We don't have to treat everything that's said—every bit of nonsense, any malicious fantasy—as though it had the same claim to be considered as anything else. If you or I think that something's crazy, or simply impermissible, not a way to behave, why not show that we do? Why be so self-denying?" I was a little disturbed with myself as I heard myself speaking. This wasn't the passive, disengaged Burgess.

I'd talked him back onto his perch. "John, we can't separate ourselves from our students that way. The problem, as I've said, is a political problem. I wish you'd give some thought to it from that point of view."

So I said I would, and meanwhile I hoped he'd be a Buddhist about the attitude I was taking. The suggestion seemed only to make him sadder, and I limped out of the office before I did anything more to destroy his faith.

The idea of a drink was beginning to seem attractive to me but I'd spent an hour being benigned at and benigning back, and it seemed out of keeping with the spirit of the occasion. So I went over to the cafeteria at the faculty club to have a green salad and some prunes. At the cafeteria I spotted Irene Howell down the line ahead of me. I maneuvered myself into position to catch her eye.

"You handed me my hat this morning," I said. "Do you think you could give me a hand now, and carry my tray?"

She carried my tray to a table, and I got her to join me for lunch. She did have eyes, nose, and mouth, just as I remembered, and, as she ate her salmon salad sandwich, I noticed that the line of her jaw had a nice, squarish look to it—definite but delicate.

"How often do you do what you did this morning?" she wanted to know.

"What part of what I did?"

"The Gary Cooper part."

"Oh. I'd hoped you hadn't noticed."

"No one could miss it. The old cowpoke, tired, knowing that gun-slinging isn't really a life for a man, but pushed onward by some principle he can't define. . . . You're good at it."

"It never happened to me before in my life, I give you my word. The occasion, if I may say so, brought out the worst in me."

"You may not say so. I'll make a bargain. If I don't say anything about Gary Cooper, you're to forget that I was laughing. I shouldn't have." She started to laugh again. "Mr. Nevis didn't laugh for the rest of the morning," she said.

She was discreet, but I inferred that a morning free from the golden laughter of Richard Nevis was a welcome experience. She'd worked until June as the assistant to James Higby —he of the big opinion-polling institute. The troubles in the spring had convinced Higby that he ought to take his institute to quieter waters, and he'd pulled up his stakes and left. His wife had been Nevis's assistant. When she left it was natural that Irene should move to Nevis's office. She didn't say anything more, which was enough to tell me that it had been a long hot summer.

She didn't really fit there, and I suspected that she knew she didn't. She'd been around—in government, *The New York Times*, half a dozen years abroad, work with other institutes before Higby's. She'd lived enough, and moved enough in a world in which words are related to things, to find her present situation a bit baffling. Why did she stay? Curiosity probably, unwillingness to leave in the middle of a crisis, perhaps a certain affection for the place. And there was something in the way she spoke that suggested she felt herself at an uncertain period, ready to change course but not quite knowing the direction in which she wanted to move. From a few scattered

things she said in a matter-of-fact tone of voice, I pieced together the fact that she'd married immediately after she'd
finished college. Her husband had been a veteran, studying on
the G.I. Bill. He'd been called back into the Air Force when
the Korean War came, and had been killed. And that was that.

When I got back to my office there was a message for me.
Elliot Wright had been trying to reach me, and if I had a
moment that afternoon could I drop in? I telephoned and went
over. I was afraid I knew what it was about, and, of course,
when I got there, that's what it was about. The Innocence of
Burgess. Would he please stand up in the public square and
say that any allegations to the effect that he wasn't Francis
of Assisi were unfounded? All that surprised me was that
Elliot Wright was the bearer of this message. But it surprised
him too.

"I'm astonished at the things I've done, at the things I've
accepted, over the last year," he said. "I don't think they've
been mistakes, I hope they haven't been, but they're not things
I would ever have anticipated my doing. Last spring I sat
down—or rather stood up—with students, twelve hundred of
them, and replied soberly to the charge that the university was
contributing to genocide because it provides living space only
for registered students and not for the people in the area who
are badly housed. Twelve hundred people in a room, half of
them hooting, isn't quite the atmosphere for analyzing a problem . . ."

"It's a damfool problem . . ."

"No doubt. But there it was, and twelve hundred students
thinking or acting as though it wasn't a damfool problem. So
I engaged in a dialogue, to use the current expression. And I
was right to do so, I think. I don't say I'm sure I was right.
But I'm damned if I can think of any alternative I had."

"You can say you're not going to play the bull in the bull-
pit."

"And the answer to that, as I'm sure you've already learned, is bullshit."

"And now it's my turn?"

"Put it that way if you want, John. The game we're playing, not only here but on every campus, is a curious game, but somehow it's been decided that it's the game to be played. It's called "Nothing to Hide." If anyone has a suspicion, out with it, we'll discuss it. If a study of the voting behavior of blacks is denounced as a contribution to the strategy of repression, very well, that's a significant idea, let's discuss that too. And if you won't play you're not as objective as you say you are, you're not working with students but against them, in fact you're not working for a better world. In all probability, you're a CIA spy."

"You've lost me, Elliot," I said. "Which side are you on?"

"I'm the stupid man with his stupid thumb in the stupid dike. Don't ask me which side I'm on. I'm trying to keep the sea from sweeping in."

"Elliot, I'm not going to explain why I don't want to do what you're asking. Up to a point, I'm sure you know why yourself. And beyond that point, I'm not sure that even I do. All I can say is that I would see myself as either ridiculous or loathsome. So much for that. But do you really think it's important? Are we facing a master plot? What in hell's the matter with everybody?"

"We don't face a plot, John. We face ten plots, fifty plots, perhaps, and no plot at all. We expect trouble."

"But why?"

"Because we expect trouble. Because everybody does. I can't tell you what the issues will be. Nobody knows now, and once the trouble begins no one will remember what the alleged issue was that began it. We make up our issues as we go along. And the only thing we can do when we see a potential issue is to try to nip it in the bud."

"I think I'll go back to Uruguay."

"They don't want you back."

"You do know, don't you, that practically everything you've said surprises me?"

"I told you at the beginning of this conversation," Wright said, "I surprise myself."

"Well, I'll think about it," I said. That isn't what I thought I was going to say. What I thought I was going to say was that I didn't like this shameful game—"Nothing To Hide," "Let's Be Sincere," "Pure Hearts and Penitent People"—whatever it was called. But what I said was, I'll think it over. I'd known him a long time, I liked him, and he was in a hole.

It was four o'clock, and Martha had said she would pick me up at the campus at that hour and drive me home. On the way home she asked me how my cold was, and I said that unfortunately I seemed to be over it. That led her to ask if I'd had a terrible day, to which I replied not at all, which led her, in turn, to remark that I seemed "grumpy." There are moments when I'm sorry that I was born in Indiana. Not that it hurt me, but it shows up from time to time in my sister's choice of words. Anyway, I spiritedly denied the allegation that I was grumpy. Lumpy was the word for the way I felt, lumpy. I insisted on it. We drove the rest of the way home in lumpy silence.

I pulled myself into the living room, poured a drink, and sat down to brood. Martha came in and said that a young man, Richard Waterman, the editor of the campus newspaper, *The Badger,* had called twice, and had left his number. He wanted me to call back, urgently. The number was alongside the phone. I grunted some kind of answer, as unintelligible to me as it was to her.

"Are you going to call?" Martha asked.

"No."

"Do you know what it's about?"

"I think I can guess. Don't ask me to tell you. It's incommunicable."

"You *are* being a lump."

"That's right."

So I sat there brooding, and Martha took to walking in and out of the room draped in a brood of her own. To make the air a little less thick I got up and went to the bookshelves for a book. I might as well look occupied. The book I chose was Saint Augustine's *Confessions*. I didn't plan to make a clean breast of things, but you could never tell: I might as well get advice from a master. I opened it at the passage where Augustine recounts his having stolen some pears from a neighbor's orchard when he was a boy. His agony about it made me want to climb the wall. I almost choked on my drink. Good God, pears were pears; the man couldn't tell them from diamonds. I had to give him credit though: he got a lot of mileage out of those pieces of fruit. I gathered that the story showed the sheer, unmotivated malice of sin, and that it was all part of the pattern that led to the fall of Rome. I drooped down in my chair, feeling more lumpish than ever.

It was then that the phone rang. It was the student newspaper editor, and he was a little sharp with me for not having called him back. So our conversation started on the wrong foot.

"We have this story about you and the CIA," the young man said. "Do you have a statement to make on it?" No reporter in Uruguay ever sounded as much like the disillusioned journalist as that young man. His voice cracked over the wire, challenging, unbelieving, all-facts-and-no-nonsense. The voice of the ugly truth, if ever I heard it.

"The story's true," I said. "Every word of it."

"Have you read the story?"

77

"No."

"Then how do you know every word in it is true?"

"It's got to be. It's coming out in your newspaper, isn't it?"

"Mr. Burgess, that story's nothing to joke about. It can do you a lot of harm."

"All right, it's false, every word of it." I kept trying to remember what it was that Elliot Wright had said to me, but I couldn't. I was thinking about knitting needles and pears.

"Mr. Burgess," the campus editor said, "you're not being cooperative at all."

"I'm sorry. Tell me what I should do to be cooperative."

"Well, we're running a series for the whole week on the CIA penetration of the universities. The story about you is part of that. If you want to issue a denial, we'll print it. If you don't, we'll have to draw our own conclusions."

The character was being so equal with me he was positively superior. Remembering all the while that I'd felt like an ass when I played Gary Cooper to Nevis's Eastern Dude, I proceeded to be a damn fool again. "College," I said, "exists for the purpose of teaching young men how to draw their own conclusions. Go right to it. I've no desire to indoctrinate you."

Young Lincoln Steffens wouldn't call it off. "Mr. Burgess," he said, "if you want to admit your CIA connection, we'll offer you the opportunity to explain it and present a defense. We want to give both sides of the issue if it has two sides. On the other hand, if you want to say the story's not true, we'd like you to give your views of the CIA."

"I charge ten dollars a word."

"Professor Burgess, I don't like to say this, but it's your funeral."

I tried to be sensible. "Forgive me," I said, "it's been a long and foolish day. I suppose, having been around this university for a long time, and having been attached to it, I just don't want to believe that this foolishness is really going on. So if I'm flippant about it, think of it as a defense mechanism. In any case, I have talked to President Nevis, and you can get my story from him. I've told him he can tell you."

"I've talked to him. He told me you denied the story. When I said that we wanted a full and formal denial, including your answering some questions we want to put to you, he said we should call you."

"Did he say anything else?"

"No, except that he understood our point of view, and that he wouldn't tolerate the CIA on the campus."

"I see. Well, I'm not going to be cross-examined, period."

"You sound very negative, Mr. Burgess."

"I feel very negative, Mr. Waterman." And so we hung up.

I went back and got another drink, and tried Saint Augustine again. It occurred to me that he wouldn't have felt so suffused with guilt if instead of having his mother peering over his shoulder he'd had Mr. Waterman of *The Badger*. I was staring at the bottom of my glass and wondering whether I ought to have yet another when Martha came in to tell me dinner was ready.

"What did you say to the young man from the newspaper?"

"I said that he should write his story as he wanted to."

"What story?"

"About me and the CIA."

"Oh for goodness sake, John."

"That's right, Martha. Join me in a drink before dinner."

"No thanks. And you're drinking quite a lot, if you don't mind my saying so."

"Am I?" I said. "Well, it helps keep body and soul together."

So we went in to dinner. My conversation with Mr. Waterman had got the adrenalin pumping in me again, and I felt much better. I got to reminiscing at the table, and told Martha about the trouble an American doctor, psychoanalytically oriented, had had with me at the hospital. He was pretty sure I wouldn't be able to face the world as a cripple unless I dug down deep and found out what might be crippling my spirit. His suggestion had been that since I had six months to lie around and not do anything except rehabilitative exercises, why not have an analysis on the side? I told him okay if he'd let me analyze his speech patterns: for example, when he used the phrase "psychological law," he didn't say "law," he said "lore." Or did he mean "lore"? My analysis never got off the ground. I think Martha was amused, but I'm not sure.

After dinner I went back to the living room, and decided that since the world seemed bent on not leaving me alone, I might as well find out what was going on in it. So I turned on the television to get the news. It was an informative half hour. The South Vietnamese Army, having won another victory, had withdrawn from previously held positions. An anti-war rally, scheduled for Bryant Park in New York that afternoon, had been rescheduled for another day. There had been an argument about who was to speak. At this point the camera panned in over the heads of the assembled crowd to the speakers' platform: bodies could be seen tumbling off. Then a skier came on, with a message about banks, I think, and I reflected that a skier couldn't have much to say to me, considering my condition, and I got up and mixed myself a brandy and soda.

When I came back, a man was going on about a breakthrough in the world of deodorants, so now there was a deodorant you could put in your shoes. On Sicily, Etna was erupting and a village at the base was imperiled. The television cameras were all in place, however, and if the village was engulfed, we'd see it happen. Then a personal message was delivered by a tough-looking hombre who strode about a half-mile down what appeared to be an airplane runway, look-ing me straight in the eye all the time. He was a man who was sick of beating around the bush, and he put the question to me straight: What did I want from an automobile? A means of transportation? Or a way of telling the world who I was?

It was strong stuff, so I turned the thing off and freshened my drink. My leg wasn't hurting any more, but the rest of me felt like my leg—cut off, being pulled along by main force. I reflected that in my own stupid, lumpish, unimaginative way, I was having a crisis of belief. I couldn't believe, I couldn't catch on. Everything around me was real: it had to be, no one could have made it up. It was dripping with reality. People were throbbing with emotion, wide-eyed with rage, indigna-tion, offended principles, driving themselves along with plots and ploys, issues, ultimatums. But for me it was a charade, a dumb-show, a put-on. I couldn't catch on to the feelings people were having, I couldn't have those feelings myself, I couldn't convince myself that they were really having them.

I had a problem, simple and ultimate—the existence of the external world. I was embarrassed to make this discovery about myself, but there it was. I didn't believe in ghosts, but ghosts were all around me. The images and sounds of the day floated through my mind, the comings and goings, the bright eyes and wan looks; I sensed the writhings in the dark; I heard the sighs and shudders. And I saw myself, standing at the side like a clod, unpersuaded that anything important, anything at all, was really happening. I felt like a eunuch at an orgy.

That simile did it. I shook off the morbid reflections and decided to call that Irene Howell and ask her to lunch. Then I got up and went to bed with Saint Augustine.

7

I spent the weekend getting ready for my courses, finished Saint Augustine's *Confessions,* and went on to De Quincey's *Confessions of an Opium-Eater.* I also called Irene Howell, and got her to say she'd have lunch with me on Wednesday. Feeling refreshed and in a positively affirmative mood, I went to my office early Monday morning. I hadn't got there early enough. There was a man there before me, a uniformed guard. President Nevis had asked him to be there.

I left him posted at the door, and went on in. Somebody had slipped a copy of *The Badger* over the sill. It was a jolly issue, which welcomed everybody back to the campus except the CIA. On the first page, center column, there was a story about me. Dorothy Bell was quoted at length. A student organization called Movement for Liberation demanded my ouster. Professor Sinclair, of the Sociology Department, was quoted as saying that he was deeply disturbed but not surprised: the CIA was ubiquitous. On the other hand, Professor Singer of the Department of English was quoted as saying that he wasn't surprised, the CIA was ubiquitous, but he was disturbed when it struck so close to home: he hoped that I would deny the story, and could only wonder why I hadn't. President Nevis said the story invited the deepest soul-searching from the university. As for the specific detail of my alleged involvement, he could only report that I had denied the charge, but he understood the anxiety that everybody felt. He had tried to prevail on me to make a public statement, and, like all my friends, he hoped I would. Elliot Wright was also quoted, but more briefly: he said I was a stubborn man.

In a signed story in the next column, Richard Waterman reported his conversation with me. He was accurate: he said that I was mystifyingly negative and flippant. There was also an editorial on the front page: the accusation was serious, it was bravado or frivolity to treat it as I was doing, and, in fact, my attitude toward the accusation presented as serious a problem as the accusation itself. The individual had an obligation to answer questions the community put to him. My attitude was part of the pattern of irresponsible individualism and moral irrelevance that had already produced the grave troubles from which the university and the society were suffering. The taste of pears came into my mouth.

The telephone rang. I thought it would be Nevis to explain the watchman at my door, but it wasn't. I didn't recognize the voice.

"Mr. Burgess? This is Otto. I've just read the story about you. I think you're tremendous."

"Otto?" I asked. "I'm not sure I . . ."

"Otto. Otto Vogel. The cat with the socks. You know."

"Oh yes, I do know. I must say I didn't expect a call like yours. Thanks."

"Why thank me? You're tremendous. I told you."

"I don't feel tremendous. I feel like a—like a cat in a doghouse."

"Yeah, that's it. It's like, you know, one man against the crowd. Socrates, James Dean, Malcolm X. Tremendous."

"Don't confuse me with the immortals. It's just a story in a campus newspaper."

"R-r-right! And that's the way you're treating it. You're fantastic. When did you say your undergraduate course was? I'm taking it."

"Did you just make up your mind?"

"Well, I was thinking about it, but this story decided me."

"It's Tuesdays and Thursdays, at ten, here in Rollins. Otto, are you sure you want to take it?"

"I'm not even sure I want to be in school. Is it a long reading list?"

"Pretty long. And when I was here before, I had a reputation as a tough grader."

"You're out of this world, Mr. Burgess. Well right, so long, I'll see you like on Thursday."

I hung up, threw *The Badger* in the wastepaper basket, and decided that the lecture I'd planned to give my first day was all wrong. I'd have a discussion: I'd ask each student to say something, and then tell him where he came from, and we'd take off from there. No, that wouldn't do. It would show Otto he could be placed, and he'd resent it. I'd resent it myself. Maybe a few historical reflections on the history of English speech . . . I was interrupted by my sentry, who stuck his head in the door and said there was a man outside, said he was a professor, name of LaRosa.

"Let him in," I said, feeling like a general in his tent.

Joe LaRosa came in, looking half-amused, half-worried. "I see you're under guard," he said.

"I don't know if he's protecting me or watching me," I said. "It's Nevis's idea."

"Have you received any threats?"

"Not that I know of. But maybe I have. Or maybe I will. People like to be prepared around here, I've noticed that."

Joe changed the subject. "John," he asked, sounding concerned in a way I'd never heard before, "are you going to make a statement?"

"I doubt it," I said.

"Don't be quixotic, John."

"Me? I'm Sancho Panza. You know that. That's my problem."

"Well, Quixote, Sancho, Puck, whoever you are, don't be stubborn."

"Stubborn? I'm not stubborn. I'm just bad-tempered."

Joe wouldn't let up. "John, you're causing trouble for yourself that you don't have to cause."

I tried to reason with him, which wasn't easy, because I hadn't really been doing much reasoning with myself. "A statement from me, Joe," I said, "will merely keep the whole thing going. I'm not going to make a mountain out of a molehill."

"But it's you who's making the mountain."

"Well, all right, have it your way. But it can't be helped. This is a mountain-building era. Snapes, over in Geology, told me about it once. I didn't realize until now that he was talking about academic politics. And anyway, you don't know what's been happening. I've got a constituency, a following. A student just called me and told me I was tremendous. He's registering for my course. A boy named Otto Vogel."

"Oh no. I know him. He's crazy."

"You mean clinically?"

"I don't know, but he's crazy. Sort of appealing, but mad. I had him in my class on the Victorians. He wrote a paper on Carlyle. Called him a bag of wind. Then he did one on Matthew Arnold; he said that 'sweetness' and 'light' were about the worst two words a man could have chosen to describe the effects of culture. Bitterness and perplexity, he thought, were much better words."

"I thought you said he was crazy."

"He is. He knows what he knows, and it's pretty good, but no one reaches him. He's a private man, wholly private, what the Greeks called an idiot. He's F crazy, or A crazy, but if he's on your side, brother, you're isolated."

"And how about you?"

"Me? I'm not crazy. Just stupid. Coming to the faculty meeting at eleven?"

I hadn't known there was one. The Humanities Division would be meeting, the agenda was the normal one for the beginning of the year, but Joe wouldn't predict what might come up. It sounded as though it was going to turn out to be a cunning form of torture, and I told Joe that I wouldn't go, I'd been to a faculty meeting. Anyway, it might cause some commotion if I came.

"I don't think, under the circumstances, that you should be absent," Joe said.

"Say I'm sick, I left my cane at the barber's, I'm in Washington checking my personnel record."

"It's quite obvious," Joe said, "that you've got to come. I'll go in with you."

So I agreed to go. But I had a busy hour before the time came to leave my office. Nevis called, his voice mellow, still hitting a constructive note, and asked me if I'd read the editorial in *The Badger*. There was some youthful overstatement in it, of course, but it had made an important point, didn't I think so? Quite a number of important points, I thought, and I asked him which one he meant. He meant the moral point: the point about an outmoded pattern of individualism, and the damage it did to the university and the society. I said that I'd been reading Saint Augustine, and I knew what Nevis meant: egoism, according to the saint, had led to the fall of Rome. But then, on the other hand, Gibbon thought that Rome fell because rational men began to take hobgoblins and the visions of frightened women seriously. What did he, President Nevis, think?

The laughter flowed through the telephone toward me like warm Pepsi Cola. "John, oh John, you do make your points, don't you? But seriously, do think about what *The Badger* says. And give them their story. I'm sure that's all that's needed to have the whole thing blow away."

"Mr. Nevis," I said, "as you know, I'm inclined to want to forget the whole thing. But if we are going to make a federal case out of it, I mean if we're going to treat it as a serious matter requiring even your attention, then why not be even-handed about it? You've had me in to talk about it: fair enough. But now why not call in this Dorothy Bell, and ask her some questions? After all, she's made a reckless statement about a member of your faculty. Isn't it reasonable that if you ask me for evidence that it's false, you also ask her for evidence that it's true?"

"I'm afraid, John," Nevis said in a tone of voice that let me know he was suppressing his sense of shock, "that such an action by me would seem very much like intimidation of a student."

I didn't say that the guard outside my door could be interpreted as intimidation of a professor. I let it go. It was my morning to be patient. So our conversation dribbled to an end. I hung up just as the guard put his head inside the door again.

I don't know if he was complaining about overwork or was just surprised that I had so many visitors, but he was beginning to sound impatient. He said that there was another man outside my door, this time by the name of Rhodes, and a professor too, so he claimed. Rhodes came in, framed in his smile, and said that now there was a double problem about the start of graduate classes in the department. It hadn't ever been quite clear that the formation of a committee to look into their grievances would be enough to keep the students from carrying out their ultimatum and boycotting classes, and now it wasn't clear that they'd even communicate with the department so long as the charges hung over my head. I tried to calm him down, but the calmer I seemed, the more frantically he smiled. He went away muttering something about the problems of being chairman when no one would be pragmatic. And then the telephone rang again, and it was Joseph Lawton, the man who'd negotiated with the students during the faculty meeting my first day back. He wanted to see me; could he come over? I said, of course.

I cleared him with my gatekeeper, and he came in looking businesslike. "Not much of a homecoming for you, is it?" he said.

"It's better than getting shot in the leg."

"Yes, I suppose that's right." He didn't laugh or even smile, and I was grateful to him. But he had a way of hanging on my words as though he wanted to let me know that each of them might bring him some ultimate piece of wisdom, and I found it a little unsettling. "Still," he went on, "it's a sticky situation. Are you really not going to make a public statement?"

"I don't think so. I think Mr. Nevis has a right to ask me about any connection with the CIA, and I've told him I don't have any. That's as far as I want to go. It's all too foolish, Lawton."

"Of course. But we're dealing with foolishness; and beneath it there's something else that isn't foolish. There are students here, faculty too, that want a reconstituted institution. They want us to start off again morally clean. You can understand that, I'm sure."

"I'm having trouble, but I'm trying."

He stopped for a moment, and seemed to be looking for words. Through his glasses his eyes smiled at me: he wanted to be helpful, his eyes were indicating, that was all he wanted to be, but I had to be willing to meet him half-way. I broke the silence.

"My own view," I said, "is that it will all blow away. People will think about something else. It's all just smoke, a silly girl's talk, a moment's excitement on a dull day."

"Perhaps. But it's one more story, one more event, that keeps this campus from being a community." He stopped, and then he put a proposition to me, his tone letting me know that he had no *arrières-pensées,* that he was only putting the proposal to me frankly: "I have an idea," he said. "If you don't want to deny it formally, publicly, in so many words—and I can understand it, there's something humiliating about doing that—then why don't we just get together a small group of people informally, faculty, some students, the *Badger* editor, a few more, and have a talk? In the course of it your story will come out, and that will be that."

"Forgive me for asking, Lawton," I said, "but has anyone—Mr. Nevis, for example—asked you to come here and propose that?" I felt embarrassed as I asked the question.

It didn't bother him at all. "Of course not," he said. "Absolutely not. And I appreciate your asking me frankly. But I'm here on my own. I just don't like to see a problem develop which can be avoided."

"Well, I'll think about it," I said. "Offhand, I don't like it at all. But I'll think about it."

"Will you?" he asked. "I do ask you to." He pinned me down. "Will you give me a call and tell me what your decision is? Sometime this week?"

I said all right once more. I was beginning to feel dangerously docile. Lawton seemed satisfied, more or less, and left, and I looked at my watch and saw that the morning had been shot. It was only twenty minutes until I'd have to leave for the faculty meeting. And then, for my sins, the damned telephone rang once more. It was Nevis again, but this time he sounded hurried.

"John," he said, "I want to talk to you, and I think I should talk to you now. Don't discommode yourself, I'll come to your office."

I told him that I had a faculty meeting to go to, but he told me that our conversation wouldn't take more than five minutes, and faculty meetings always started late anyway. His laugh at the end was more abbreviated than usual and he hung up. When he arrived, he wasn't alone. He had the campus newspaper editor with him, Richard Waterman, who turned out to be a somewhat overstuffed young man whose build didn't go with the tough, flinty voice he used on the telephone.

"Well, we're here," Nevis said, warbling like a cheerful bird in the morning. "John, it's really time this nonsense stopped. I've told Mr. Waterman that you say you're innocent, and all he wants is to hear you say that yourself."

I was tired of being massaged, I suppose. I turned to Mr. Waterman, who had his notebook ready. "I am not innocent," I said. "I am a grown man."

"You misunderstand," Mr. Waterman said.

"I do not misunderstand," I said. "And please take this down carefully. I don't want you to miss a word. I have some revelations to offer. The fact is, I have been, one might say, an aboriginal member of the CIA, for I was in the OSS, its predecessor organization. That was how I spent the war. Please tell the readers of *The Badger* that it is still my considered opinion that it was a necessary war, and that the OSS was a necessary organization. I was happy to be part of it."

"And the CIA?"

"Ah, the CIA. Well, I no doubt speak from what might be called a paternal point of view, but is it possible that it, too, has its points? I merely ask. Is it possible that men have served it out of a sense of purpose as overwhelming as that which leads you to ask whether I've been associated with it? I'll tell you something I shouldn't: some of my best friends went into the CIA right out of the OSS."

"And you?" Mr. Waterman asked.

"Me? I came to this university."

"But associated with the CIA?"

"Guess, Mr. Waterman, guess."

Nevis stood up, and he wasn't laughing. He took Mr. Waterman almost roughly by the arm, and strode out of the office, brushing past Joe LaRosa at the door, who was just entering to take me to the faculty meeting. The door slammed behind him, and it wasn't necessary for me to fill in the details for Joe to understand what had happened.

"You're a stubborn case," Joe said.

"I'm a man at peace with himself," I answered.

8

On the way to the meeting I asked Joe about Lawton. What was his interest in what was happening? Why had he intervened?

"I don't know," Joe said. "He does that. Somehow he was in the middle of all the events last spring. Between the two sides, or so he claimed. He says he likes to bring people together."

"I don't remember ever seeing him three years ago. Was he here?"

"Oh yes, but not many people knew it. You'd be astonished how many people came out of obscure corners last spring and suddenly made themselves felt. He's one of them. He seems to think he's got a function now that he didn't have before. And many people seem to agree with him. He's the official unofficial mediator, the peace-maker."

"And it works?"

LaRosa shrugged. "I'll tell you one thing it does. It makes force and threats seem kosher. And it puts the two sides on an equal basis, like two sovereign states. To me, it's a formula for perpetual war. But you're asking a pessimist. I can't judge."

My uniformed aide hadn't accompanied me to the meeting, so my entrance didn't cause much comment so far as I could judge. I walked in through a door in the front of the room and took a seat, Joe next to me, in the second row. Across the aisle Godderer shook his finger at me in mock accusation, and seemed much amused. Other than that, however, I seemed to be just one of the boys. Elliot Wright wasn't there, and Knapp chaired the meeting for him. You can't ever tell about faculty meetings. This one, as it started off, had the timeless quality I'd come to know and hate over the years. Formal motions were presented to put us in a position to start another year officially, no one said anything except "Aye," and I was beginning to nod a little when, at the point in the agenda marked "New Business," Knapp said he had a statement to make.

"As you know," he said, "the dormitories are only half-occupied during the summer. Some of the people in town, mainly on welfare, moved in and took over a number of rooms. At the risk of being challenged again about the facts," he stopped and looked around for a moment, but the room was silent, "there is little doubt that they came at the invitation of some of our students. In any case, the problem now is what to do about them. They appear not to be leaving. President Nevis hasn't wished to have a confrontation on this matter, and I hope you will agree that this is wise. We are, however, talking to their leaders. In the meantime, some of our students, for whom we'd hoped to provide space, will have to make other arrangements. They'll either live in town or double up with others in the dormitories. We'll do the best we can for them. As a purely practical matter, it's not too serious a problem. There aren't more than twenty or thirty outsiders in the dormitories." He stopped for a moment, and then said, "We think."

Tom Hilary, from the French Department, stood up and asked, "Do you mean you're not sure how many outsiders are there?"

"That's right," Knapp sighed. "We can't line them up for a head count. They come and go. The figure I gave you is a guess. It's about right." He smiled again, the smile of a man in a minor automobile accident who's been in accidents before. "I think."

"Did the administration," Hilary asked, "make any effort to remove these people during the summer?"

There was a snort from the row just behind me, and one of the younger men stood up. "Why should it have done anything like that?" he asked. "The dormitories are half empty during the summer. Why shouldn't they have been used?"

"That is a good part of your answer, Mr. Hilary," Knapp said. "We didn't think ourselves in a good position to ask these people to leave."

"But might it not have been expected," asked Hilary, "that when the fall rolled around these people, having established themselves, would be even harder to move?"

Knapp shrugged. "We had to weigh risks, values, the feelings of the people involved. I'm sure you can see that."

Hilary shrugged. "I suppose I can," he said.

Knapp recognized someone else. It was Ralph Singer. "Has the faculty been asked—will it be asked—to express its point of view about these events in the dormitories?"

"I take it," said Knapp, "that it's in the process of expressing its point of view right now."

"I move," said Singer, "that we express our sympathy with the people who have moved in, and our approval of a policy of providing them with shelter."

That started quite a discussion. Someone said that we could express approval or disapproval as individuals, but it wasn't the faculty's business to take a corporate position. Someone else said he'd agree if the question was Vietnam, but not this. Someone else stood up and tried to split the difference: could we perhaps simply take an unofficial straw vote? No, somebody else said, wouldn't it be better to have a vote on whether to have a vote? As for me, I was thinking that perhaps I should stand up and move for adjournment, but when I looked around at my colleagues I could see this would be unkind. Too many of them were waiting to get up to bat. But Knapp didn't call on any of them. He recognized a young man in the back, with boots on his feet and a Fidel Castro beard.

"Who's that?" I asked LaRosa.

"One of the three student representatives who attend faculty meetings. We started the system last spring. They don't vote, but they can take part in the debate."

". . . the contemptible spinelessness of this faculty," the young man was saying as I turned to listen to him. "Shut up with your books, you don't know what reality is. And now reality has moved into the dormitories. I move that this faculty instruct the administration to provide a minimum of a hundred rooms in the dormitories for the housing of oppressed people."

"No, no," shouted Dieter Wisniewski, "this student is not permitted to make a motion."

"I can make a motion even if I can't vote on it," the young man said.

"Let him speak," someone shouted. It wasn't necessary. Nobody, certainly not Dieter Wisniewski, was going to shut him up. "This university," he zoomed on, "has been part of a pattern of repression. It is time to pay reparations. If you don't do so willingly, the people will find a way to make you do it unwillingly. If there is inadequate housing in this town, why should students here not share the burden? We students have no desire to live separately from the poor, or better." His voice rose in volume, and it had been pretty loud from the beginning. "Is it the policy of this university to ignore injustice and oppression?" He let the question settle down over us, and sat down.

I couldn't think how to answer his question. I couldn't think: I was suffering from the sensation of having been joined by the supernatural again. I turned and looked around at the faculty to see what their reactions were. They were sitting there mesmerized, like participants in a séance. Most of the younger ones were dressed in their Russian student costumes, and half the types my age and station were wearing love beads; scattered among them were a few, like Wisniewski and old Shanley, wearing stiff collars and looking like Herbert Hoover. Next to the student who was speaking there was another, also a Cuban revolutionary. It occurred to me that Castillo had never dressed like that—he believed in disguise.

Another student—non-Cuban—stood up. He was dressed like a businessman. That obviously required me to figure out what he really was, and it didn't take long to recognize that he was the elder statesman in the room. A couple of meetings, equal to equal, with the faculty in the spring, three months to think about his experience, and he'd made it to elder statesman. What we needed, he told us, what was regrettably lacking in our deliberations, was historical perspective. He had a little pot belly, and his clasped hands rested on it as he spoke.

His words were measured: "This is not a time," he said, "for abstract statements or impetuous actions." But he didn't quite say that. For emphasis, he put a vowel between each consonant, and what he said was, "This is not a time for abasteract stataments or imapetuous akshyons."

He went on to rebuke his fellow student mildly for his overly excited utterances, though, of course, he shared his fellow student's feelings, as did all concerned individuals. He then called on the faculty to face the future with equanimity, and suggested that it need do nothing but accept the inevitable. No decision from us was necessary; history was taking charge. New forces were at work, and we should let them unfold. "Afater much refalekshyon," he said, "I hava come to the conacalusyon that the path of wisadom lies in not attempating to block the currents of change moving among us. It is perahaps too much to exapect this faculty to be acativaly perogeressive, but it can at least be passivaly perogeressive."

No one said anything when he was finished. Singer simply moved for adjournment, and we went out into the fresh air. LaRosa was silent, and so was I. The morning's music was still in our ears. I went home and had lunch, and decided to stay there.

On Tuesday, back in my office, the watchman still at my door, I had a brief, inconclusive talk with Elliot Wright. What with everything else happening, I told him, people might forget about me. *The Badger* didn't even have a story on me that day. He agreed, more or less, that it was possible, and hung up. He sounded harassed.

On Wednesday I lunched with Irene Howell at a restaurant in town. The food wasn't much good, and we didn't have as good a time as I'd hoped. The only solid thing that came out of our rather listless conversation was that she liked wine, and had a favorite wine shop on Madison Avenue in New York where she bought her wine when she could. But on the whole she seemed distracted. As for me, I was trying to sound sweet-tempered, and it didn't get across.

During the afternoon, she called me with an official communication from the president. It was a little hard for him to speak to me personally, but he hoped that I would recollect that I had some obligations to the university. She told me this without undue expression in her voice, and then proceeded to the specific point. There was a small alumni committee in New York involved in fund-raising, chaired by a man named Wilson Dowd. They were having a dinner meeting on Friday, and wondered if I could join them. Mr. Nevis would be grateful if I did.

I groaned and growled, and Irene said she was glad I accepted, Mr. Nevis would be very pleased. Also, there was an important trustee in New York, a man named Walter Izard, active in banks and foundations. He hoped I might drop in to see him in the early afternoon. I grumbled, and she said she knew I'd have an interesting day, she'd let Mr. Izard know I'd be in to see him at two-thirty. A good train to New York left at ten. It was fortunate, too, that I didn't have any classes on Friday.

"How did you know?" I asked.

"I checked before I called," she said. She was a competent woman, and I didn't like it. I'd had enough trouble during lunch trying not to notice the way her jaw curved up toward her ear.

9

On Thursday, classes began. I hadn't been doing much staring into the bottom of a whisky glass during the week, and, as she drove me to the campus, Martha seemed to be feeling pretty good about me, all things considered. The sun was out as I scratched down the path to Rollins. I noticed a few more uniformed guards around, and through the arch at one of the side entrances to the campus I thought I spotted what looked like a couple of police cars from town. At the entrance to Rollins there were pickets, Hedge and Sledge among them. They greeted me uncomfortably.

"Graduate classes in English are off," Sledge said.

"Does everybody know?" I asked. "The professors, the students?"

"The point is," said Hedge, "that we're not meeting in Rollins."

"Gentlemen, I'm a new man around here," I said. "Explain the system."

"Well, we're meeting, sort of," Hedge said. "But we're meeting in professors' houses. That makes it unofficial. The committee worked it out."

"When did I invite my graduate class to my house?" I asked. "Not that I'm arguing. I'd just like to know."

They looked more embarrassed than ever. "You don't have a graduate class," Sledge said.

"I thought I did," I said.

"Only in the catalogue. But, er, Dorothy Bell said we couldn't recognize your courses until you were cleared, if ever."

"Oh, I see," I said. "I'm here, but until full confession I'm not officially here."

"The point is," said Hedge, and I thought he might faint from embarrassment, "it would only make trouble."

"It sure would," I said. "A bunch of students cluttering up my house, and I hadn't even warned my sister Martha. Could you tell me, though, do I have an undergraduate class?"

"As far as we know," said Sledge, and he seemed happy to give me the news. I started in through the door, and then a question occurred to me, and I turned back.

"How about Professor Wisniewski?" I asked. "Is he meeting his students at his home?"

Hedge and Sledge scraped their feet in the gravel. Finally Sledge said, regretfully, "He insists he'll meet his class in Rollins."

"Well, thanks for talking to me," I said. "I hope you don't get into trouble for communicating with the enemy."

"Oh, Professor Burgess, it's not like that at all," Sledge said. He sounded as though he was calling for help, but he was a big boy now, and on his own, and I, of all people, wasn't the one who could do anything to help. So I turned and went into the building and down to my office, where my sentry was standing. He was a little happier than usual. There were more people in the building, and he had more to observe.

At ten, I went down to my classroom at the end of the corridor. There were ten or twelve undergraduates waiting for me—about a third of the registration I'd had before I left—but Otto was there, sitting in the first row, his hair around his face, his bare arms, thin and white, gleaming in the light coming through the window. He smiled at me happily when I came in. The rest of the students looked cautious and careful—the usual undergraduate look on the first day of a course, but with a little extra something added. One or two, I guessed from looking them over, had come out of curiosity about me; perhaps half the class was interested, some mildly, a few more strongly, in the oddities of English speech; the remainder were there because the course came at ten on Tuesdays and Thursdays, and gave them two points credit. It fit their schedules, so it was what they needed.

I got through the first ten minutes without trouble because I spent them taking down names, handing out reading lists, and talking about examinations and papers. Then I got down to some questions about language and speech, and ran into rougher sailing. No one in the class wanted to speculate about the origins of language, and I couldn't get them to take the bait even when I asked them to pay attention to some of the oddities of the human tongue and lips. They weren't taking any chances, and Otto in particular was holding himself back. But he seemed to feel the class slipping away from me, and came to the rescue.

"Professor Burgess," he asked, "has anybody in your field considered the possibility that speech was invented, I mean by an actual person?"

"Not to my knowledge," I said. "Anyway, who'd do a thing like that? And why?"

"Well, I don't know who," Otto said, "but I can speculate about why. He couldn't stand all the noise—like the roars and cries and bird-calls—it was too much pressure on him. He thought maybe if people tried to talk, to actually say something, they'd be quieter. But it didn't work out."

"I don't follow you," I said. It was true, I didn't.

"What I mean is, people think speech is for communicating something. That's what you've been implying. But it isn't. It's for making noises so we won't feel lonesome in the dark."

Perhaps it wasn't much to start with, but it was enough. The others in the class gradually unwound, and when the bell rang I suspect half of them were looking forward to the next meeting. Otto followed me down the hall, and into my office. "I didn't mean a word I said," he said to me.

"That's too bad," I said. "You made a kind of sense."

"It was nonsense," he said. "Nonsense. I don't know why I have to like talk all the time. It's a disease. In fact, that's what speech is in general. It's a disease."

"Do you mean what you're saying?" I asked.

A laugh broke out of him. It was like a bark, exhilarated, relieved, and yet with an undertone of worry still there. "Right," he said, "right. I don't mean what I'm saying now."

"Have you thought that perhaps you mean everything you say?"

The laugh again. "I hope not," he said. "I hope not." He turned abruptly and left the office. A moment later he put his head in. "I usually forget to say good-bye," he said, "but good-bye. I mean till Tuesday." He closed the door again; in fact, he more than closed it, he slammed it. He must have been feeling exhilarated.

LaRosa caught me as I was preparing to go out for lunch. "Join us at the Faculty Club," he said. "Some of us meet there regularly twice a week—Moses Epstein, Tom Hilary, Shanley, Knowles from the History Department, Elliot Wright when he can make it. They asked me to bring you along. If you can't make it today, then let's do it next week, but we'd like to have you. As a matter of fact, we hoped to have a sort of welcome-home party for you. Not much, I admit, but something."

It wasn't a hard invitation to accept, and I went along. Joe made for a table in the corner of the dining room. Moses, Hilary, Shanley, and Knowles were already there. I began to feel that perhaps the university was recognizable after all. The morning's class hadn't been bad, and now I was having lunch with my friends.

We made a party of it, ordering the Faculty Club's best dish, an Irish stew that was pretty good, and Moses picked up where he'd left off the evening he'd spent at my house. In our talk about student preoccupations, he said, well, basically he'd been right in maintaining that the world hadn't changed very much, but he had to admit that maybe there was a qualification.

"Only a qualification?" Shanley said sadly. "Believe me, the world's changed drastically. At the Faculty Club these days, all we talk about are the students and their preoccupations. We didn't do much of that before."

"That may be a small improvement," Knowles said. "There've been students around all these years."

"Are you going to let me go on," Moses wanted to know, "or are you going to deny yourselves enlightenment? Here's my qualification: the world's changed in one respect. In our day we raised hell outdoors—parades, demonstrations, Oxford oaths—but we didn't raise hell indoors. Indoors was sacred: it was for love, books, talk, privacy. Outdoors was for changing the world. It's like a shift in incest taboos."

"And what produced the change?" LaRosa asked.

"Why ask me?" Moses said. "I'm just a geneticist. Maybe these kids don't know about the outdoors. A change in the way the way they were brought up. That's it: too much television."

"Don't ask him any more questions," Hilary said. "He's just a geneticist,"

"You know," Knowles said, "perhaps we take it all much too seriously. A boy doesn't see why he's required to study French, and before we know it we've got a battle on our hands over the rights of man. But maybe all that's involved is a change in rhetorical style, something that's here today and gone tomorrow."

"I know a lot of students who don't like the style," Hilary said. "Why, then, the general commotion?"

"It's like fat girls in miniskirts," Knowles said. "They'd look better if they didn't wear them, they'd feel better, but they don't want to admit in public, they don't want to admit to themselves, that they don't have the right legs. So they go along. It's the same with all these ideologies and performances on the campus. When trouble comes the students who waver are told that they don't have guts, or that their wavering shows that they're on the fence, they're not really committed morally. So the style prevails and picks up momentum. That's how styles work, in clothes, ideas, politics, name it. And when the style changes, the crowd goes along with the change."

"And what makes styles change?" Hilary asked.

Knowles shrugged.

"Don't ask him," LaRosa said. "He's just a historian."

"And don't ask me," a voice said. "I'm just an administrator." It was Elliot Wright. He looked harassed. He sat down, noticed my presence, shook his head at me ruefully, and then said that despite all the help I'd been to the university administration lately, he was glad to see me back. He couldn't think why, but he was. He looked around at the Irish stew, grimaced, and ordered a cheese sandwich. When it came, he bit into it absentmindedly.

"So what's new?" Moses asked.

There was, though it's hard to believe, something new. Elliot sighed and told us about it. It seemed that there was a young soldier who'd gone AWOL and taken refuge in the Student Union in Godfrey Hall. About fifty students were sitting in the auditorium with him, and Elliot expected that once the first few days of classes were over he'd have even more company. Elliot had tried to talk to the soldier just to get a closer understanding of the situation, but the students hadn't let him.

"And now what?" Knowles asked.

Wright sighed again. "And now I don't know. We've announced that for the moment there will be no official exercises in Godfrey Auditorium. Other than that, we're not doing anything."

"And the Army?" Shanley asked. "It won't come after the boy?"

"God forbid," Wright said. "Nevis is working to prevent it. I hope he makes it."

"Leaving the boy out of it for the moment," Hilary said, "doesn't this create quite a precedent?"

"You can't leave the boy out of it," Wright said. "And we're already overloaded with embarrassing precedents. What's one more? Anyway, we're always saying the university's a sanctuary of freedom, aren't we? So now we've got a sanctuary. We're as good as our word."

"I've got a new theory," Moses said. "It's not styles, and it's not politics, and it's not human nature. If some of the people at this table won't mind my saying so, it's literary conventions. You know: the individual against the massed forces of evil; innocence, lost causes, youth, the night, the moon. The young believe in that sort of thing. Adults too, if they read the wrong books, novels for instance. And what people believe, that's what they see, and that's how they act. They fix their experiences up so that it fits their expectations."

"Maybe," Wright said, "but I know that compared to us when we were their age, these students have it rough."

Shanley looked at him almost paternally. "Come, Elliot," he said, "I was a man when you were a boy, and I seem to remember that you had a depression, a war, the McCarthy period. Most of you were poorer than our students are now. Many more of you spent years of your lives on real battle-fields."

Elliot said doggedly, "And that's why, in a way, we were better off. We had usable outlets for our feelings. What do these characters have today? A lousy, shaming war. And for the rest, what they've got around them is a lot of smiling, adjustable adult types, sopping wet with goodness, saying all the right things, and certainly never saying no to them in so many words. And nothing happens, the society drifts, the stink gets worse. I had friends who were killed in the war. All right. But those of us who survived the war had had an experience. Why do you think our students take the chances with themselves that they do? The drugs, the riots? They want an experience. The organism needs exercise. If a man doesn't have an outlet he makes one."

"And what about the people our age, on this faculty, who take it all in stride?" Hilary asked. "They're looking for outlets too?"

Elliot had turned weary. "I suppose so. Anyway, I don't have that privilege. The faculty can explain, understand, sympathize, and over a cheese sandwich I can do the same. But back in my office, I've got to say no. Not that I mind making the decisions; it's the vetos. I've got a boss: he's got one. Then there's the faculty, and the trustees, who don't know what's going on, and the press. Tell the press that you understand what's bugging the students, and they paint you a permissive educator. Tell them you're opposed to what the students are doing, and they make you sound like a troglodyte. They've got the veto too."

"It's been a hard morning, Elliot, has it?" LaRosa asked.

"Not much worse than usual," Elliot said. "I suppose seeing you all here, eating Irish stew, made me feel a little sorry for myself. I take it all back."

"Don't," said LaRosa. "Just tell us whether you're saying that nothing can be done about the sanctuary, the dormitories, all the rest."

"Well, what should we do about the sanctuary?" Wright said. "Run the boy out? We'd have a fine time living with ourselves, wouldn't we?" He shrugged. "I wish I knew what to do," he said. "The whole thing seems to have a life of its own."

Moses had the good sense to change the subject, and we got off into a discussion of eighteenth-century medical practices. "A perfectly plausible idea, leeching," Moses insisted. "The body's a hydraulic system. If you're sick, the pumps are under too much pressure. So you relieve the pressure by bleeding the invalid."

10

When I got back to Rollins it was two o'clock, and time for the graduate class I was scheduled to have, if I had a class. I decided it was my duty to show up even if nobody else did, and I made my way to the third floor. There were about a dozen students standing about in front of the classroom when I limped up to it, Dorothy Bell among them. Her knitting needles were nowhere in sight.

"There's no class in this room," a sweet young thing said to me, and I recognized Gloria God's Hawk, the orator.

"There's a class scheduled here," I said, "and it's my duty to be here to meet it." I wasn't feeling combative. Just the roulette ball on the wheel, going through its motions.

"There's no class here," the boy standing next to Gloria

said. He was broad-shouldered and angry-looking. "It's been cancelled."

"I haven't cancelled it," I said.

The group began to move in on me. I wasn't angry, and I wasn't frightened, and I didn't want to make an issue of it. I would have backed up and gone away if I could, but what with my leg I couldn't back up. I would have had to make a full turn, and I didn't think I could pull it off with dignity, so I simply stood there, and repeated, "It's my duty to go inside that room."

"Let him go in if he wants to," a voice said indifferently. It was the Bell girl, of course. "He won't have any company."

The group divided, and formed an aisle for me. I walked down it toward the classroom door. There was an amazon of a female, wearing a wool cap on her head, in the middle of the line on my left. She was grinding her teeth as I walked past her. At the end of the line a boy spoke up as I turned the knob of the door and walked in. "I don't know how you live with your conscience," he said. Somebody slammed the door closed behind me.

I waited in the room a while, and nobody did come. But I could still see the shadows of the group outside through the frosted pane on the door, and I didn't feel like walking out past them. I looked through the books I'd brought, trying to outwait them, and then I heard a sudden sound in the hall, as though something heavy had hit the floor. The shadows at the door moved away fast, and Dieter Wisniewski's voice, down at the other end of the corridor, came down to me: "I will have you arrested," he was shouting, "I will have you arrested."

I got up and opened the door. Thirty feet away, in front of a classroom, Dieter and a student were wrestling for his briefcase. The group that had been in front of my door were watching silently. And on the edge of the crowd, there were Singer and Rhodes and Godderer. They were watching silently too. Dieter was weeping with rage. With a sudden jerk he pulled the briefcase from the student's hands, and waved it around threateningly.

"I shall use this bag again," he panted. "I demand my right to enter this room."

"You've been using violence," Dorothy Bell, standing in the rear, said.

She'd pressed the right button. Dieter's eyes grew wide, he let out a brief, muffled groan, and brought his bag down in the direction of the nearest head. The boy who owned it got out of the way nimbly. "No violence," he said, shaking his finger, "no violence."

"I shall use violence," said Dieter, "I have warned everybody I shall, if I am denied my rights."

"What rights?" the Amazon said. "The right to be a fascist?"

I started to move down the hall as fast as I could to try to stop the bear-baiting. But before I got there Joe LaRosa came bounding up the stairs, and broke through the crowd to stand at Dieter's side. "Stop it," he said, "stop it."

"We've done nothing," the Amazon said. "We simply told him he couldn't have his class in this building. Then he started to use force."

Dieter started to swing out with his bag again, but LaRosa caught his arm. "Dieter, go away," he said. "Go away."

Dieter looked around, puzzled. The tears were coming down his face harder than ever. "You'd better go, Dieter," LaRosa said softly. "Donald," he said to Rhodes, standing in the rear, "lend a hand. Go along with Dieter. Take him home."

But Dieter suddenly wrenched himself loose from LaRosa's

grip, broke through the crowd, and lurched down the stairs. Some students laughed, whether in amusement or nervousness I'll never know. And Rhodes stood his ground. He didn't go after Wisniewski; he stayed and looked concerned.

LaRosa faced the crowd. "You oughtn't to use the word fascist so loosely," he said to the Amazon, almost gently.

"And when the chips are down," she said, "you go along with him. You're a good German, Professor LaRosa. You stay with the system, even when it's violent."

LaRosa sighed. "This good German," he said, "spent four years in the army being shot at by good Germans. And Professor Wisniewski was a hero of the anti-fascist resistance."

"Fascism has many forms," somebody in the middle of the crowd shouted.

LaRosa was silent for a long moment. Then he shrugged his shoulders and said, "You're a bunch of young thugs. Your motives, I know, are what are today described as idealistic. You want the war to end; so do I. You say you can't stand the lies that are fed to you every day. I don't blame you. But you're doing nothing about any of these things. You're strutting around bullying people. And you've just done great harm to one man. I think you'll regret it, not when you're standing together in this crowd, but when you're alone. I hope you will."

"And with all that's wrong, you just want business as usual?" the Amazon asked. "There are people dying. In this town, a hundred yards from this campus, they're dying."

LaRosa took a deep breath. He walked through the crowd and down the stairs. Godderer, Singer, and Rhodes still didn't move. I made my way to the elevator, and got in, and went down to the first floor and got out of the building. I hailed a taxi at an entrance to the campus, and asked him to drive me home. Perhaps because I hadn't been directly involved, and hadn't done anything, I found that I was a lot more aroused than when Castillo had come for me in the night. I sat against the leather back of the seat, and I heard myself breathing hard, and felt drops of sweat running down my back.

"What's going on around this dump now?" the taxi driver asked.

"Oh, some students picketing some classes," I muttered.

"No, I mean the cops. They're around one of the dormitories. Somebody said they found somebody pushing drugs in there, and wanted to bring him out, but the students wouldn't let them."

"Well, well, it's great to have the kids off the streets and back in school, isn't it?"

"This goddam place is breaking all records," the driver said. "Usually trouble doesn't start for a month or so, and no real trouble until the spring, when the little fuckers get hot pants. You a professor here?"

"I'm just starting," I said.

"Godspeed," he said, and let me off in front of my door.

I paid him, and went into the house, and called LaRosa's home. He wasn't there, so I called Wisniewski's. Dieter's wife answered, and she was distraught. Dieter wasn't home, and she'd known he was heading for trouble. I didn't tell her much about what had happened, but I said I suspected that LaRosa was with him. I hung up, poured myself a double Scotch, and ten minutes later tried LaRosa again. This time he was there. He'd caught up with Wisniewski, and had taken him to his house to let him cool off before he went home. LaRosa sounded very subdued. "I think he ought to go away for the year," he said, speaking in a low tone. "Far away. Work on a book. He'll never make it through the year. He's pretty far gone now."

"Is there anything I can do?" I asked.

"Yes, stay far away. All Dieter needs is to get aid and comfort from the CIA."

"Okay," I said. "And if you find a way to get Dieter a grant, get me one too. I'd like to go far away too."

"Get your own grants," LaRosa said. "After Dieter, I'm next in line. And take care. Did any students, by the way, come to your graduate class?"

"I wouldn't know. No one got through the people blocking the door. No one but me."

"It's not a bad job. They cut down your hours of labor and think that they're hurting you. Look at it that way." LaRosa hung up, and I went back and had another drink.

When Martha came home I was, I believe, drunk. I could tell because I didn't want to risk standing up, and she could tell, she said, because I looked so damnably solemn. I was beginning to tell her the story of my day, by way of explanation, when the telephone rang. Martha answered it, said with a touch of surprise, "Yes, he's here," and brought the phone over to me. I took it, put the wrong end to my ear, had some trouble straightening it out, but finally got squared away. It was the distinguished president of my distinguished institution of learning, Richard Nevis.

The call presented a kind of technical problem to him. He wasn't exactly on speaking terms with me, but, on the other hand, here he was speaking to me. So after his first tentative hello, there was what I would call an unpregnant silence. It was rather agreeable in a way, but I can stand only so much time for meditation, and I finally took the initiative.

"Good afternoon," I said, trying to sound chipper, which took an effort. "Or good evening, as the case may be. Well, it's been quite a day, hasn't it?"

It seemed to ease matters a bit. A sound that I interpreted

as his clearing an obstacle from his throat came over the phone. "Another day another problem," he said. "There'll be many more days like this. We take them in stride."

To keep him striding I said, "Did you hear that Dietrich Wisniewski was shut out of his class this afternoon, and that the situation got pretty tense?"

"No, is that so? Well, I don't hear everything. I've been rather on the move myself." Another sound came over the phone, a kind of strangled chuckle. "The fact is," he said, "that some students have occupied my office. They won't go away until the police stop besieging the dormitories."

In front of me a fly had settled on the lampshade. "And how are you, John?" Nevis asked, beginning to warm to the cause of brotherly love.

"Oh, I'm fine," I said. "Is that what you called to find out?" Nevis laughed, and the fly, which had settled on the phone, shot up into the air, hovered a moment, and settled back.

"There I go joking again," I said into the phone. "I don't know what gets into me."

"Were you joking, John?" Nevis asked.

"I guess so. Weren't you laughing?"

"Oh." I had him in full form again. His laughter tick-tocked through the wire. "No, no," he said, "I wasn't laughing because you were joking, I was just laughing."

"It's a good thing to be able to do," I said. The fly had taken off and was walking on the ceiling, and I wished I could join him. "Professors kept out of their classes, the student union a sanctuary, squatters in the dormitories, the police besieging them, maybe a little dope-pushing going on inside, and you're calling from a phone booth because they're sitting in your office. It's for laughs, you can't deny it." My friend, the fly, came back and settled on the back of my hand.

"Well, we swim along," Nevis said. I thought for a moment there was a catch in his voice, and I remembered his Adam's apple and the independent life it lived. But he went on joyously. "If you're an educator," he said, "if you believe in education, there have never been better times, more propitious circumstances, for education."

The fly on the back of my hand was beginning to worry me. His mood seemed to have changed. He was twirling his front legs busily, as though he were working a pair of knitting needles. "No doubt," I said to Nevis. Was I supposed to sit here all night, giving a hand to an insect and an ear to an educator? I wanted one of them to get to the point.

"Are you with somebody?" Nevis wanted to know.

"What?"

"Well, you just said, won't one of you get to the point?"

"Oh." I shook the fly off my hand. "It was just a manner of speaking. I was wondering, what with all you had to do, why you'd called me."

"Well, the fact is," Nevis said, "that you're going down to see some alumni and a trustee tomorrow. And I know you don't mean it, but you enjoy sounding—well, I may as well say it—just a bit negative sometimes. I was hoping you'd remember to accentuate the positive."

"Professors can't teach, students can't sleep, cops can't arrest pushers, presidents can't get into their offices: tell me what's positive."

"Classes are running, John. The institution is essentially normal. These are fringe problems."

"I'll try to be positive," I said.

"I know you will, John. We all count on you."

"Yes sir," I said. We hung up.

The fly was over at the window, trying to get out. Defeated, he limped back to my hand and licked it. "Well," I said to him, "I've had my briefing." I stood up, didn't like the way I felt, and sat down again. The fly held on fast with all four feet. How many feet does a fly have?

"Turn over," I said. "I want to count your paws."

He started to knit again.

"Go away. Out!" I said, and pointed with my free hand toward the door.

He got up and left.

I decided I ought to call Nevis back, maybe I hadn't been altogether responsive, but I remembered I didn't know where he was, he didn't have an office. He was on the loose, like the fly, like me.

11

My head was heavy the next morning, and there was unswept refuse in the gutter as I stepped out of the house to go to the station. The pages from an old newspaper were blowing down the street. A car came along the street moving in the direction of the campus, its motor sounding reluctant. The man behind the wheel had a fixed, hurt look on his face. Martha didn't say much on the way to the station, and I was just as pleased.

The train trip down wasn't too bad. I slept part of the way, and read the paper desultorily. In New York the crowds seemed to be slogging along without much spirit, but I said to myself that that was me, not them. I ate something tasteless at a restaurant near Grand Central, and took a cab down to Wall Street to see Walter Izard. His office was at a bank, where he was chairman of the board. One girl took my hat and raincoat, another led me down a carpeted corridor, a third opened the door to his office for me and led me in. Izard was waiting for me.

I couldn't tell his age. He was maybe fifty, maybe sixty, but he had that young look of people who have had servants all their lives. They don't have to worry about the details of staying alive. He must have had servants to handle his desk too. There wasn't a thing on it except one piece of paper in front of him. It was swept clean. So was his face, the hair perfectly combed back, a good healthy tan, shining cheeks, boyish eyes. He was an uncluttered man. The main lines of a problem, the long view, that was his bag: the specifics were for his assistants. He greeted me cheerfully, and I could see he was taking a long view of me too: he wasn't really aware of me, but he was aware of what I represented.

"I'm very glad to meet you, Professor Burgess," he said. "We all read a good deal about you, of course, last year, when you had your terrible adventure. And we've been hearing a little about you over the past week."

"It's a little surprising," I said. "I've been quiet as a lamb."

"Yes, I suppose that's what's made the commotion. You don't want coffee or tea, do you?" I said no, but he ordered some for himself, and we made small talk—where did I live, where were my children, what his children were up to—until one of the girls brought him his tea. "Sure you don't want some?" he said. It smelled as though it might do me some good, and I changed my mind and asked for some. He seemed pleased.

He stirred his tea, and took the paper in front of him and held it up to me. "You have had, you know, a most interesting career: Princeton; a Rhodes Scholar; an outstanding war record; a good solid list of articles, not too many but all, I'm told, of unusual competence; and two elegantly written books. And you've been active on the outside too—two educational commissions, a number of advisory positions, your work in Uruguay. You make professoring seem like a very satisfying way of life. I take it that it is?"

"It has been," I said. "Of course, my life hasn't been quite normal these past years. My wife died, as you probably know, I've been away, and now that I'm back I've got quite a lot to readjust to, beginning with being a one-legged man."

He asked me some tactful questions about my leg, and then turned to my problem. "You don't need to tell me," he said, "that you've had no contact with the CIA. If you had, I'm sure you would have said so."

I nodded, and he went on. "It's a curious world. The CIA is a government agency. It exists by virtue of a national policy. And yet one would think it were a crime to be associated with it."

"Curious as it may seem," I said, "I don't think professors should be involved with the CIA. I'm not passing judgment on whether it's a good agency or not: it's probably good in some ways and very bad in others. But the essence of the problem, so far as a teacher or scholar is concerned, is that it's secret. I don't like that."

He looked at me with interest. "You mean you approve of the concern being shown on the campus about it?"

"Yes in principle, no in concrete fact. Forgive me, but the concern seems a little excessive, a little factitious. I'm in a curious spot. I don't like professors with secrets, but I don't like witch hunts either, or having to go on public trial to prove one's innocence." I was trying to talk to him decently, but I felt a bit hypocritical as I delivered myself of these abstract reflections. They were all after the fact: I'd hardly given them a thought before I entered his office. I'd taken the line I had out of sheer cussedness, and I knew it. No, not cussedness only. I didn't want to go through the forms people were asking me to go through because I didn't want to be dragged into playing a part in a farce: I was trying to keep my lifelines to reality. But I didn't say any of that to Izard. Though the tea was easing my head and warming my stomach, I didn't feel that open with him. So I confined myself to the platitudes.

"I do understand your situation very well," he said. "But there is another side, you know. It seems to me that the young today are full of suspicion, and that they want us to communicate with them, honestly and openly, with none of the old pretences. I don't say that you have any—you obviously don't—but if you hold back when they've asked a question, a quite reasonable question, if you give them an answer, but only through another person, and don't seem to want to go into the subject fully, to join them in their concern about it, then . . ." He stopped and shrugged. His eyes were gentle and friendly, but puzzled and a little worried.

"Young people like to talk about themselves, Mr. Izard," I said, trying to keep up with him. "They stay up all night revealing themselves, or thinking they are. They don't really reveal themselves, of course, not usually. Most of the time, I think, they're trying to make the others see them as they want to be seen; in fact, they're trying to persuade themselves that they are that image of themselves that they've created. No, not created—that they're creating. They're working themselves out. And I suppose that's desirable; anyway it's unavoidable. But I'm not young people, Mr. Izard. It's not my métier to stay up all night in public confession. If you want, that's what I'm communicating to them by not playing their game. I have my secrets, my privacies, I have no desire to lose myself to a community; I pick the people to whom I talk or give the story of my life."

"Oh quite, quite," he said. I could see he wasn't on my wave-length at all. "But you're not getting my point. What they want from their professors is less reserve, more openness. They want to feel the professor's there as a person."

"Well, perhaps some professors aren't persons. And those who are, they'll be there, and I think they'll communicate that fact. But must they be twenty-year-old persons? Or characters out of a Dostoevski novel?"

"I'm afraid I'm not doing very well saying what I want to say, Mr. Burgess. Let me put it this way: it's a question of style, of the approach to the educational process. A scholar— let me be frank, a scholar like the one sitting in front of me— can think that truth is entirely a matter of what can be put into sentences, what can be argued, what you can produce evidence for in a linear mode of communication. He's likely to forget the emotional side of education, that it's a process of communication, and communication is a personal thing. I don't know, perhaps I'm groping to say something that can't be put into words, but there's a kind of truth we've been neglecting with our emphasis on the intellectual side of education. We've pushed that side too far. I think that's one of the things students are trying to tell us."

The tea was turning cold, and the stale feeling in my head was coming back, "We don't entirely neglect the emotional side of education, Mr. Izard," I said, feeling all the while how lame my reply was. "We teach Sophocles, the Bible, Shakespeare, Mozart, even Wagner and Kandinsky."

"There you are. You teach them, you talk about them. You don't enter into your students' emotions directly, you don't offer yours to the process. Education should have qualities of openness, intimacy, warmth."

I had a vision of holding my class in a sauna bath. "Mr. Izard," I said, with what struck me at the moment as admirable diffidence, "might I ask a question? Not to compare a bank to a university, but do you run your bank that way? Everybody letting his hair down all the time, undressing his soul in public?"

He looked at me sadly, guiltily. "Well, perhaps that's the trouble. Perhaps we should." I'd never seen a man look so pleased to be sad, so proud to feel guilty.

"I think I see a bit of what you mean," I said. "Professors and bank executives can be awful stuffed shirts. And they can let themselves turn cold. Obviously, we ought to do more at the university to be sure that students don't feel like IBM cards. We ought to be ready to listen to them and talk with them, and not just about course work. I recall the university before I left. It was going downhill. It was too big, the people in it were too harassed, not enough of them cared about teaching. The academic bureaucracy, the departmental lines, all that was becoming stifling." My God, I was trying to be affirmative. Nevis would have been pleased with me.

Izard nodded appreciatively, but I hadn't won him over. "That's part of it, but only a small part. You're speaking of reforms, of incremental changes. I'm talking about something much more fundamental, a tidal change, something spiritual."

"A cultural revolution?" I asked.

He shrugged. "If you want."

I thought of the man I'd read about in the paper coming down on the train. He imported dolls from Hong Kong, and when you pressed a button on their backs their bellies opened and out popped Mao's Little Red Book. The man was making himself a pile. "Well, a cultural revolution's a big theme," I said. "And the practical fact is that a university like ours is a fairly big place. It's got lots of odd types in it, a large number of them are loners, and a reasonable number of them, though they're excellent scholars, aren't people I'd want children of mine to hold hands with. They're not going to be made over, and while I'd like a university that was more open, intimate, and warm, to use your words, I don't think it can be turned into a big, sheltering, communal bed, and I don't think it should be."

He shrugged. "You're pushing it too far. I'm talking about the old principles like yours: logic, evidence, orderly statement, individual freedom, the cherishing of your privacy. And I'm saying that perhaps there are new principles to which we ought to give more attention: emotion, vision, spontaneity, a sense of belonging, a willingness to let oneself go. Maybe any large organization, a bank, a university, requires rules, as you imply. Maybe we have to live, when we're inside an institution, at some emotional distance from most of the people we meet. But perhaps in a university we can try something else, another life-style, something more human. I'm chairman of the board of a foundation, you know; and I'm on two or three other foundation boards. On all of them we've been going over the programs we've been supporting. Frankly, I've been shocked at what, in the past, I've been ready to endorse: it's all been along the scientific, the intellectual, line: the arithmetic of things, not their reality. We haven't thought about people enough."

I sat there thinking about people, about Nevis's pomposities, and Rhodes's Buddhism, and Dieter Wisniewski with his back to the wall, at no emotional distance at all from the people around him. I thought about all the people I knew, young and old, lame in one way or another, who got through life because the conventions gave them a cane to lean on. And here I was, sitting in an office at a Wall Street bank, the air-purification system humming just perceptibly in the background, and a millionaire was talking to me about the horror of institutions. I took it that his bank didn't think arithmetic was unreal; I hoped it didn't.

"Mr. Izard," I said, "this conversation is a far cry from me and the CIA, which is, I suspect, the reason you asked to see me. But I'm glad you've been talking to me as you have. I'm grateful, in fact. I'm back from Uruguay not quite two weeks, I'd been shut off in a hospital, living pretty much a hothouse existence, until three weeks ago, and all sorts of confusing things have been happening to me since. This conversation has helped me quite a bit to straighten things out. First of all, the problem about me and the CIA: I gather that the apparent issue—whether I have any obligation to respond to a malicious lie about me if I don't want to—isn't the real issue. The real issue is the philosophy of education, and maybe a whole cultural revolution. So let's turn to the philosophy of education: what's the issue there? If I follow, and I admit that I'm not really quick about such matters, the question is whether we can turn the university into a hotbed of to-getherness, a fine, large, pillowing, old-style family. Not the kind of family, of course, that ever gets in your hair, or with a grandparent who's sick that you've got to take care of. A family without obligations, not even with any clear business, except to love one another, and communicate. Well, I don't think the university can be turned into that, and I don't think it should be. And if that's what this ridiculous tempest in a teapot about the CIA is all about, well . . ." I subsided. "Well," I concluded, laughing at myself, and hoping he'd laugh with me, "I'm a slow-witted man, and I just don't follow."

He was tolerant, he was downright forgiving, but laughing with me was something else. "You've tried to put it all in logical form," he said, "and that's not what I had in mind. I was simply trying to put the problem in its emotional context. And to appeal to your instincts as a teacher. You'll think about it from that point of view, won't you?"

I said I would. I'd made a lot of promises to think about "it" over the last few days, even if I wasn't sure that there was any "it," and I felt I might as well give my promissory note to a bank. Izard changed the subject. "Other than your own personal problem, things are pretty quiet at the university, are they?"

I wondered if he'd been in touch with Nevis at all. "Well, you do know," I said, "that Mr. Nevis's office has been occupied?"

He knew. He nodded, unperturbed. "And the Student Union's been turned into a sanctuary?" I went on.

He knew that too. "I've been talking to friends in the Pentagon," he said, "suggesting they not send the military police for the boy in there. I think the situation will iron itself out on its own."

"How about the police around the dormitory, and the talk about drug-pushers in residence?"

"Oh, it's not just talk. There's at least one there, that's fairly certain. He's not one of the welfare people, in fact he's been there for a year."

"Why are the students protecting him?"

"Well, as I understand it, they view the arrival of the police at this point not as an effort to get the pusher, but as a pretext to get the welfare people out. After all, the pusher's been there a year, and they left him there."

"Could they have got him?"

"Well, there would have been a problem, undoubtedly, going into the dormitory after him. No one likes to see the police on the campus. The fact is, they're just not very good at their job. They might have picked him up when he went out to get supplies."

"But apparently the evidence is in the room where he's living, or am I guessing wrong?"

Izard shrugged. His forehead remained as golden as ever, his eyes as boyish. "It's all a bit complicated," he said. "But manageable. The important thing is to remember that we're running an educational institution, and to keep our sense of purpose clear. President Nevis is talking to the police. I think he'll work something out."

"And whether students are using hard drugs, whether the university provides a sanctuary for them to do so, that doesn't affect the purpose of an educational institution?"

"Well, it's nothing anyone approves of, of course. But I don't think authoritarian methods are the way to handle it. For one thing, they don't fit in a university. For another, they don't work. If we don't have the students with us, we're lost."

I agreed with that, but it was a pretty negative proposition to chew on. "Mr. Izard," I said, "it's not every day I talk to a trustee, and of course I'm a new boy around here in a way, so I may be talking through my hat, but I can't help but ask you a question. We talk of *the* students wanting this or not wanting that as though they were a homogeneous group. But that's not true, is it?"

"Oh, not at all. They're all kinds, obviously."

"And a certain proportion of them, maybe most of them, really don't mind going to classes, and rather enjoy studying, within limits, is that right?" He agreed, and I went on full steam. "And though they're not politically apathetic, they don't see why the university has to be a revolutionary commune; and while they don't mind knowing a professor intimately, they'd really like to be friends on a selective basis, and don't feel like cozying up indiscriminately to the whole damn faculty. Is that right too? I've been away, but I can't believe life has changed even these elementary truths."

"Perhaps you're right," said Izard, "but it's not important. You'll find that when an issue arises, the students will stand together pretty much. There'll be some who disagree, and a larger number who are apathetic, but if there's a confrontation you're facing a pretty solid mass against you. So the idea is to avoid the confrontation if you can. And the students—all right, the articulate students, the leaders—are really trying to tell us something important. I've been on committees with some of those boys; the ones I've met are wonderful without exception. They've got a lot to teach our generation."

"But mightn't we state some positions of our own, just to give thoughtful students another point of view? Just to show that we have a point of view too? I've only been back, as I've said, a couple of weeks, but the air is pretty thick on campus. If you judged by what comes to the surface, you'd think the range of opinion up there was about as diversified as at a meeting of Holy Rollers. And just about the same intellectual content. That can't be so. Don't you suspect there's some intimidation perhaps? And certainly some psychology of the mob? I don't like to think that that's happening to the university."

"Nor do I. But you're looking at things apocalyptically, Mr. Burgess. And perhaps just a bit from a middle-aged man's point of view. What's interesting on the campus is all the new ideas that are emerging. It's those ideas that we must listen to. I don't approve of the violence that sometimes accompanies them, of course, but we mustn't mistake occasional aberrations for the central issue. On the whole, what's been happening has been very healthy. Those boys and girls have shaken us up, and that's always a good thing, isn't it?"

It was just too damned air-purified in that room, so I told him about the incident with Dietrich Wisniewski that I'd witnessed. "But apparently it was the professor who was violent," Izard observed.

"Yes, that's true," I said.

"The best thing," he continued, "would be not to pay attention to what happened. It will mean less trouble for all concerned. These things blow over."

I thought that pretty much exhausted the subject so far as we were concerned, and I made a move to get up. But he had something more on his mind. He was looking at me quizzically.

"Professor Burgess," he said, "I'm going to put it to you differently. You have some principles for which I feel some sympathy . . ."

"Not principles, Mr. Izard," I said, "just reactions, gut feelings."

"Call them whatever you want. In any case, don't assume I don't have them myself. And for all I know, they may be right in the abstract. I don't quarrel with your having them. But I'll tell you what you don't have. You don't have the troops to back them up." He was keeping his voice under control, but there was a sharp edge to it. I must have said something, I thought. I've got under his skin. I liked him a lot better now that he was hitting me with something more than generalized benevolence.

"Troops?" I said, not feeling as smart as I had, "I don't follow."

"Let's just review some facts," he said, "some plain, inescapable facts. How many people on the faculty would you think share your gut feelings?"

"I don't know," I said. "I'd be surprised if it wasn't the majority. The senior people, the permanent faculty, anyway."

"I imagine you're right. But now let's look over that group. You already admit that in the senior faculty there are twenty percent, thirty percent, who are opposed to you, or sitting on the fence, or bewildered, or what have you. And now let's look at the people who agree with you. A tenth of them, perhaps, are on sabbatical leave, and another tenth on special leave. They're not around. And will you give me another twenty percent who are there in body but not in spirit? The ones who think they've got better things to do than get involved in campus haggles? For all I know, they may be right to think so, but it means they're not much use when trouble comes. If classes are called off, that's all right as far as they're concerned, they have more time to spend on their books or experiments. And if a fight starts about making educational standards easier, that's all right too. They've never cared about more than a few students, and as far as the rest are concerned, their feeling has always been to let them slide through. Anything just so long as they wouldn't be bothered by them. And once again, I don't say they're wrong. It may well be that they're using their time better, using the university's resources better, doing first-class research instead of wasting time and resources on second-class students. But you're not going to count on them for support, are you?"

"I'm not counting on anyone for support, Mr. Izard," I protested. "I'm not organizing anything. I just seem to have got my leg caught in a trap."

"And that's just it," said Izard. "You treat your problem as though it were a purely personal and individual one. But from where I sit, I've got to look at the problem as an organizational one. I have to consider your position as one on which, as you've suggested, the trustees, the university, I myself, should also act. And when I think of it that way, it doesn't recommend itself to me." He was beginning to have a hell of a good time at my expense. I had the impulse to grasp his hand and greet him as though I'd just met him, but I restrained myself: I feared that if I got his hand in mine, I might give it a sharp twist too. "From a practical point of view," he went on, digging the knife in deeper, "your position doesn't amount to much if the faculty won't support it. And we've already got pretty close to half the senior faculty who are either in disagreement with you or are absentees, physically or psychologically. And now shall we think of some of the others?"

"Let's not," I said.

"No, let's," he said. "Just a quick rundown. The people on the faculty who are just like many of the students: they don't like what the more extreme militants are doing, but when it comes to lining up on one side or the other they find that they can't line up against people who are against what they're against. They don't like the war, they don't like the situation of the blacks, they don't like police violence, and so they'd rather sit on the fence than make those people who have the same ideals they have suffer. How many of the faculty are like that, would you say, Mr. Burgess?"

"I don't know," I said. "I haven't been doing my research." I held my hands out imploringly. "Is it all right if I surrender now?"

I must have been looking at him with something that resembled affection. At any rate, that's the way he was looking at me. "No, not yet, if you don't mind," he said. "Let me just name some of the others on the faculty. The professors with children of their own who are part of the Movement. The professors who think that if they come down sharply against any students, they'll never be able to reach their own students again. And I hardly mention the great fact about almost all professors: I saw it last spring. If there's an emergency, a number of them will come forward and do what needs to be done quite admirably. But they can't wait to be released from the meetings and committees. Professors, intellectuals—on the whole they're good for one-day demonstrations. But working away at a practical problem day after day, the awful boring grind of committees, that's not for them. So they pull out, and the action flows back into the hands of the people who have a burning cause, or who just happen to like committees. And that's why you're barking up the wrong tree, Mr. Burgess. You don't have the troops, not enough of them, not enough who'll stick it out through the long cold winter."

"I can only repeat," I said, "I'm not looking for troops. Nor am I looking for support from Mr. Nevis or the trustees. I didn't ask to see you, you know, even though I'm now rather glad I came. I'm just being stubborn, I suppose."

"And making trouble for a lot of us in the process," he said. He didn't accuse me, he just stated the fact. "And when I look at where you stand, and have to decide whether to bet on you, I think about it the way I think about investing money. You don't invest money in a firm, certainly not other people's money, just because you admire what it stands for. You look at its resources."

"Mr. Izard," I said, "forgive me for asking, but if I may put a fashionable question to you, Who is the real you? The progressive educator or the banker? Rousseau or Rothschild?"

"Can't I be both?" he said. "You were getting a little superior, you know, and I wanted you to look at the problem of governing a university as I have to. But it happens that I do think we've overemphasized the cognitive side of education. If we haven't, then why is it that professors don't do better when they face political problems in their own back yard?"

I said I'd settle for another cup of tea. He poured it, I sipped it, and said to him, "I still think you're wrong, but don't ask me why. I'm an irrational professor."

He let it go at that and I got up to leave, but he asked whether he couldn't have one of his people call a taxi for me.

I said it wasn't necessary, but he shrugged me off and put in the order. While we waited he looked at me, a touch of amusement coming back to his eyes, and said that he understood I was seeing Wilson Dowd that evening.

"You'll find him not exactly in tune with the kind of thing I've been talking about," Izard said. "He's invaluable to the university, of course, and he's quite a character, but Richard Nevis and he are at opposite ends of the spectrum politically, educationally, every way. He doesn't think much of me either." He grinned cheerfully. "But perhaps you and he will hit it off. To tell you the truth, I'd rather you two didn't get together. Once he said he wanted to have you talk with his committee, however, there wasn't anything we could do." The buzzer sounded softly on his desk; the taxi was waiting. "So you're warned," he said.

He patted me on the shoulder lightly, and said good-bye. I left his office, feeling like a boy who'd just had a chastening talk with his school principal.

12

The middle-aged woman in a midi who ushered me out of Izard's office passed me on to a gal about thirty, skirt just above the knees, who led me down the corridor and passed me on to a young thing in a mini, who guided me to the street. The taxi driver was in a foul temper when I got there: he'd been waiting too long. I told him that I was glad he told me he was mad, because one thing I liked was sincerity. That made him madder, which settled me down a bit, and I asked him meekly to drive me to the hotel where I was going to spend the night. He got me there, rolling me around quite a lot, so I didn't ask him to wait. I checked in, left my bag at the desk, and limped over on foot to the Princeton Club a couple of blocks away. It was only four-thirty, but it felt a lot later to me. I needed a drink, maybe two, and a little quiet until six, when I was scheduled to meet with Dowd and his crew.

I sat over in a corner near the bar, and drank Scotch, and reflected that I hadn't done so well in Izard's office. I spent some time thinking of what I should have said to him. No troops, Mr. Izard? What do you mean, no troops? Did you ever hear of a fellow named Castillo? A friend of mine. Which leads me to the analogy you draw between banks and universities. A most unsavory analogy, I don't approve of it, and I'm ashamed of you, Mr. Izard. Mr. Izard just sat there grinning cheerfully at me and I realized I wasn't laying a glove on him. I decided I'd better look for a more promising line of thought.

So I took to brooding over the system. This goddam country, I thought, they won't even let you have a revolution. They don't get mad, they love you for it, and thank you for your advice. If you've got the troops anyway. It was maddening: you hit out at the buggers and they give you a fellowship and tell you you're a good investment. If I were twenty, I'd feel absolutely hopeless. Then a newsboy came through and I bought a paper from him. It had some news about Attorney General Mitchell, and I cheered up. I decided that maybe I was taking a one-sided view of things, the system wasn't so goddam lovable after all.

In that spirit, and with a resolution to be mellow if it killed me, I took off to meet Wilson Dowd. As I stepped out into the street, I realized that my hangover from the evening before had finally left me; thanks to dear old Princeton, it was superseded by a new glow. I decided that I'd better not trust myself to walk, I'd been walking too much anyway, and took a cab.

This time the driver was a philosopher. "You want to know why the traffic's all crapped up?" he asked me. "It's because people want it. They don't think they do, but they do. You want to know about the war? People want that too. You can't let twenty years go by and not have a war; people need excitement. They say they want peace, but they don't. You want to know about pollution? They want that too. They want the automobiles, don't they? They want the aluminum, and the chrome, and the Corfam shoes, don't they? So then they want all this piss in the air. They don't think they do, but they do. I'm telling you. And what is it you don't think you want?"

There's nothing like being mellow. I said what I didn't want was bitterness between two human beings.

He turned around to look at me. "You try to talk to some people," he said, "but they're too goddam smart to listen. They don't want to know. They'd rather be smart guys, which is being stupid, you see what I mean?"

It was ten blocks to the club where Dowd's committee was meeting, and the traffic was heavy, but it was a short and enjoyable ride. The meeting, I was told at the desk, was in a private dining room on the third floor.

Wilson Dowd, no, Bill Dowd, none of this Mr. Dowd stuff, and for god's sakes don't call me Wilson, was waiting for me, and how was I, Jack, and what was my poison, Scotch? he thought so, and I had some Scotch in my hand. The glow I was wearing as I entered broke apart into little piercing points of light that darted back and forth in front of my eyes. Hell, Bill was glad to see me. Did the leg give me much trouble? Yeah, he figured I wouldn't complain. Just the same, put your tail down in that chair, Jack, no point being brave.

So I sat down in the chair and tried to get used to being Jack. A moment or two later, two of Dowd's henchmen came in, and I judged that, like me, they had a wee drop taken on the way over. One was a tall, stout man named Stuttle, I mean Wally. The other was a tall, stout man named Biggy Butler. Their arrival gave me a chance to look at Dowd. Up to that point he'd only let me use my ears; I'd had the impression of having been caught in a tornado with a voice. He was built close to the ground, short and solid, and his head was as bald as a billiard ball.

"I can't tell you how good it is to have you here," Dowd said to me, after downing half his glass in one swallow. "It's about time we had a man up there on the faculty, one solitary, two-balled man. I'm glad you're taking a stand."

"I think you're handling it real well," Biggy Butler said. "Deny the story and then let it ride. Start talking and too much will come out, though I guess you probably know how to conduct yourself in that kind of situation."

"What was that son of a bitch Castillo like?" Wally Stuttle wanted to know. "I've certainly been anxious to meet you. I've wanted to hear what one of those terrorists is like from somebody who really knows."

"Take it easy, Wally," Dowd said. "One question at a time. Let the man have a drink. Can't you see he's wounded? I'm sure he'll tell us what he can, and what he can't tell us he won't."

The points of light were now coming together in front of my face in a bluish glow. And an uncomfortable inference was beginning to crawl up my spine. But I didn't get a chance to pursue it because at that moment the final two members of the committee arrived. The larger of the two men, tall and every-day-in-the-gymnasium trim, was named Alfred Boggs. He brought a sterner note to the proceedings. He looked angry, not at me or anybody else in particular, just on general principle. The other chap, who'd met him just outside the door, was a small man, younger than the others, and a lot frailer. He didn't look angry, but he didn't look happy

either. I judged he was the minority member of the committee. His name was Jackson Jacobson; Dowd called him Son-
Son. Each of them took a drink, and Dowd filled my glass to
the top again. I was looking over at the table longingly, thinking I'd better get something to eat, but I had the feeling it
was going to be a long wait.

"Now that we're all here," said Dowd, "let me just tell you
what the drill for the evening is, Jack. As that character,
what's his name, Nipple, Nobble, no Nevis, probably told
you, we're an alumni committee that's busy raising funds for
the place. And I don't mind telling you we've been doing a
good job. Last year our annual giving program finished
right behind Yale, and that's good. Good? It's miraculous.
But that was before the shit hit the fan in the spring. I don't
know how we're going to do this year; I'm not even sure I
care. It's going to take somebody to convince us we ought
to continue to work as hard as we have. But that's not you:
you don't have to convince us. We're on your side. We just
thought we'd have a talk, nothing formal, just give-and-take,
and you could tell us about Uruguay, we're dying to hear
about it, and then, if you cared to, we'd like to have your
views on the revolutionary situation in Latin America, and
then, I know you're only back a couple of weeks, but if you've
got any reflections about the situation on the campus and
how to deal with it, we'd like those too. To sum it up, we
just want to have a talk. We thought we'd enjoy it, and we'd
like one honest-to-god objective, hard-boiled view of what's
really going on on the campus. And don't let's be formal
about it. And also, if we ask you any questions that are out
of bounds, just say so. We'll understand, we're men of the
world."

I'd got my drink down to where it was before Dowd had
refilled it, and I decided there wasn't enough in the glass.
I held it out to him. "Refill?" I said. He couldn't have been

happier. Biggy Butler turned to me while Dowd was over at the liquor table, and said, "What I can't figure out is how this Bell girl got hold of the story."

Dowd put the glass back in my hand, and I sipped it reflectively. "I can't figure it out either," I said, "because there isn't any story."

"I told you, Biggy, you weren't going to be able to make him talk about it," Wally Stuttle said.

"You don't have to answer me if you don't want to," said Biggy Butler. "It's like Bill said. If you can't say anything, we understand. I'm just poking around to see what I can find out." He waved his glass convivially under my nose. "You can't blame me for that, Jack, can you? I'm a tax-payer."

"No, I don't blame you at all, Mr. Stutler," I said.

"Butler," he said. "Biggy."

"Biggy. I don't blame you at all, Biggy. I just wish I had something to tell you. But I'm getting the impression you think I'm a CIA man. I'm not. Can't help it, but I'm not. I swear it."

"Well, why did those terrorists pick you up?" Wally Stuttle asked.

"So far as I could figure out, they thought I was a nice guy," I said. "Be pleasanter to have around."

Dowd clapped me on the back. "Goddam, you're tough," he said approvingly.

"No, but it's a fact," I said. "If I ever talked to a CIA man in Uruguay, I was unaware of it. My job was what it was advertised to be."

"I believe him," Stuttle said. He sounded hurt.

"I don't know if I believe him or not," Dowd said. "But what the hell, I don't care. He got kidnapped by Reds, he almost lost a leg, he's come back here and taken a tough line. He's my boy."

"What are you doing about that sanctuary with the de-serter in it?" The question came at me softly, testingly. It was Boggs.

"Me? I haven't done anything."

"Why doesn't the Army send the military police in and take him out?"

"Nevis won't let them," Biggy said.

"He doesn't have to let them," Boggs said. "They can just go in."

"They'll be stepping over five hundred bodies," I said.

"Let 'em step," said Boggs.

"The press will be there, the television. It won't do the Army any good, and it's not doing so well these days anyway. And it certainly won't do the university any good. Besides they won't know how to recognize the boy in the crowd, and by the time they find him he'll be gone." That was me talking. I hadn't known that I'd thought about the whole scenario before, and there it was, coming out of me one, two, three, four. I began to think I'd better be careful and not talk too much.

Wally Stuttle was upset. "But what happens to the law?" he said.

"You see what's happening to it," I said. I felt a pulse beating at the side of my neck.

"Oh crap, let's get something to eat," Dowd said. It was like a rescuing shout to a man who'd fallen off a ship at sea. We all got up and went to the table. I speared two clams on my fork fast, and stuffed them in my mouth.

"Where do these student movements get their money from?" Biggy Butler asked. "What's your idea, Jack?"

I had two more clams in my mouth, and waved my fork at him apologetically.

"They get it where that kind of money always comes from,"

Dowd said. "Where those revolutionaries in Uruguay get it, where Castro gets it."

I'd got the clams down. "Maybe we can tap into some of that dough for the university," I said, and jammed two more clams into my mouth.

Dowd signaled the waiter, who walked around the table and put more Scotch in everybody's glass. From the end of the table, Son-Son spoke up. "Do you think the militant students on the campus are being directed from the outside, Professor Burgess?" he asked.

I'd finished the clams. "I don't know," I said. "I'm fresh back, I haven't thought about it much." Boggs looked so impatiently at me that I hurried on. "No doubt, there's a grapevine that runs between campuses. And probably there are outsiders who make it their business to fish in troubled waters. You don't have to know any secrets to know that. Some of the same people show up wherever there's a serious campus crisis. But I don't think they can create these problems by themselves. Money and agitators aren't enough to get students acting as they are now; they're already agitated, and that's that."

"But why?" Wally Stuttle asked. He sounded so perplexed that I wanted to put my hand around his shoulder and comfort him.

"Because it's an agitated world," Son-Son ventured. The words just popped out of him, and he cringed a little in his chair as Boggs stared down the table at him.

"He's our liberal," Bill Dowd said good-naturedly. "We're bi-partisan, Jack." We were eating vichyssoise.

"There are outside forces that contribute to the trouble," I said. I was trying to divert the fire from Son-Son. "The press, the television. The student movement—the movements, really, because there are a number of them—don't need couriers. The system does their work for them. Blame it on the system, I say."

"The goddam system," Dowd said. "I tell you we're going to hell."

"We're going someplace," I said, "and it sure looks like hell." That seemed to please Boggs. I could see I was working my way back into his good graces. The waiter came in with the steaks. I was feeling definitely better, beginning to get into the swing of things.

"What I don't get," said Biggy Butler, finishing his soup, "is the way these goddam kids dress."

"There's a lot of sex up there, isn't there?" The words formed in neat black and white block letters above Wally Stuttle's head.

"I don't know," I said, "I think some of the students are against it."

"Why the hell don't they just kick the troublemakers out?" That was Biggy. The letters were blinking on and off.

"They do sometimes," I said. "Not that it's easy. But you kick them out, and then there are others. It's like a super-market: you can't get to the bottom of the shelf."

"It's the goddam system." Dowd. The words were in red.

"Drugs?" That was all, just "drugs?" Over Boggs's head. In Baskerville, I think.

I nodded wisely, and filled my mouth with watercress.

"Terrible." Biggy.

"I can't figure it out." Wally.

"I agree." Son-Son.

"Something the matter with your eyes, Jack." That was Bill Dowd.

"No, why?"

"You're squinting."

"Oh. Smoke in the room maybe."

The voices came on again, loud. "Why do they let this stuff go on in the dormitories?" Dowd was saying. "I understand there's even a couple of whores, I mean real professionals, living there."

Biggy Butler said, "That's the first good thing I've heard."

"What would you do, Jack?" Dowd was looking down the table at me expectantly. I reflected that I'd work it out as I talked, and rose to the challenge.

"I'd sell the dormitories," I said. "Get rid of them."

"Say that again." It was Boggs.

I stood up to him: I didn't say it again. I took some steak into my mouth, chewed it slowly, swallowed it, and took another piece. Everybody was waiting to hear what I had to say. So was I.

"Where the hell's the Scotch?" I said, holding up my glass aggressively.

"Yeah, my God, where the hell's the Scotch?" Dowd said. "We got a two-fisted drinker here." The waiter came hurrying over, and filled my glass. I turned it in the light, admired the color, swallowed some, and felt the glow settling down on top of my head again.

"The students," I said, "want to live by their own rules. They don't want the university to be in loco parentis. And in the dormitories, the university can't enforce any rules it makes, anyway."

"They should never have given up parietals," Wally said.

I ignored the remark and went on. "All right, let's take them at their word. Let's really turn them loose on their own, and not continue to stand in for them as their protectors. Let them form cooperatives, or hire hotel managers, I don't care what, but sell the dormitories to them. Then let them set up rooming houses and get licenses from the town. If they want to do things there that you can't do anyplace else without having to deal with the police, let them work that out with the mayor's office. Keep the university out of it. Give them their independence, and the problems that go with it. They're grown up, they say. Okay, they're grown up, I say. Take them at their word."

"You're not kidding, Jack?" Dowd said. He sounded worried.

"I don't know. I don't think so."

"But that would be the end of college life," said Biggy.

I don't recall too much about what happened after that. Toward the end of the evening I remember Dowd saying to me that he didn't agree with everything I said, in fact I was softer on some matters than he'd thought I'd be. He was pretty sure there was a conspiracy, and we were looking in the wrong place for the cause of the trouble when we looked inside this country. I half remember saying that nobody was smart enough to plot the kind of trouble we were in, and Dowd's replying that those Russians and Chinese were pretty smart, and they were working together, and the fact that they put on a show of arguing only proved how smart they were. That led, I think, to a rather repetitive colloquy in which I said I thought the Russians and Chinese were as stupid as we were, and Dowd kept insisting, no, they were smarter. He seemed to think I was unpatriotic to deny the point.

But he'd made up his mind that I was the man he had to count on, so he didn't push the argument too far. Fundamentally, he said, he agreed with me: the goddam system was all wrong, or maybe the wrong people had wormed their way into positions of power in it. He didn't have to agree with me, as he said, one hundred percent. It was a free country, anyway it used to be. He was on my side, and he appreciated what I was trying to do. While I was trying to figure out what I was trying to do, Biggy and Wally chimed in and said they agreed, and Son-Son piped up and thanked me too. Boggs just kept on looking at me suspiciously, but by that time I was inured to it.

We left together. They went off in their different directions, and I stood in front of the club waiting for a cab to come by. I waited I don't know how long, time not meaning much to me at that point, and after a while a car came along and pulled to a stop at the curb in front of the door. It was Son-Son. He'd got his car out of the garage, was driving past, and had seen me waiting. He drove me back to my hotel.

"You did pretty well," he said. "I don't know how, but you did."

I wasn't feeling very steady, and I didn't say much. "I can't figure how I got involved in that committee," Son-Son said. "I guess it's my feeling for the university." I don't know why, I wasn't really feeling sad, but I felt like weeping. "When I'm with Nevis," Son-Son said, "I feel I ought to be with Dowd. When I'm with Dowd, I see Nevis's point." He sounded like a member of a small conspiratorial group talking to a comrade on a dark corner. I almost heard the whisper: Some of us survive; pass it on.

We shook hands wordlessly in front of the hotel entrance, and I got myself through the lobby and up to my room. As I struggled to get my pants off, I reflected that it was a tricky world. You don't like to be blocked on your way into a classroom, and that makes you a fascist. You feel a little queasy about policemen stepping on people, and that makes you an apostle of permissiveness. There wasn't a lot of space left for most of the human race, it seemed to me. Or was I wrong? Were the people who felt as I did all unhooked, like Wisniewski, or trapped, like Elliot Wright, or weary, like LaRosa, or furtive, frightened characters, like Son-Son, or drunks, like me?

13

I awakened the next morning feeling lots better than I'd thought I would when I'd gone to sleep. Maybe it was that I'd weighted down the Scotch with steak. Maybe it was that handclasp in the dark that Son-Son had given me. Anyway, I didn't feel great, but I didn't feel awful. I dawdled around the room, waiting to take the eleven o'clock train. Then I said to myself, No, why hurry back to madness? and decided to catch the four o'clock. In an effort to cow myself into a completely cheerful mood I put on an orange paisley tie, the broad-beamed kind, and wandered out into the street.

Saturday in downtown New York isn't bad. There's something contemplative about the streets, the air is fresher, and you can see the city. You can almost see what it might be.

I put my free hand in my pocket, and, doing my best to imi-
tate a saunter, I scraped across Madison Avenue. I remembered that Irene had mentioned a wine shop in the neighborhood, and decided to look for it. Wine, I thought, I've liked
wine very much, and I've been neglecting it. And maybe I
ought to find something to take the place of Scotch in my
life. I found the shop, brooded over the bottles in the window,
then went in.

The place was empty, and the salesman had nothing to do
but take care of me. They did ship wine, indeed they did.
We studied the catalogue together, and he followed me,
pad in hand, as I looked around the shop. I'd ordered some
Chambertins, some Bâtard-Montrachets, and taken a fling on
a Richebourg. I was pondering what next to order when the
salesman drifted away to wait on a woman who'd just come
in. While he was gone, I wandered over to the clarets, and
picked up a bottle to examine it. I suppose it may have been
the restless night I'd had; anyway, I dropped it. Fortunately
it didn't smash. It just rolled tantalizingly across the floor,
with me behind it pursuing it as best I could.

I caught up with it in a corner, and bent down to pick it
up. As I began to straighten up, I found myself looking at
a delightful pair of legs. I tried not to pause too long but
pulled myself up all the way to find myself looking down
into the face of a very pretty woman, who was laughing very
prettily at me. She was the customer who had just come in,
and I wondered how I could have failed to take full notice
of her when she'd entered. I mustn't allow wine to become
an obsession, I thought.

"Perhaps you'd better hold this bottle," I said to her. "I'm
not to be trusted with it."

She took the bottle from me, and little expectant lines
formed at the corner of her eyes as she waited for me to go

146

on. She was a lady, that was plain, but playful. "Do you know much about wine?" I pursued the subject. "Can I throw myself in your hands and get some advice?"

"I know a little," she said, "perhaps not enough." She had an accent, not French, Belgian perhaps, or Dutch. The United Nations, I thought, has done a great deal for New York.

"Hello, John," a woman's voice said behind me. I turned around. It was Irene Howell. She looked playful too. "I'm glad you took my advice," she said. "It's nice to see you here." Then I saw it dawn on her that I was otherwise occupied, and she flushed. I put my hand out quickly and took hers so she wouldn't go.

"I've been asking for help," I said. "Come and help."

"I think you shouldn't have too much help," the United Nations representative said, not at all irritably, not even very disappointedly, I'm sorry to say. She nodded companionably to Irene, and wandered off with the salesman.

"I think I interrupted an important maneuver," Irene said softly to me.

"Could be," I said. "And now I'll be a broken and rejected man unless you stay." Her legs were excellent too, I noticed. And there I was again, I also noticed, foolishly admiring her ears. "I'm ordering wine," I said, "and turning to kind faces to help me. Do stay and help."

She was willing. We spent another ten minutes in the shop, made our selections, and stepped out into the street.

"Irene," I said, "I was just beginning to get a bright idea when you came in, just about the brightest idea I've had since coming home. And you've made it brighter. Will you come to lunch with me?" And then it occurred to me that she might, after all, have plans of her own. It was my turn to flush. "I suppose you have other plans," I said. I don't know how I sounded to her, but I sounded miserable to myself.

"No," she said. "I had no other plans. Are you inviting me to lunch?"

"Yes," I said. "With me." I picked up courage again. "And if you don't come, I'm going back in that shop and throw myself at that doll."

"No, don't do that," she said. "I'll have lunch with you."

We went to a restaurant I remembered, off First Avenue. I hadn't been there in years and had forgotten about it, but Irene's presence was a stimulant. It was the right place to choose. We ate snails, and had a bottle of Pommard to go along with them. Irene, it turned out, had come to town the night before. Just to get away, she said. The air was pretty thick at the university. Besides, she didn't have an office for the moment, and Nevis was closeted with faculty or downtown with the police. He'd said she could go if she wanted. She wanted. So she was spending the weekend in New York, on her own. And what about me? she wanted to know. She'd supposed I'd be taking the night train back after dinner the evening before.

"No," I said, "taking the night train back means that Martha has to stay up for me, to drive me from the station. I thought I'd wait until this morning, and then this morning I thought I'd wait until this afternoon." The Pommard was going to her cheeks, which were turning a lovely pink. "Irene," I said, "I've suddenly discovered something about myself. I don't like Saturday trains, I like Sunday trains. So if you have a good idea on how we might spend this afternoon and this evening, if you have one-tenth of a good idea, I'll stay over tonight and go back with you tomorrow." I was going too fast again. "Unless of course you have other plans," I finished foolishly.

She took pity on me. "I'm full of plans," she said, "but as it happens, not for this weekend." She said she'd been looking at the paper, and had been thinking of going to a three o'clock matinee at a theatre near Cooper Union. A play based on Dostoevski's *The Idiot* was there. Clive Barnes had given it an enthusiastic review.

I called my hotel and asked them to keep my room for me, and called Martha too, like a good little brother, to say I'd be back the next day. Irene and I went to the play. It was a revelation to me. I discovered that, with a little effort, you can turn even Dostoevski into a bore. The fellow playing Prince Myshkin acted like an embarrassed draftee from Kansas on his first day in the Army. He kept giggling, which was meant to show his goodness, I take it, but it came across to me that he was apologizing for taking up my time. I thought that a decent gesture. The actress who played the *femme fatale* was more persuasive. There were a lot of men flapping around her threatening suicide, and I could understand how they felt. Still, I got the idea of the play. The idea was that it was a Significant Play. It had about as much shape as a fog, but beads of higher meaning glinted through it. It was like *Hellzapoppin* with a message.

You're being negative again, I said to myself, you're not letting yourself get the vibrations. I looked around at the audience and so far as I could see, they were sitting there obediently, trying to soak up the significance of it all. Out of the corner of my eye I glanced at Irene. I sensed she was sitting there trying to keep her face straight so she wouldn't spoil it for me. I fixed my own face up, tightened the muscles in the back of my neck, and looked at the stage again. I must have drifted off into a half-doze: I saw myself as Prince Myshkin, the university idiot, standing between Izard and Dowd, and trying to bring them together with my simple love. But Prince Myshkin, on the stage, fell to the floor in a shuddering fit, and the first act clanged to an end.

We both seemed to want to get out to the lobby for the intermission. "Unless Clive Barnes is subject to fits," I said, "his advice is unintelligible. I'm going to write him a letter. What has he got against Dostoevski?"

"Maybe there's more to the play than you see," Irene said.

"Maybe, but what?"

"I don't know. But maybe there's more to it than I see."

"New York is outside," I said. "Let's go outside and not come back."

"We may miss something," Irene said.

"That's my hope," I answered.

We walked out into the light of the late afternoon. I found the play hadn't done my mood any harm at all, or maybe it was the decision to walk out on it. I felt free and easy, and Irene did too. A bus came by, and not thinking much about it, we got into it. In the fifties, near the East River, we got off, and found a bench looking out over the river. We sat down and watched the freighters go by, and speculated on the lives people lived on them. A man came along selling roses, and I bought Irene one.

I proposed a short walk, and Irene asked if I should. I insisted. "Do you know, it's supposed to be a law of nature that you can't walk with both a scratch and a clump. Either you drag your bad leg behind you or you put it down stiffly from above. But me, I seem to have found a way to break that law." It was true. When I walked, I put my cane forward, dragged my leg part of the way, swiveled, swung it out and forward, and then came down on it. "There must be a better way to do this," I said to Irene. "Let's see."

She got up and coached me. I found that with a little concentration I could do lots better than I'd been doing. I could be either a scratcher or a clumper, one or the other.

I didn't have to be both. On the whole, clumping seemed better.

Around six-thirty I reminded Irene that we didn't have a plan for the evening. "Dinner and the theater," I proposed. "There's a play based on *The Idiot* . . ."

"Is there something else we'd like to see?" she asked, "and can we get in on a Saturday night?"

"I'll handle it," I said. "But first let's have dinner."

I took her to another restaurant I suddenly remembered. That woman had the same effect on me, there's no doubt about it, that *madeleine* had on Proust. The restaurant was a small one, and there weren't many people in it when we came in. We forgot to get up and go to the theater. I got to talking to Irene about my sons, and my wife, and my rather rambling life since she'd died. Irene told me something about her husband. We didn't mention the university once. After dinner, over brandy, our conversation turned to Uruguay.

"The men who kidnapped you," Irene asked, "what were they like?"

"What you'd expect," I said, "which is to say, what you wouldn't expect. Most of them were gentle in a rough sort of way. Given the rather unusual circumstances, they were decent to me. But most of them were desperate, of course. Frightened and desperate."

"Not fanatics?"

"I suppose so, one or two of them. But that doesn't catch their quality. Fanaticism in Latin America isn't what it is here. Down there it fits the scene better. It matches what people are up against—the Church, the Army, the landholders, the apathy and sickness. It takes less effort at self-persuasion to be a fanatic there than up here. So the fanatics there aren't as grim. They seem less fierce, more humorous.

151

Anyway, *my* fanatics, the ones who put me to bed every night, did. And perhaps I'm giving general reasons for their behavior when I don't have to. There was a particular reason why they were relatively decent: their leader, Castillo, was an unusual man."

"You sound as though you liked him, John."

"Oddly, I liked him very much. I would like to have met him under other circumstances. Of course, I might not have noticed him then. Maybe it was just the circumstances. Anyway, I liked him. It doesn't do much good to give reasons. He was the man he was and I was the man I was. I wanted to get out of that hole, but it wasn't bad while I was there." I described Castillo to her, and repeated some of the conversations I'd had with him. It was the first time I'd ever told anyone that much of the story.

Around eleven Irene said that it was time for me to take her home. "Shall we ask them to telephone for a taxi?" she asked.

"Haven't you heard of walking?" I said.

She looked at me doubtfully. "It's half a mile," she said.

"I need the practice," I insisted. We went out, and I walked all of six blocks with her. "That's enough for demonstration purposes," I said, and looked around for a cab. It had been a good day in New York, and it was a good night. A cab was right there, pulling up to the curb. I walked into the lobby with her at her hotel, and said I'd be over in the morning and have breakfast with her. I felt the pull toward her as I was saying good-bye, and wondered whether I ought to wait for an invitation not to go. But I decided not to press my luck. Maybe she had other plans. I turned and left, trying my new walk.

Back at my hotel, I noticed that the orange paisley tie had come a little loose, and that the button on my collar was showing. Oh, well, I thought, a man can't be any better than he is. I looked at myself in the mirror, expecting that I'd be looking rather cheerful, even foolish, and was startled to see that I looked rather grim. But I slept very well.

We had breakfast near Central Park the next morning, and afterward we went over to the park and watched the touch football games. We talked, but not much. The Sunday train left right after lunch, and we arrived home around five. I felt I'd been away for weeks. Martha told me a Mr. Lawton had called, and had said that I'd promised to call him. I'd completely forgotten about it. That woman, I reflected, had a perfectly wonderful effect on my memory. I decided just to forget about Mr. Lawton.

14

Monday noon there was a departmental meeting with the graduate students. I didn't go because it would have complicated things. LaRosa dropped in during the afternoon to tell me about it. Nothing much had happened to change the situation, he said, but the meeting had taken three hours.

"We went over the list of student complaints," LaRosa said. "Not only complaints. Their proposals for reform, their ideas, the general sources of their uneasiness. We listened, they talked. Shanley and I asked a few questions, but not many. Godderer made jokes, but nobody enjoyed them. It was a solemn occasion."

"Well, what were the suggestions?"

LaRosa sounded worn out. "Well, a major one, as I expected, was that we cut out all examinations, not only the comprehensives but the examinations in course. Cut out grades too. The whole process is demeaning. People should study without being whipped."

"They should too. But what does the faculty do with its evaluations of the students? Keep them secret, even from the student concerned?"

"Stop interrupting, John," LaRosa said. "You're just not in touch. The complaint was that they should be evaluated at all. That's professionalism, and it's wrong. It fits the individual into a niche, assigns him a role, suppresses his individuality. Now just let me go on, and maybe you'll follow. Another idea was that we break the classroom pattern: go out into the town with our students, and study the patterns of living English in the ghettos."

"Did the ghettos invite us?"

"You continue to interrupt. The question you ask didn't come up. Another proposal was that the department as a whole devote itself during the next month to a study of the internal structure of the university: we should find out where the seats of power are, as I recall the phrase, and expose them. Godderer snickered at the thought. And oh yes, I almost forgot. Your friend Dorothy Bell had a proposal: the department as such should be disbanded, and we should all form a commune. Live together, talk about English literature when we wished, and anything else we wanted to talk about when we wished. Shanley said it wasn't a practical idea, he had a wife. Miss Bell looked scornful."

"Was she knitting?"

"Yes. And there were other ideas too: when job offers for new Ph.D.'s come in, they should be assigned by lot; new professorial appointments, of course, should be made with the consent of the students; the department should conduct classes in the dormitories for the people from the town who are living there; the department should pass a resolution condemning the war. That one, of course, was easy. We did it right away."

"Has the Pentagon answered yet?"

"Not to my knowledge. But we're for the People's Treaty, if you want to know. And oh yes, I forgot: we may cut out all the foreign language requirements for the degree. We agreed to study the possibility, as Rhodes said, affirmatively."

"But why?"

LaRosa looked irritated. "You ask why. You assume there has to be a why." He shrugged wearily. "We'd been saying no, more or less, for two and a half hours straight. Somehow it seemed time to say yes. Otherwise we're entirely negative."

"It's like water on a rock. Bit by bit, the rock gives."

"I suppose we did decide something moderately important, didn't we?" LaRosa said. "I must say I hardly noticed at the time. I was too worn out." He looked up ruefully. "You know, I think it's the haggling I can't stand, more than anything else. No, it's the vulgarity, the cheapness of the ideas we have to listen to, the cheapness of having to listen to them. After a while I get to think that it doesn't make any difference what we concede. We can't ruin the education of people who are approaching their education as these students do. So let them have what they want. Not that I really mean that. But I don't know why I don't mean it."

"Was anything said about the Wisniewski incident?" I asked him.

"Yes. I brought it up. I said that he was a distinguished man, that he'd suffered a great deal, and that what people had done to him last week was cruel. And I said that even if his past had been quite different, it was still intolerable to shut a man out of his classroom and to prevent people from hearing him if they wished. I thought we couldn't go on if that sort of thing was accepted."

"What happened?"

"Well, one student said that I was just articulating platitudes, and of course everybody was for motherhood. Another
got up and gave me a little lecture: freedom of speech, he
told me—and he said that he was surprised that he had to
tell me because he was only repeating what everyone knew—
freedom of speech never included the right to cry fire in a
public hall, and that's what Professor Wisniewski was doing.
I'm afraid I was stupid and got into an argument with him."

He looked up at me, and I'd never seen him look so defeated. "I'm in terrible shape. That young man was a cretin;
there wasn't any point arguing with him. And it certainly
wasn't the occasion; no one was doing any thinking. It was a
prayer meeting, or a talk show. And yet there he was, and he
was a student, and I can't think of a student as a cretin. So I
tried to reason with him. As I say, I'm a fool; I can't remember that we're in a political situation, not an intellectual one.
Anyway, I said to him that there was no evidence, so far as
I knew, that Professor Wisniewski had shouted 'Fire' anywhere, and he told me that I was being too literal, and he
was, of course, only speaking metaphorically. Professor Wisniewski had been saying things that made the community very
mad. There was, so help me, a general buzz of approval in the
room. It was too much: I said that there were always people
who selected themselves to be protectors of the community,
spokesmen for its outraged feelings, and that they were
known as vigilantes, Ku Kluxers, Pharisees; and I said that
civil liberty existed precisely in order to protect the right to
speak and be heard of people who make 'the community'
mad. So that led another student to lecture me, thankfully
more briefly, on the realities: he said that I was living in an
ivory tower and didn't know what was going on. There was
repression all over the country: outright repression, Nixon,
Mitchell, J. Edgar Hoover; and also my kind, the liberal kind,

repressive tolerance. The question was whether, for a change, one was going to take a moral position or go on talking about sham freedoms."

"Did all the students feel that way?"

"I hope not, I suppose not, but how would I know? They didn't speak up."

"And the faculty?"

"Singer said that when people had very strong moral feelings the traditional niceties were obviously a little beside the point. Anyway, no one had prevented Wisniewski from teaching; the only issue was whether he should teach in a formal classroom or in his home. He also reminded me that it wasn't the picketers who were violent, at most they'd done a little heckling; the violence, unfortunately, came from Professor Wisniewski. Donald Rhodes, and may the devil take him, came in at that point, and said to me that I was digressing into matters of abstract principle, which wasn't very profitable, and that we'd come together to discuss more practical matters."

"Like turning a specialist in romantic poetry loose in the ghetto with a dozen students to conduct a sensitivity session."

"Now you're with it, John. You've caught the spirit of the meeting. So far as practical ideas are concerned, we covered every one there is. No, not every one. Nobody mentioned reading books."

"But anyway, except for the language requirement, nothing else was decided. That's a gain, isn't it?" I asked.

"Well, as a matter of fact, something else was decided," LaRosa said uncomfortably. "After the students left, we stayed on for a little private meeting of the senior people. It was decided that we'd ask the administration to give Wisniewski a special leave of absence. Rhodes called his wife over the weekend. She's agreed to take him away."

"Where?"

"To a sanatorium probably. And Nevis, of course, approved the proposal in advance. I understand Elliot Wright showed more hesitation but went along." He looked up at me. "And John, I have a confession to make. I didn't say a word against it. I think it's probably what has to be done. It may kill Dieter, but staying here will certainly kill him."

"Have you talked to him?"

"No. His wife's keeping him away from the phone. She's going to make the proposal as though it comes from her, and as though she worked out the arrangement with the university on her own. It's probably best."

"Yes, it's probably best. And who's next on the list to be badgered to distraction?"

"Not you, John. You've got a naturally bad temper, and it's a protection. Not me: if a man has given up hope, it's hard to reach him."

On Tuesday things seemed a little better. I arrived at my office, and the sentry, who now greeted me like an old friend, handed me a copy of *The Badger*, which he'd been holding for me. I took it inside and read it. There'd been a break in the situation at the dormitories. A group of black students had broken into the room where the pusher was holed up, and carried him, kicking, out of the building. They'd taken him across the street, where the three police cars were, and delivered him to the cops. So now there was only one police car stationed there, not three.

Nevis was quoted as saying that the event proved the wisdom of a policy of relying on students to govern their own affairs. This seemed to me to leave out a little bit of the problem: if people have to be carried out of buildings kicking, I'd rather cops did it than private citizens. But I had to agree that Nevis's policy of not forcing the issue had worked, and that he'd got the break he was playing for. One gold star for him. And certainly *The Badger*, that morning, seemed less exasperated with the state of the campus or the world. There wasn't any mention of me in the paper.

I had friends too, it turned out. Godderer worked his way past the sentry, and came into my office looking mischievous.

"Is that fellow there to keep us out or keep you in?" he wanted to know.

I shrugged. The subject was beginning to be a boring one.

"Enjoying being back?" Godderer asked. "Despite the, er, somewhat unusual circumstances?"

I shrugged some more. "I'm still deciding, I suppose," I said.

"You've been too much by yourself," Godderer said. "How about coming to my house Saturday night? Bring Martha."

I thought about it for a second. Why did I want to spend an evening with Godderer? I'd been thinking of calling Irene. But then I thought, he's trying to show I'm not isolated, and colleagues are colleagues, you can't cut yourself off from them. So I thanked him and said yes.

"Good," he said. "I'll try to keep you entertained." We chatted a bit about university affairs: Godderer seemed to think that most of what was happening was amusing. The place had been pretty dull, it wasn't any longer. The events last spring had been "lively." That was the word he used. Not that he'd played any part in them, but, as a spectator, he'd enjoyed them. The bell rang for class just as he was on the point of telling me about a Talmud class he'd attended on the lawn during the week that "free university" classes had popped up all over the campus.

My class that morning was a pleasure. Otto had a lot to do with it, but the other students, most of them, contributed too. I asked them why people who may live no farther than a hundred yards apart talk differently. They speak as their parents did, a boy named McHugh volunteered. That's right,

I said, but only part right. McHugh's eyes clouded over in disappointment. Very often, especially in America, I said, people don't speak just as their parents do. Well, of course, a girl named Elizabeth David said, just a little impatiently, they also pick up the mannerisms of the people around them. And when they grow up, I asked, do they change their speech patterns? I saw Otto, in the front row, beginning to squirm: I could tell that he was thinking that the whole dialogue was infantile. A young fellow named Grimaldi saw a chance to speak, however, and answered my question. Sometimes people change their speech patterns, he said. Then he decided he'd said too much: "I mean they change more or less, sort of," he added.

Then Otto came in. He wasn't going to wait for me to develop my point, he saw it coming, and he didn't think it was all that great.

"Are you trying to say," he asked, "that people's speech shows their regional origins, and not only that but their class origins, and not only that but the experience they've had in life, and not only that," and here he stopped and looked at me in mild accusation, "but the experience they want to have in life, the social class they want to get into, the class they want you to think they belong to?"

"Yes, that's what I'm trying to say, more or less, mostly more," I replied. "But you don't seem to agree, Mr. Vogel. Am I wrong?"

"No, I agree. Of course. I was just wondering, well, why you didn't just say it. I mean all those questions you were asking."

"Well, you know, a teacher. He doesn't want to tell students things. He wants to get the answers out of them."

Otto snorted. "Socrates. Well, all right, but it takes much longer that way."

"If I just told you what I knew, just like that," I said, rather amused at him, "this whole course might last perhaps two weeks."

"Well," said Otto, "I doubt that that's true for you. You're more modest maybe than you should be. But that's a fact about a lot of courses. And if a professor's wisdom adds up to two weeks, that's all right with me. Let him give a course for two weeks. Why insist he be a fifteen-week man? It's like socks, shoes, and bare feet. People are different."

It was an opening, and I seized it, for he was talking too much, more than he himself wanted to, and the rest of the class was becoming uneasy. "Mr. Vogel," I said, "what you say is true, but what's also true is that people talk alike, and that they make an effort to talk alike. Often a man will talk a little like a truck driver if he's with truck drivers, and he'll try to sound like a Brahmin if he's with Brahmins. People don't want to stand out, they don't want to be different, not always. Speech patterns tell you more about that than what people actually say."

"I know," said Otto, and he was way ahead of me again. "The desire to conform. It's very confusing for everybody."

"But do you think that's right?" Miss David wanted to know. "I mean that people should want to conform?"

"It's not a question of right or wrong," said Otto. "Professor Burgess is just talking about facts."

"But is it right?" Miss David persisted. She looked straight at Otto across the aisle, her blue eyes challenging. "Do *you* want to conform?" she asked.

Otto looked for an avenue of retreat, but there was no way out. "Of course I want to conform," he finally said. "Why do you think I'm dressed like this? But I like to be different too. Why do you think I'm dressed like this?"

That confused Miss David, and she didn't like to be confused. "I don't think that that makes sense," she snapped at Otto.

"That proves it's true," said Otto, standing his ground but wishing he could run away.

I broke in at that point, and plunged ahead into a lecture. The Socratic method hadn't been devised, I reflected, with Otto and Miss David in mind. I spent the rest of the hour not beating around the bush but telling the class what I knew. I must say a number of them seemed grateful. There was a happy clicking of notebook binders at the end of the hour as the class closed up shop. They finally had me where they wanted me—right down there in their notebooks, in black and white, clean and neat, and no taking back what I'd said.

After the class Otto followed me down the hall as he had after the first class. "Am I getting to be a pest?" he asked.

"Not at all. Really."

"I'm enjoying the class. At least I think so. That girl though, I don't know."

"Let's not talk about your fellow students."

"That's a good idea. They're a bunch of Huns and Huns' concubines."

"Well, let's not talk about them."

"I'm only talking about them in general, not in particular." He seemed jazzed up, alternately gay and depressed. "Mr. Burgess, how would you like to do something with me? I'd like to take you over to the sanctuary."

"The sanctuary?"

"Where the AWOL soldier is. I'd like to see your reaction."

"Do you think, in view of things that have been said about me, that I'm exactly the person to go in there?"

"Mr. Burgess," he laughed, "you don't have to take all that

seriously. Half the students don't even read *The Badger*. And the people who read it don't necessarily believe it. There are more people than me on this campus who like you. And anyway, you'll be with me, and I'm a student, so that gives you a passport."

He seemed eager about it, and I agreed. I dutifully went to my no-class in the afternoon, was greeted in silence by those outside, waited fifteen minutes for somebody to come, and then left. On the whole, it was more encouraging than not: life had settled down to a predictable routine. At four, Otto met me in front of Rollins, and we went over to Godfrey together. His excitement and talkativeness of the morning had disappeared. He seemed moody, and a little wary of me.

The auditorium at Godfrey is one of those all-purpose rooms that are built for student centers, the kind of room into which you can put chairs or horses. I use this particular example because, as we entered, the sense-datum wafted to me was that horses were there. But it was only all the bodies in the room. There must have been three or four hundred and they were all packed together up front near the stage. The windows were closed, I suppose to make anybody who wanted to enter use the door, where he could be observed. There was an air of siege about the place, though people were walking in and out as freely as they pleased.

As we walked in the people in the room were rising to their feet. They stood together and began to sing; some raised fists over their heads, and then almost everyone did. I thought at first they were singing an old psalm, and then I recognized "We Shall Overcome." I had the sense, again, of not being where in fact I was. This was a hideaway of early Christians; at the very least, it was a hideaway of early

Christians in the mind of Cecil B. DeMille. The slow, solemn, passionate singing; the men with their unshorn hair, their beards, their muddy sandals; the women with their flowing hair and long skirts, except for those whose clothes had been half torn away in struggles with Roman legionaries: it was all there, even the slave girls with the slave chains around their waists.

Otto joined in the singing, his face unusually grave. I suppose my face was grave too. The scene was overpowering. I'm embarrassed to have to say it, I was embarrassed at the time that it had that effect on me, but it did. A man would have had to turn himself into a stone to walk through that crowd on his own business. There was no other business there but the business of that crowd. If soldiers had broken in to find the runaway, they would have had to brutalize themselves, to turn all their senses off, to feel like fierce animals or to see only fierce animals in front of them, to do what they'd been ordered to do. There weren't only four hundred bodies in that room. There was a spirit there, another presence, which no one could say no to. I couldn't see it, but I could almost touch it. Even I, Sancho Panza. Not that I liked it. But that extra presence, that immanent collective ego, was there. A fact is a fact.

Otto was looking at me. "Do you feel it?" he asked.

"The spirit in the room?"

"Yes," he said eagerly, gratefully. Then he pulled back as though he wasn't sure we were understanding each other. "I'm not talking about, like, there's a good feeling in the room," he said almost pedantically. "I mean something else."

"You mean there's a Spirit in the room. Spirit. Capital S. I know what you mean. I've been feeling it myself. And if I feel it, it's there, Otto, objectively there. I'm the ultimate test."

"It's as though all the people here, by getting together," Otto said, "made another person. God, I hate words." His voice had a hoarse note in it.

"Don't try to explain it, Otto," I said. "Just enjoy it, if you can."

"Do you?" asked Otto.

"No, but I'm a sonuvabitch."

"Do you hate it?" asked Otto. "Do you hate the spirit here?"

"No, that's too strong. I don't hate it. No, that's too weak. I'm impressed, and it also gives me the shudders."

"It's a spirit that's got many sides," said Otto. "Sometimes it's full of crap."

The singing stopped, and somebody began to talk hoarsely through a microphone. I couldn't see who it was because the crowd was too thick, and I couldn't make out most of what he said because he wasn't talking to the crowd, he was talking to the Spirit, rapidly, mechanically, as in a memorized prayer. I caught only a few phrases: "life rather than death," "the liberation of all of us, the poor, the young, the black," "the butchers in the Pentagon and Prindle." Nevis inhabited Prindle, when they let him.

"You see what I mean about the crap?" Otto said.

"You were singing before," I said to Otto. "Why, if you don't like the slogans?"

"Singing is one thing," Otto said, "talking's another. And he's talking in like English. Hebrew or Latin, that'd be different."

"Otto, don't tell me you're a traditionalist."

"I'm not telling you I'm anything," Otto said, and his voice made me turn and look down at him. He was talking with a passion that surprised me. "I'm not anything," he repeated. "That's what I am. A not anything."

I smelled something sweetish in the air, and Otto noticed.

"Grass," he said.

The speech-maker stopped and music began. Hard rock. One of the slave girls began to move to the rhythm, and two of the men rose and squirmed in time with her. Around the room dancing began, the people dancing to themselves, enclosed within themselves, no one touching anyone else, everyone alone with that common Presence that was there. And the music, impossibly, grew louder. I felt as though someone had inserted a trip-hammer in my head, and turned it on.

"Saint Paul," Otto said to me, and then I couldn't hear the rest.

"What?" I shouted to him.

"Saint Paul," he bawled. "I said Saint Paul."

"All right, Saint Paul. What about him?"

"Let's get out of here," Otto shouted.

We went outdoors and a great silence seemed to descend on us. Otto was almost gibbering with impatience to talk. "Saint Paul," he shouted, "didn't Saint Paul . . ." And then he realized he didn't have to shout, and he brought his voice down. "Didn't Saint Paul write some early Christians and tell them it was wrong to think they could sin just because the Kingdom of Heaven was at hand and the world was at its end? And didn't he say that maybe the Kingdom wasn't so imminent?"

"Something like that."

"They've got this world and the next mixed up," Otto said. "Those types in there. They don't know where they are."

"I thought you would have some sympathy with them, Otto."

"I do." His voice was strident, and he heard it himself and tried to control it. "Mr. Burgess," he asked, "what did you think?"

"I don't know that it much matters," I said. "I'm an old

man, a native unbelieving type. That scene in there, it's not for me." I shrugged. "But I can't pass judgment on it."

Otto took his dark glasses off. His eyes were wide with anger. "Why not?" he shouted. "Why can't you pass judgment?"

"Easy, Otto," I said. I took his arm and turned and started down the path with him, hoping he'd calm down. He came along, almost hopping in rage. "Otto," I said, "that happening in there, it all began with the right idea, didn't it? The war's abominable, there's a boy who's been caught up in it, they want to help him."

"Do you know where that boy was in the room?" Otto cried. "Did you even think about him? Was anybody thinking about him? Do you know what they're doing to him? They're hardly aware he's there. They're using him so they can dance all night."

"Well, all right, Otto," I said, "if that's the way you see it. What do you want me to do?"

"I want you to judge it," said Otto. "I don't want you to say, Well, that's their style, and you've got another, and everyone to his taste. Why do you play at being objective? You're not. You're you."

I stopped and sat down on a bench along the path. He stood over me looking down at me.

"And do you have a judgment?" I asked him.

"I have four, five, six judgments about it. I think it's out of this world, I think it's diabolical. I feel that spirit, I want it, and I hate it. I told you: I'm a not anything."

"And you want me to make you a something?"

"No," said Otto. He sat down next to me. His voice changed. "No," he said, "I'm not that foolish. I don't want anything from you, I suppose."

"I'm sorry, Otto," I said. "No, that's not just polite talk.

I'm sorry, apologetic, unhappy. Maybe what I saw in there was too much for me. When you're in the path of a tidal wave, perhaps you start to look for something good in it. Don't ask me to be too specific, but I don't think that many of the people who were in that room are ever going to believe that a new diet soft drink is the greatest achievement in the history of civilization."

"No, they think it's the electric guitar," Otto said. "They say they're for peace and wear military boots. They say they're for gentleness and give you all that *machismo*. And then they talk about sincerity. What's got into you, Professor Burgess? I didn't think you were going to be tolerant." He sounded miserable.

I felt miserable myself. "About passing judgment, Otto," I said, "let me explain. I'm a middle-aged man, and I don't like the feeling that nothing that's happening is for me. The world's rolling past me. Maybe it's the instinct for survival, and I'm only trying to hang on, but I tell myself that if I'm not catching the vibrations around me, perhaps the fault's with me."

"It's got nothing to do with being middle-aged," said Otto. "I'm trying to hang on too. Why do you think I dress the way I do?" He began to smile, the same smile he'd shown me the first day we met. "Also, if we're going to hell, these are good going-to-hell clothes. And wow, do they make my father mad." His face lit up with pleasure. "It's the way you make *The Badger* mad by refusing to talk."

"That's not my object, Otto," I said reproachfully.

"Oh yes it is," he said. "One thing you're not is universal love." He got up. "So don't be so middle-aged tolerant. It doesn't fit you. Bye-bye." He wandered off down the path.

I had dinner with Irene that evening, at a diner downtown. It was better than the chi-chi restaurant we'd tried the week before—the food, the service, the decor, everything. As I dug into my french fries I told her about the sanctuary and my conversation with Otto.

"What I didn't see then but I see now," I said, "is that those kids in the room weren't doing what they were doing as a means to an end. It wasn't part of a struggle against the war, and it wasn't a preparation for a liberated world. It *was* that world, right here and now. It's all very foolish perhaps, but it made me not want to come down on them hard. I should have said that to Otto."

"No, you did much better," Irene said. "You said the world was pushing you off the edge, and he said the same thing himself. You avoided all the nonsense about a generation gap."

"Is it nonsense, do you think?"

"The important difference," said Irene, "is the one between the men and the boys, and that's not got much to do with the generations."

"Do you know," I said, "we didn't talk about this kind of thing at all over the weekend."

"It was a lovely weekend, wasn't it?" Irene said.

15

Wednesday dawned cold and gray, and when I got to my office I discovered there'd been some happenings overnight. LaRosa came in to tell me about them. The pusher who'd been delivered to the police by the black students had done a lot of talking, and it turned out that there were two more pushers in the dormitories, and two prostitutes from town whom the police knew rather well. Nobody was sure whether the chief of police had talked to Nevis or not; the bets were he probably hadn't. The cops had gone into the dormitories at midnight, found one of the pushers and both of the girls and pulled them out. There'd been a certain amount of commotion. Eight students had been arrested for obstructing the police, and three of the welfare people had got mixed up in the action, which led to their being arrested too. And, oh yes: in the boy's wing of the dormitory—it's hard to know which is which, of course, said LaRosa—they'd found one little number entertaining a group of boys, and decided she was a whore they hadn't been told about. So they'd taken her in too, but she turned out to be a student who'd graduated last year. She'd just neglected to leave.

"All in all," said LaRosa, "quite a night, and quite a bag."

"And now what's happening?"

"Elliot Wright, I understand, is down at the jail trying to get the students out. He'll probably succeed. There are pro-test meetings in the dormitories. Nevis is over at one of them. And there are a dozen police cars on guard just off the cam-pus."

"What got into the cops?" I asked.

"Force of habit, I suppose," LaRosa shrugged. "They knew where the pusher was, they wanted to get him. And they don't like the whores operating on protected ground. It's not playing the game. So the cops did what comes naturally, and went in. Also, I suppose their patience was wearing out. They get called names from the dormitory windows all day and all night."

"It rather upsets Nevis's plan, doesn't it?"

"We'll see. He has a way of coming out of these things in one piece."

My guardian opened the door and passed in *The Badger*, which had just been delivered. It was late that morning. It carried a description of the night's events, and a couple of pictures featuring nightsticks. The editorial said that the police action was the opening of a planned action to break the peace movement. It took Nevis to task for having spent so much time during the week talking with the police. Either he had consented to the police action, the paper said, or he'd allowed himself to be fooled. A man his age, who had lived through Munich, ought to know better than to try to do business with fascists.

Still, the campus seemed quiet. LaRosa and I looked out the window and saw half a dozen students on the lawn tossing Frisbees back and forth. I spent most of the morning putting a preliminary bibliography together for a paper I wanted to write, and, after lunch, went to the library to continue the job. When I got home that evening, I felt almost like a professor again. After dinner, I was back at work at my desk when LaRosa called to bring me up to date. The students were out of jail, all but two of them—a boy accused of having hit one cop with a chair and a girl they said had kneed another in the groin. Elliot Wright, apparently, had thought they should be handled in the normal way—bail, lawyers, the whole bit. Those two were still in the jug, and Nevis, according to the rumors, was upset with Wright. I gave up working and went to bed.

Some time during the night the telephone rang, and I reached out in my sleep, grabbed the thing, and answered in the dark. A woman's voice was at the other end.

"Mr. Burgess?" she asked.

"Yes."

"We don't want you around. We don't want you around at all."

I was still half asleep. "Around where?" I asked.

"You don't belong here," the voice said. "Not with your associations. Not after what you've done."

"Who is this?" I asked, much more awake.

"A member of this university. Someone who only wants the right to live." Then she hung up.

Martha had heard the phone ring and came in to ask who had called. When I told her, it shook her badly, much worse than I would have expected. But anonymous phone calls in the middle of the night weren't part of her usual routine. We spent an hour in the kitchen together drinking tea before she was ready to go back to bed.

At breakfast the phone rang again. This time it was a man. The message was the same, but he delivered it more enthusiastically. He had a foul mouth, and I hung up feeling angry and dirty. His last words were that there'd be more calls like his. I called the telephone company and told them to give me a new number, unlisted. They said they'd get to it later in the day. I left the phone off the hook, and suggested to Martha, as she was driving me to the campus, that she stay away from the house. She dropped me at the campus and drove away. I could tell from the angle at which she was holding her head that she wasn't sure just where she ought to be going.

Crossing the campus, I felt a kind of heaviness in the air, but tried to tell myself it was only the telephone calls I'd received. In front of Godfrey a satchel of students were standing, locked in what seemed like a debate; from the sanctuary came the sounds of hard rock. Through one of the arches I saw the police cars. A sheet was strung between two windows on the campus side of a dormitory, and on it was painted the words, "Off the pig!" When I arrived at Rollins the pickets were still there. Everything quite normal, I said to myself; everyone in his place, and a place for everyone: the perfect university, everyone occupied, everyone doing his thing. But the atmosphere had something new in it. There was a kind of brooding hush in the air. I had the feeling that people were watching from windows. It wasn't true, I suppose, but the feeling was there.

I went past the pickets and down the corridor to my office. I said good morning to my sentry, and went on in. There was a leaflet on the floor, which had been pushed under the door.

It solved the mystery, at any rate part of the mystery, of the telephone calls. It said: "Know your professors, and use your right of free speech to tell them what you think of them. John Burgess, Professor of English, has been a CIA spy. He refuses to divulge his present relations with this notorious death-dealing agency. Telephone him and tell him he has no place in this community." My number was at the bottom of the sheet. The only name on it was mine, but running across the top was the heading "Committee for an Unpolluted University."

I sat down at my desk, and I think I was half amused, but decided that I ought to inform Nevis. I called his office, but got only a crackling sound in the phone. Then I remembered that, of course, he wasn't in his office, which was occupied by students, and the telephone had probably been cut off. I got the central board at the university, and asked how to reach the president. They put me through, and, a bit to my surprise, found Nevis himself.

"Yes, yes," he said, after I told him my story, "it was inevitable. It would all have been so much simpler if you'd made a statement."

"Well, maybe so, maybe not," I said, "but what does the university propose to do about it?"

"What can we do about it?" he said. "For that matter, what should we do about it?" He wasn't being young, affirmative, and charming that morning, not at all.

"I suppose you could try to find out who's doing it. Or you, or I, could call the police."

"The police. That's a remarkable thought." He was in such a bad mood that I was beginning to think more kindly of him. "I don't think the police can do anything but make matters worse," he said.

"In short, you're telling me I have to put up with anonymous telephone calls in the night."

"No," he said, "you don't have to. You can make a statement." He hung up, and I found myself grinning. If the man hated you enough, he was agreeably honest. Downright caustic. Still, it didn't solve my problem.

It certainly didn't. The phone rang and it was another caller with a dirty mouth. He was also a thinking man's dirty mouth. He suggested to me that if I cut off my phones, the community would find other ways of getting its message to me. After all, my sister went out shopping, didn't she?

I didn't reply, there wasn't any point; I simply put the phone back on the hook. I was worried about Martha, and wished I knew where she was. The phone rang again a moment or so later, I picked it up hesitantly, and it was Martha. She'd recognized I'd be wondering where she was, and had phoned to tell me. She hadn't liked floating around making up errands, and had gone home.

"I think you ought to go down to New York and spend the weekend there," I said.

"And leave you here alone?" She was dubious.

"I'll get Joe LaRosa to invite me to spend the next few nights at his house."

"John, I don't know what all this means, but I don't like it."

"It's disagreeable, that's all," I said, "and I don't see why you have to be exposed to it." It took a little work, but in the end she agreed to take the late morning train to New York. If nothing happened to change our plans, she'd be back Monday.

"Give my apologies to Godderer for my missing the party," Martha said. "And for goodness sakes, John, don't make a joke out of all this. Be careful."

I hunched down the corridor to LaRosa's office, and asked him to invite me to stay with him. He said, Of course, and looked curious, and I told him why, trying to make as minor a matter of it as I could. Joe looked angry and then thoughtful.

"I'll call Ruth," he said. "We'd been thinking of going up to the lake, to our cabin, for the weekend. But we'll stay with you."

"If you do that," I said to him, "I won't come. It's Thursday. I'll move in this evening, we'll have dinner together, and tomorrow evening you two can go off as planned. Nobody'll know where I am. I can spend the weekend at your house alone. In fact, it'll be pleasanter without you. I was hoping you'd have plans to be away." He argued a bit more, but he gave in, and I went back down to my office and saw it was time for my class.

The attendance was down, but Otto was there. He'd done something to his hair, not quite combed it, but moved it off his face. And he was wearing shoes. It was a morning when nobody was very focused, and we stumbled through the hour. Otto walked down the corridor with me toward my office.

"Shoes?" I asked, pointing at his feet.

"It's the influence of your course," he said. "People have always wanted to be noticed as different. Today they do it with clothes, but clothes offer limited alternatives. They fall into patterns, and it's not very creative. It takes more wit to work up a style of speech. If you're going to be affected, do it with your accent."

"Are you working on one, Otto? What kind?"

"I'm reflecting," he said. "Black is out: it's pathetic when whites try to talk that way. Finnish, maybe. Yes, Finnish."

"Otto, you're pulling a one-legged man's leg," I said.

He reflected on it. "Yeah, maybe I am. And my own. I don't know." He smiled at me. If he'd been irritated with me, he'd forgiven me. "Ta ta, Professor Burgess," he said, and turned and left.

I walked past the guard and into my office, and tried to reach LaRosa on the phone. The phone didn't work. I was about to get up and go down to the departmental secretary's office to report it when I noticed a slip of paper on my desk.

It was from the departmental secretary. On advice from President Nevis, she said, my telephone had been cut off for my protection. I sat there, and the feeling was exactly like the feeling of being kidnapped: I was shut in a room, cut off from communication, a guard outside my door, and forces beyond my control were deciding whether I'd ever get out. I yearned for Castillo. If you're going to be kidnapped, you need a man who gives the impression that he knows what he's doing.

I was aroused from these reflections by loud noises at my door. Some sort of meeting seemed to be going on. And then I heard my name being repeated. The man who was doing the talking was putting on the manner of a tour guide. He was showing people the various landmarks on the campus, and one of them was me. There was no question at all, he was saying, that I had organized an institute for teaching English in Uruguay. That, at least, was uncontested public knowledge; I admitted it myself. And so I admitted that I'd been an agent of an expansionist American foreign policy. But now the question was, What more had I done? And I wouldn't say. Here, ladies and gentlemen, the speaker said, is an office full of secrets. It's classified. It's not for you and me, the people, the citizens, to know what's going on in there. We must pass it by, knowing only that some things in this university are not our business."

"Why not?" someone shouted.

"Let's go in," someone else said.

"No, no," the speaker said, "secrets are secrets. And government secrets are sacred. Nixon, Kissinger, Mitchell, LBJ, Dean Rusk, they all say so. What more need I say?"

"I think we should go in," an older voice said. His tone was different—quiet, reasonable, placating.

"You can't go in." That was my sentry.

The door opened and they came in, sweeping my man in

with them. There were about a dozen of them, males and females. No one seemed very threatening. They were laughing. It was a lark. From the center of the group a man came forward, gray-haired, fiftyish, wearing a white laboratory smock over an open-collared shirt. He was smiling in as friendly a fashion as anyone could want, but he was serious. I could tell that.

"Professor Burgess, how do you do?" he said.

"Who the hell are you?" I said.

He looked hurt, and looked around at the others to share his hurt.

"Now, now," he said, "we come as neighbors. We simply want to remove the distrust and suspicion that are in the air."

"I said," I repeated, "who the hell are you?"

"No," the man said, "the question that brings us here is, Who the hell are *you?*"

There were titters, and a cry of "Right on." My man smiled more happily than ever.

"I would suggest you all get out," a voice said. It was La-Rosa. He had entered the room and was standing in the rear. Singer was standing next to him. "This is atrocious," LaRosa said. "Not funny at all. Go out and play with Frisbees."

The man in the laboratory smock turned red with anger. "We have the right to ask questions," he said. "Or do you deny even that?"

"Professor Inkelmann," said LaRosa, "I'm almost embarrassed to remind you that this is not the way colleagues should behave toward one another."

"Should they keep secrets?" Inkelmann said. "Should they engage in covert activities?"

"You don't know anything about that," LaRosa said, "and it's not your business to be the investigator."

"Whom shall we leave the investigation to?" Inkelmann

asked. "The government? The clean, honest, no-secrets government?" He was vastly amused.

"What is it you want?" I asked.

"We want to look through your files," Inkelmann said. "We
intend to."

"You do that," I said, "and I'll prefer charges against you."

It must have been very funny. General hilarity broke loose.
Inkelmann had come into my office in such a good mood that
it was difficult to think it could have been any better, but I
was certainly improving it. He beamed at me, and went to the
files.

"Now wait a minute," my sentry said, despair in his voice.

More cheerful sounds, more general amusement. Inkelmann
opened the files and began to look through them. There wasn't
anything I could do at the moment but let him. He took fifteen
minutes, the crowd around him going through my letters and
notes. Somebody said at one point, looking over a letter of
recommendation I'd sent, "That's a lousy letter to have written
about a student." But there weren't any other comments.

Inkelmann turned to me when he'd finished, and said, "These
files are all four years old, and all purely academic."

"I apologize," I said. "I haven't moved my more recent files
in here yet. They're the ones with the letters in code."

LaRosa had worked his way forward to stand next to me.
Singer was still in the back of the room, looking on silently.
LaRosa said, "Inkelmann, I'm going to request a faculty committee be formed to examine your conduct. You ought to be
kicked out."

"The CIA belongs, and those who protest don't, is that it?"
said Inkelmann.

"He could have given the files to LaRosa," a young man in
an old army jacket said.

"Let's look at his files," another boy, with blond hair to his shoulders, his blue eyes incongruously fierce, said.

The group turned and ran down the hall to LaRosa's office. Singer went with them. LaRosa and I waited in my office in silence. After ten minutes or so we heard them leave, and Singer came back.

"I'm afraid they left your papers around the room," he said to LaRosa.

Neither of us said anything.

Singer didn't like the silence. "It's the kind of thing that can't be helped," he said. He looked at me. "You've invited it, Burgess."

"That's right. You heard me invite them," I said.

"They can't help but be suspicious," Singer said. "No one has ever told them the truth."

"It's not suspicion that brought them here," said LaRosa. "It's the pleasure of being in the crowd that watches a hanging. Did you enjoy yourself too, Singer?"

Singer flushed with rage. "I don't approve of what they did," he said. "But I don't approve of your self-righteousness either. Your problem, LaRosa, is that you hate students."

"No, I hate thugs."

"Are you calling me a thug?" Singer said, his voice low. He walked up to LaRosa grimly.

"No," said LaRosa, "I'm calling you the man who stands on the sidelines watching while the thugs do their work. Watching and excusing."

"There are no sidelines," said Singer. "You're in one camp or the other."

LaRosa started to answer and thought better of it. Singer and he stared at each other in silence for a long moment, and then Singer turned on his heel and left.

"That son of a bitch," said LaRosa after Singer had closed the door on us. "That pious prick." He shook himself and brought his voice down. "It's too much," he said. "It's too much. And yet I feel stupid, cheap, getting into an argument like that."

"Who's that apparition, Inkelmann?" I asked.

"A very distinguished chemist. He came here a couple of years ago. They say he's going to win a Nobel Prize one of these days."

"What's his interest in all this?"

LaRosa shrugged. "How would anyone know? He goes off on a binge like this every once in a while. Something grabs him, and he doesn't think, he acts. But what's your interest, John? Why are you so damnably stubborn? And what's my interest? We act, all of us, from the seat of our pants."

16

We went out and had a couple of drinks together, and roast beef sandwiches on rye. I thought of going home and packing a few things to take over to LaRosa's, but remembered the charade I was playing with my graduate class that never met, and decided, from the seat of my pants, that since I was scheduled to appear in that room, I would. LaRosa said he'd join me in an hour and come home with me to help pack, and I worked my way back to Rollins.

There's no telling what a day will bring. I went to the classroom, and Dorothy Bell and half a dozen other protesters were in front of the room, the awe-inspiring Amazon among them. But when I went into the room, there were Hedge and Sledge, and two other students they'd brought along.

"Are you sure you're in the right room?" I asked them.

"Yeah, we're sure," said Sledge. "This thing's gone too far. We thought we'd come to your class."

"We don't like breaking solidarity," said Hedge, "but . . ." He stopped, and looked abashed.

"But what?" I asked.

"But." He smiled. "It's a long story. Just but."

"Well, this is a little surprising," I said, "but I'm naturally pleased.

"The trouble is," said Sledge ruefully, "I never had the slightest intention of taking this damn course."

"I know how you feel," I said. "It's a tough world."

"Tough?" said Hedge. "It's crazy. It's not here. First you don't do something on principle, then you do something on principle. You never just do something because it makes sense. You get my point?"

I allowed that I did, and moved on to the business of the class. Afterward, LaRosa drove me home, I threw a few things in a suitcase, and we went to his house. We told Ruth LaRosa about the day's events, and she became so angry we had to drive twenty miles into the country to a pretty good restaurant to calm her down. We spent the evening talking about the good old days. Not that we believed much of what we said, but it helped us to drive home feeling somewhat less drained.

The next day was Friday, and I was glad it was the end of the week. LaRosa and I drove to the campus together, and we heard the sirens a quarter of a mile away. At Hodgkin Street, the main intersection before you get to the campus gate, a police car was on its side, the flames still smoldering. The police, forty or fifty of them, were drawn up in a solid line in front of the main gate. Inside the gate the students were milling around, the front line facing the police with elbows locked. It looked as though half the student body was there, but I suppose it was less.

LaRosa and I could have turned around and gone home, and I don't know why, but we didn't. We stopped, drove around a corner, found a place to park the car a block or two away, and made our way back to the campus gate. The shop windows on the street facing the campus were all smashed. We picked our way through the broken glass, and came to the police line. One of the cops, looking harassed, asked where the hell we thought we were going, and we said we thought we were going to work. He asked for our identification. We showed him our faculty cards.

"God be with you," he said, and patted me on the back as he signaled us to go ahead. The boys in the front line saw us coming, and greeted us cheerfully.

"It's two professors," one of them called out, "let them through." On this day, apparently, anyone was accepted, even LaRosa and me. The line opened up, and we went on through.

In the crowd behind the front line I saw the boy in the army jacket who had been in the group that had invaded my office. "Hi, professor," he said. I was an old friend. No hard feelings, no more suspicions. The Day of Love had come.

"What's happened?" I asked.

"Nothing yet," he said.

"All this?" I waved my cane around, pointing.

"Oh. The pigs tried to bust one of us. Around midnight. They said he spit on one of them. We blocked the car, then turned it over. A little trashing took place." He smiled and shrugged.

"I see. But nothing happened."

"Not much yet."

I looked around at the crowd. Quite a number had red bands around their sleeves. I saw Inkelmann with one on, and standing in the front line, arms locked with the others, was Sinclair, from the Sociology Department, a red bandanna around his forehead. Behind them was a ragged circle of students, and in the middle, holding forth, his shirt sleeves rolled up and a piece of red cloth in his belt, was Pritchard the Protestant counselor.

"Join us," said the army jacket hospitably.

"No thanks," I said. "I'm a cripple. Also an agent provocateur."

Army jacket looked surprised, and then caught on. "You'd better come over to our side, professor," he said, not threateningly, just factually. "There isn't going to be any other side."

LaRosa and I went on. Across the campus, in front of the administration building, there was another large crowd. I said to LaRosa that I thought I could make it, and we walked over. A fellow in an old football jersey, No. 33, was haranguing the populace through a bull-horn. "Pringle is ours," he was saying, "and it stays ours. *We're* going to run this goddam place, not Nixon Nevis. We've taken over. I ask for a vote on that. How many for taking over the whole fucking place?"

He got the vote. There were a lot of people milling around, some looking amused, some worried, some angry. But no one said nay. It wasn't that kind of public exercise.

"And now another motion," said No. 33. "Nevis can stop pussy-footing with the pigs. Let's tell him that it's the vote of this meeting that he tell the police to stay a quarter of a mile from this campus. It's our community. We don't want an occupying force around it." A woman stopped No. 33, and whispered something urgently into his ear.

"Well, well," LaRosa said to me, "it's Dorothy Bell." And so it was. No knitting, just a pretty red kerchief around her neck.

No. 33 nodded in understanding, and put the bull-horn to his mouth again. "We're going to tell Nevis something more. *We* don't want an occupying army harassing us, and neither do the people in the ghetto. We demand that Nevis demand that the pig police stay out of the ghetto."

"Off the pigs!" came a shout.

"Up against the wall, Nevis," somebody else shouted.

"Do I get a vote?" asked No. 33.

"What are we voting on?" the boy in front of me called. His friend next to him boxed his ears, and, in high spirits, they wrestled each other to the lawn.

"Do I get a vote?" No 33 repeated.

The crowd responded, clenched fists in the air.

"Had enough?" LaRosa asked me.

We were turning to leave when I spied Ralph Singer a few steps off. He hesitated and then came up to us. He must have had the same thought in his mind that I had in mine—that we were colleagues, that we mustn't allow a permanent rupture between us. When he spoke, his tone was careful but friendly.

"I'm afraid everything's come loose again," he said.

I took the peace pipe he was tendering and puffed on it. "Yes, it looks that way," I said.

"And on the whole," he went on, taking the pipe back gratefully from me and puffing on it in his turn, "it may be that students learn as much from this kind of experience as they do in the classroom."

"They learn how to be a Nazi mob," LaRosa said.

The peace pipe lay in fragments at his feet, but Singer, I give him credit, persisted. "No, Joe," he said, "there's nothing in common between these young people and Nazis." I think he was mainly interested in keeping the conversation between us going. There was a note of entreaty in his voice, as though he were begging us not to argue back. Still, he felt impelled to make his point. "No resemblance at all. The spirit is different, the intention. These students are telling us something valuable."

The valuable thing that No. 33 was telling us at the moment was that the People, now that they had taken the machinery of power into their hands, were going to choose the professors. No more faculty tyranny. No more irrelevant course work. No more crap about professionalism. No more tenure. No more nothing. Just Democracy, one and indivisible, now and forever.

In its own way it was a soothing thought: if the People were going to choose the professors, then the People, not me, would have to attend committee meetings. I turned to share this cheerful reaction with LaRosa, but he was staring moodily at Singer.

"Do you hear the useful program that they're offering us?" he asked Singer. "Or does your ear screen out all such disagreeable sounds? I think you'd hear celestial music in Pandemonium."

Singer flushed. He'd made an effort to patch things up and been rebuffed; the disappointment, humiliation, resentment, showed in his face. As for LaRosa, his face was red, and he gave the general impression of a fighter circling his foe to land another blow. I was thinking that I might have to bind and gag him when I heard a pleasant voice at my ear.

"Hello, Mr. Burgess." I turned to find Walter Izard standing next to me, his face swept free from care, just as though he were sitting behind his desk at his bank. I introduced him to LaRosa and Singer, who reluctantly gave up glaring at each other in order to greet him.

"Colleagues?" Izard asked.

"Colleagues," I said. "Fellow workers. Members of the same department."

Izard nodded. "Troops," he said, slipping the knife in gently.

I asked him whether he was on the campus to take part in the festivities. No, he'd come up for the trustees' meeting that afternoon, but the goings-on at the moment were certainly livelier. He was evidently in excellent spirits. When No. 33, moving on to the next item on the agenda, called for an investigation of the trustees, Izard said to us equably that it was a good idea, any group was helped by friendly investigation.

I thought LaRosa would go up in smoke. "Mr. Izard," he said, "what do the trustees propose to do about all this?"

Izard seemed almost unhappy to have his attention turned away from No. 33. "All this?" he asked, gesturing around him. He shrugged. "It will pass. It's a mere surface phenomenon. The real problem's the long-range one: where is the university going, what is its mission?" I think he was only half listening to his words.

There was a vein running down LaRosa's forehead that I'd never noticed before. "I have a mission here," he said. "A job. I'm supposed to teach here." I realized suddenly how much anger he'd been suppressing for how long. "And the trustees have a responsibility to insure that I do teach. Not in the long run. Today. What are you going to do about it?"

He'd caught Izard's attention. "It's for you," Izard said, looking LaRosa in the eye, "to work out the ways that will let you teach. We can't create the conditions by fiat. Look around: quite plainly these students are starved for another kind of experience than they get in the classroom. We've deified the cognitive and ignored the affective. But nature will out."

Nature, No. 33, was now shouting that for every student busted the People were going to exact ten thousand dollars' worth of damage in broken windows and furnishings from the university.

LaRosa let go. "In other words, you're not going to do anything." I put my hand on his sleeve to try to lead him away, but the light of battle was in his eye. "Isn't there anything that people have to know, and that they can only learn in the classroom?" he shouted at Izard.

The conversation, at this point, headed for the upper regions. Singer, now aroused on his side, broke in to say that it was less important for a student to know what Kant thought than what he himself thought. Izard agreed, saying something about putting aside the pablum of the past. Singer came back with a remark about the mystique or mistake of this culture, I couldn't tell which, and LaRosa, now almost weeping with rage, pronounced maledictions on people who thought they could learn the history of the solar system by contemplating their navels, to which Izard responded by asking if facts were as important as ideas, or the solar system as significant as a single soul.

I wanted to be far away. I was bored with Singer, impatient with Izard, angry with LaRosa. It was as though, in a madhouse, they'd climbed into their own closet, hearing nothing, seeing nothing, so that they could have their own separate, mad quarrel.

All at once the noise from the speakers' stand stopped. The bull-horn had gone on the blink, and No. 33 and a couple of other students were trying to fix it. Blessed silence hung over the lawn.

I seized the opening. "Mr. Izard, Ralph," I said, "you don't want to push things too far. Those characters up there want to run a university and they can't even find anybody who knows how to fix a bullhorn. The lack of objective knowledge is stopping a revolution." I laughed, weakly.

"That's why I don't worry too much about the short run," said Izard. "There're no troops on one side and there's no know-how on the other. We can weather the storm. The real question is what lies on the other side of the storm, what we'll see when the storm's over."

"It won't be a university," said LaRosa. "Not like anything we've known by the name."

"Evolution," Izard said.

I led LaRosa away as gently as I could. I was in such a hurry to get away, in fact, that I headed in the wrong direction, away from Rollins, and we had to circle back furtively to escape Izard's and Singer's eyes. But the walk did LaRosa good. A quarter of an hour later he turned to me and said that he'd probably made a fool of himself. The walk made me feel better too. What had seemed like a generalized ache settled down to a quite specific ache in my leg.

"That trustee, that banker," LaRosa said, "with his talk of the wave of the future. Does he like the wave or does he just accept it?"

I didn't know, and we finished the walk to Rollins in silence. There weren't any pickets at the door—they'd gone on to bigger things, obviously. And the guard had gone from my office.

Inside my office, Otto was waiting, looking agitated.

"He's left," he said.

"Who's left?"

"The boy. The AWOL soldier who was in the sanctuary. He couldn't stand it any more. The noise, not sleeping. He took off."

"But we passed the place a half-hour ago, and the music was still coming out of it."

"Oh sure. They're still dancing. Most of them haven't even noticed."

"Do you know where he's going?"

"No." He seemed less agitated, now that he'd told me. He pointed out the window. "The sap's rising," he said. "Did you notice?"

"We noticed."

"The cops, the kids, the administration, the faculty, everybody's spaced out."

"What are you going to do, Otto?"

"Me?" He shrugged. "I'm collecting impressions. Everybody's coming unraveled. Maybe I'll go home. I don't know."

"Tell me if you go," I said.

"Okay," he said, and left.

Joe and I sat in my office and looked at each other, and after a while LaRosa began to laugh softly, shaking his head in disbelief. The bell signaling the end of a classroom hour rang. LaRosa went to the door and looked down the hall.

"Do you know," he said, coming back, "there are actually students going to class. Even today. Seekers of cognitivity."

"Lost souls," I said. "Everyone of them with a hang-up. Finks."

"That man Izard," Joe asked, "do you suppose he really likes anything? I mean, genuinely cares for it, takes it seriously?"

"Why?"

"Because if he did, he couldn't talk that way. If he cares for football, he recognizes, surely, that there are good football players and bad ones. If he's not a eunuch he knows there are warm women and cold ones. When people say that everything's the same, everything's equal, there are no distinctions to be made, they're only speaking about things they don't think very important. All this self-expression, each man slopping over and calling his slop the truth—you believe in that only when you haven't found out what to believe in, only if you don't care about anything."

"Not enough affectivity, that's his trouble," I said.

LaRosa went off to teach a class. And, having mentioned affectivity, I tracked Irene down, using a phone booth down the hall, and we went out to lunch together. The trustees, she told me, were meeting this afternoon.

"Where?" I asked. "The Trustees' Room is occupied by students, isn't it?"

"Yes. So the trustees are meeting in a room at the Student Union."

"Every man in his place," I said.

"Better than that," Irene said, "every man getting what he wants. The students want to run the place, the trustees want to be students again."

"Paradise unlimited. How do people arrange it?"

"It's not hard. Nevis called Lawton the mediator, Lawton interceded with the students, and the students said, Yes, they thought they could accommodate Nevis." She finished her flounder. "You see," she said, "with a little good will, everything can be worked out."

17

Joe and Ruth LaRosa went off that evening. They puzzled me. They seemed tense and distracted, and it wasn't due only to the events of the day. They had something else on their minds, something ahead of them.

Though they were clearly eager to go, Joe asked me once again whether I'd be all right alone.

I tried to reassure him. "A lot's been happening," I said. "The people who've been calling me will have other things on their minds. Larger historical forces are at work." Ruth and he continued to look uncertain, unhappy. "Has something happened to you two?" I asked.

"No, nothing in particular. Ruth and I have to have a long talk, that's all." Joe caught my glance and smiled. "No, we're not in the middle of a marital problem. Nothing like that, not faintly. But we've got a problem of sorts, and some thinking to do. We'll tell you about it when we get back."

"Well, fine. Then go."

"But will you be all right?"

"If I'm not here when you get back, look up a chap named Castillo."

A half hour later they were off. I slept pretty well, and woke up to find that a sullen Saturday rain was falling. I spent the morning writing, had some scrambled eggs for lunch, and enjoyed a fine solitary afternoon poking around Joe's library. No one telephoned, and the rain came down, no longer sullen but sheltering. I settled down with Rousseau's *Confessions;* who knows, I thought, maybe I'll give a course on confessions.

Toward the end of the afternoon someone rang the doorbell obstreperously. I opened it carefully, and there was Moses Epstein. Joe had whispered the secret to him that I'd be there, and he was checking up. He came in and we had a drink together. I asked him how things were on the campus.

"Quiet," he said. "What did you expect, John? It's raining. Revolution is for sunny days. Sunny weekdays."

"What's on the books for this week, do you think?"

"I should know? I keep telling you, I'm a geneticist. It can all die out as quickly as it started. When I get back next Thursday you can tell me all about it. I'm going to a conference in Boston. I leave tomorrow morning."

"You chose a good time to be away."

"It chose me." Moses shrugged. "The work of the world can't stop because students are playing games."

After Moses left, I called Martha in New York, as I'd said I would. She was fine, and I told her so was I, and would see her Monday. I hung up, and then called Irene, as I hadn't said I would, but there wasn't any answer. I whipped up something in the kitchen for myself, and while it was cooking I called

Godderer to tell him that Martha wouldn't be coming with me.

"Am I still invited?" I asked.

"Oh dear yes," he said. "By all means." I wondered why he sounded so urgent. Around eight-thirty I called a taxi, and it drove me to Godderer's place.

He'd moved out of town, where he'd built a new house. He was a bachelor, and the house, I'd heard, was his own creation, from the first plans on paper down to, or up to, the church-bell he'd put on the roof. According to the story, he'd done very little else for two years but fuss over the house and chirrup at the workers. It was a wooden house, long and low, the wood its natural color. To get to the front door I walked between a pair of carved swans whose necks stretched out insinuatingly toward me. Godderer opened the door, and I stepped into a dimly lit foyer covered with tatami. Behind him I could see a large sunken living room. Two thirds of it was sunken-sunken, forming a conversation-pit in which a herd of buffalo could have grazed.

Buffalo were grazing. Over Godderer's shoulder I could make out Lawton, Sinclair, from the Sociology Department, and three or four others, male and female.

"Come in, come in, John," Godderer said, helping me off with my raincoat. He was trying to control an attack of the titters. "We've been waiting for you. It's a coming-home party. Surprise, surprise." The titters erupted.

I planted my cane firmly on the floor. "I'm not sure the people here even knew I was gone," I said.

"They've wanted badly to get to know you, John," Godderer said. "I thought it would be good to break the ice, and amusing. N'est-ce pas?" Now that I was there he seemed not so sure it was going to be amusing. Titters came again.

I felt something give beneath me and looked down. I'd

pressed so hard on my cane that it had gone through the straw matting, making a neat incision.

"I'm already breaking up your place," I said. "I'd better go."

Godderer turned tremulous with concern. "Oh dear no. We absolutely won't permit you, John. You're our prisoner now. And we're so happy to have you."

I smiled a wan *cher collègue* smile at him, extracted my cane from the mat, and permitted him to lead me down the three steps into the living room, and then down the four steps into the pit. Three large lamps were placed at strategic points around the plain. They set up pools of light, like oases, against the surrounding shadows. At the center of one pool there was a low chair, and Godderer established me in it.

"Scotch?" he asked, and answered the question for himself. "Of course." He wafted off.

I blinked a little under the light but gradually my eyes came into focus, and there was Pritchard, he of the pear-shaped tones, sitting on the floor in front of me, his eyes like tubs of warm water, beckoning me to come in. He had his arms curled around his knees, and a long drink was in his hands. He made a small round bundle. Once again I was surprised to see how short he was. Somehow I'd stretched him out in my mind.

"John Burgess," he crooned, "John Burgess. Well well." His voice cuddled up to me, whispered in my ear, ruffled my hair. He put his glass down on the floor, worked himself with difficulty to one knee, and grasped my right hand. He repeated the message: "Well well."

"Well well well," I said. I could give him as good as he gave.

"So the moment of truth has come," he said. I thought I heard drums roll. I looked up to see what was producing the effect, and into the floodlight above me. Blinded, I turned my head down quickly, and, as I did, something wet and cold was inserted into my left hand. Godderer, I inferred, had delivered the Scotch. Bubbles of light were in front of my eyes. Through them I made out Pritchard's face, soaked in sincerity. The glass in my hand was slowly but steadily sliding out of it.

I wriggled my right hand loose from Pritchard's grasp just in time to catch my drink before it hit the floor. I swallowed some of it before I turned back to him.

"You were saying?" I said.

"I was saying," he intoned, "that the moment of truth has come at last." An eternity had passed, I'd been struck blind, transfixed and paralyzed, but back there where Pritchard had been while I was undergoing this test of character, apparently nothing much had been happening. We were still astride the moment of truth.

It wasn't bright but it was the only thought I could find in my mind. "To the supernatural," I said, and raised my glass to him.

His eyes, which had been pools of love, turned into archers' quivers. "Not at all," he said, "if you will permit me, not at all. On the contrary, to the natural." He lifted a finger to chide me, and the truth sped from his eyes to mine, riding on an arrow. "God is natural," he intoned. "He is of this world. He is immanent."

"That's a disturbing thought," I said.

"It is," he bugled. "It is meant to be." The man was more than a voice. He was eyes. The whites flashed, the pupils glinted, flicking indignation at me and then forgiveness. We sat in silence for a moment or two while the display continued. Then he took dead aim with his finger at a spot between my eyes. "God is here," he said.

I felt a slight burning sensation at the spot he had singled out. "I'm sorry," I said, "I didn't realize."

Godderer saved me from getting in deeper by bringing over the Sinclairs at that moment. From my low chair I raised my hand vertically over my head and shook hands with them. Sinclair was a nodder. He said hello, nodded, remarked that he'd certainly been eager to meet me, nodded some more, added that we ought to have lunch together to discuss, in an objective spirit, nod, the revolutionary movement in South America, and tailed off into a slow, sustained, sage nod. It wasn't a nervous tic, it was a method of punctuation. After his full-stop nod, Mrs. Sinclair took over. She weighed two hundred pounds neat, and her voice came up like thunder out of China 'cross the bay.

"So you're John Burgess," she rumbled.

I remembered how I'd felt my first day in school being introduced to the teacher. "How do you do, Mrs. Sinclair," I said.

"Ottilie," she rasped. Her voice sounded like a bulldozer starting up on a cold morning. "The name's Ottilie."

"Ottilie," I said, recognizing an order when I heard it.

"What have you been up to?" she asked. There wasn't any point in answering. Like my teacher that first day, she knew what I'd been up to. I waved my glass at her in a self-deprecating fashion, and finished my drink. She settled down to the floor in front of me, producing the general effect of a parachute bellying down to earth. As a matter of fact, she was dressed, as best I could make out, *in* a parachute, square blue and red patches over the white.

Then Godderer brought over the Lawtons. Lawton threw a knowing wink at me, and his wife, an underfed, tall woman, said hello with a nervous half-laugh. Somewhere in the middle of all this a priest made his appearance. Sitting on my low chair, I felt a pair of knees pressing into my shoulder, and looked up to see a collar turned backwards, and a profoundly melancholy face above it. The man was trapped. Ottilie Sinclair, reclining on the floor, was using his legs as a back-rest. His name was Cantwell.

We were waiting for others to arrive and we spent our time making contributions to the advancement of thought. Pritchard observed that what counts is the revolution as revelation, and Ottilie Sinclair remarked that it was a mistake to ask the Movement for a definition of its goals because in a time when all the old categories—class, sexist, racist—have been exposed, definition is impossible. Sinclair, with a nod, summed it up: "We begin at scratch, existentially. What we offer is something fluid and unstatable but real."

That led to a discussion of words and logic and how misleading they are, and Pritchard told us that Western secular civilization rested on the great lie of objectivity. True knowledge was something else, a feeling in one's bones. My own bones were feeling like dead weights, so I kept out of the conversation, and we tripped on gaily to a discussion of Western civilization's guilt feelings about the body. Sinclair brought out a book he had with him, and asked us to listen.

"It's called *Bodies in Revolt*," Sinclair explained, nodding three times slowly for emphasis. "It's by a professor of philosophy from Florida. It's a quite remarkable work." He began to read: " 'If one's conditioning is in the traditional kind of perception and behavior typical of the Western fear-aggression approach of constrictive conscious control, then an attempt to cultivate the somatic experience of accommodative, sensual behavior will be somatically repulsive if not literally convulsive. It will be so because the avenues of parasympathetic energy expression have been so long atrophied and constricted that the musculature is incapable of relaxing and becoming a medium for sensual-accommodative energy expression.'"

Sinclair looked up and nodded at me. "What's your reaction?"

I felt my musculature twitching a bit. "It's a new thought in a new language," I said. "I'd have to study it a bit."

"Do," said Ottilie Sinclair. She pulled the book from her husband's hands and wedged it into my pocket. "Take it and read it," she said. "We'll talk about it next time we meet." I was sure we would.

"I fear, John Burgess, that you are a rationalist, verbally oriented." It was Pritchard.

"What's the alternative?" I knew it was a mistake to ask, but I couldn't help wondering.

"Other forms of communication, non-linear, non-verbal."

"Oh I'm for those," I said. "Always have been." I hoped he'd let me shut up soon. I hoped he'd shut up. After all, he was a non-verbal type.

Father Cantwell, standing in the shadows beyond the pool of light, spoke up for the first time. "You don't expect Mr. Burgess to go along with you, Pritchard, do you?" he said. I couldn't see his face, but his tone was dry. "After all, he makes his living from studying human speech. He's got a professional interest in words."

"Words, turds," Ottilie Sinclair said. Her laughter ripped across the pit like a shell from a howitzer.

"Western secular civilization," Pritchard said, "rests on a verbal-cognitive obsession. The whole thing has to be rejected."

"What do we do, take it back to the store like a pair of shoes that don't fit?" I asked. "You can't just reject a civilization, the whole thing, can you?"

"Why not?" Pritchard asked. He had me there. I couldn't think of an answer.

There's nothing like small talk to take one's mind off one's troubles. After getting rid of Western civilization we moved on to how we'd do it, and that naturally brought up the subject of violence. Sinclair referred to something out of Simone de Beauvoir. If I followed, violence was the proof of each individual's loyalty to himself: you don't really believe in something unless the belief gets into your muscles and you're prepared to use them. The alternative was inauthenticity, frustration: you don't register your feelings on the fact of the world.

Well said, Simone; well done, Ku Klux Klan, I was thinking, when I realized that Pritchard was visiting me with his eyes again. "And what is your reaction to that?" he asked me. He was still tapping me fore and aft to see if I had a soul.

"There's a lot in what Beauvoir says," I replied ruminatively. "That's why exercise is so important. Four times around the track and cold showers every morning. I've long believed it should be compulsory for everybody. Gets rid of the vapors."

It never pays when I try to be conciliatory. Sparks from Pritchard's eyes sprayed all over me. "Be relevant," he said.

"Public executions," I continued, "that's the ticket, with every citizen getting his chance to wield the knife. There's nothing like registering one's feelings upon the fact of the world."

Sitting at my left knee, Pritchard turned on the illuminated signs. The messages came fast: be careful, God is here, God lives. At my right knee, I heard a snort. It was Ottilie Sinclair.

"Are you capable of being serious?" she asked.

"I thought I was being serious. The intellectuals' love affair with violence, it's savage, gratuitous, and comfortable. I don't like it."

She found me quite amusing. "Don't tell me," she said, "that you've got the liberal hang-up against violence."

"I've got quite a hang-up against it," I said. "It hurts."

"And what exists, apparently so unviolently, hurts too," Sinclair said. "And if you aren't prepared to oppose it physically, violently, you smudge the evil, deny your own feelings, and become inauthentic."

I felt damned inauthentic. I pulled myself up from my torture seat, asked Godderer to help me find another drink, and followed him into the kitchen, intending to tell him that I'd only been there fifteen minutes and I'd had enough amusement to last me for a month, and I was leaving. Lawton came sailing in after me.

"Don't be too impatient with them," he said. "Their bark is worse than their bite, I assure you."

"Then they should stop barking," I said. I looked at him and then at Godderer. "This has been a light-spirited evening, gentlemen, and I owe it all to you, but I'm afraid I must leave it."

Godderer said, "No, don't go. You mustn't shut yourself off from the world, John. That's a no-no."

Lawton intervened quickly. "I thought I'd better take the bull by the horns, John. You didn't call me back, and so I went ahead and worked this party out with Godderer. He thought it would be amusing, to use his word, and I thought it would clear the air. Remove misunderstandings, and perhaps set up better lines of communication. We've too much factionalism on this campus."

"So you planned it just as it's happened?" I asked.

"Well, not exactly as it's happened, but more or less." He shrugged, looked sympathetic, and gave me his honest man's look. "The evening need only be as difficult as you make it. It fits your needs too, you know. You're at an informal party with colleagues, something in your honor, and it's the most natural thing in the world that you should tell your story. You haven't had to grant a point you didn't want to. You're not making a formal public statement. It's a perfect compromise."

"Better than perfect," I said. "You even have clergy here to take the confession."

Lawton never raised his voice. "I can assure you that if you persuade these people—and I know you will—your problems on the campus will be over. We're even expecting some students, the editor of *The Badger* among them."

"The press too," I said. "You do arrange things."

He smiled, taking me into his confidence. "The good always takes arranging." Honesty, helpfulness, civic purpose, a little bent by the thick lenses of his glasses, shone from his eyes. He was putting his cards on the table, what more could I ask? It was sheer churlishness to object.

I was churlish. "You're a candidate for the junior Nobel Prize," I said, "a wheeler-dealer, a country boy from the Pedernales."

His glasses shone; his innocence was unassailable. "I try," he said. "All in a good cause."

"To all good causes," I said, and lifted my glass to him.

"I don't do it for fun," he said. "I do it for the university."

"To the good old university," I said, and took a drink. His spectacles glinted in the light. I winked at him like a fellow conspirator. He winked back. We were fellow conspirators.

"Do stay," said Godderer. "It's going to be a great party yet, I promise." I thought for a moment he was going to weep.

All right, I thought, I'd tried walking out of gatherings, I'd try something else. I'd stay, another ten minutes anyway. I left the kitchen and wandered back into the living room. Seeing the Sinclairs, Pritchard, and Mrs. Lawton sitting in the glow of the lamp near the chair I'd abandoned, I decided to take reimmersion in slow stages, and stopped to look at the books on Godderer's shelves. I was reaching for one, a book on Ecstasy and Something, I forget exactly what, when I felt someone at my side. It was Father Cantwell.

"In case you're wondering why I came," he said, "it was to give this affair some class. I come from a long line of inquisitors. We know how to do these things more suavely."

"Did Pritchard ask you?"

"Yes. I didn't see why you should have all the fun to yourself."

His face was like a fortress, locked-in, brooding. At each corner of his mouth a deep line, like a trench, was etched. I think he was smiling at me, but I'm not sure. His mouth moved out in a kind of exploratory way, hit the moats at each side, and snapped back. He must have been around fifty.

"Is Sainte Simone de Beauvoir one of your favorites, Father?" I asked.

"She helps one to understand nunneries, doesn't she?" he said. "Monasteries too. There exists a kind of passion to redeem the world that you can't let roam around freely. But put it under a firm rule, mix it with penitence, prayer, and charity, add a regular routine, of course, of physical exercise, and you've got a potent source of energy."

"You're sure you're not describing Mao's medicine for intellectuals?"

"I don't keep up with the news. I wouldn't know." You couldn't say his eyes were twinkling, but the melancholy in them had turned softer.

I went back down into the pit feeling a little quieter, and my spirits picked up still more a moment later. Richard Waterman, the *Badger* editor, another young man, and a blonde young woman came in. They greeted the others, and Godderer brought them over to me.

"This," said Godderer, presenting a tall young man, "is

Henry Rule." I'd seen the young man before, I knew, but couldn't place him.

"Paleased to meet you," he said, and took my hand in both of his, squeezing it avuncularly. Then he folded his hands on top of a little pot belly. I placed him. He was the students' elder statesman, the orator with the intersyllabic delivery who had addressed the faculty meeting.

"And this," said Godderer, indicating the young woman, "is Sheila Sanders." His voice had a high pitch to it. He was working hard to show me that it was good I'd stayed. "And you know Mr. Waterman, I think." His hand, on top of a limp wrist, waved from one to the other. "Sheila is Mr. Waterman's," he said, trying to sound benign and sounding salacious, "or Mr. Waterman is Sheila's."

Sheila was long and pale, a princess out of an Icelandic saga wearing a Mexican poncho with fringes. "I'm glad we're getting together this way," said Mr. Waterman. He was trying to sound crisp, but his eyes were big and anxious. He reminded me of someone, but I couldn't think whom. "Do you have a new statement to make?" he asked. He had a pencil, ready for use, sticking out of his breast pocket.

"Now, now," Godderer said, "all in good time, Richard. Don't press Professor Burgess. He'll tell his story when he wishes in his own way."

"But I've got the right to ask questions," Mr. Waterman said. He didn't sound aggressive; he sounded as though he were hounded by a sense of duty. And then it came over me; he reminded me of Spout, a dog in Indiana to whom I'd been much attached, who had the eyes of a police dog, the mouth and ears of a beagle, and the body of an underexercised bull terrier. I'd loved Spout, but he was difficult to live with, he was such a welter of inner conflicts. He had pride and he hated himself because he also needed affection badly. He was prudent and intelligent and knew his limits, and so was afraid of a dog-fight, but he was also too vain to run away. I didn't have the words at the time, not yet having been enlightened by sociology, but I now realize that he was an outer-directed dog trying to be inner-directed. My feeling for Mr. Waterman mellowed.

"Sit down, sit down," said Godderer. Sheila Sanders sat down on the floor next to Ottilie Sinclair, displaying a startling length of leg. Spout plunked down next to her like a tub of butter. Henry Rule kept his emotional distance. He remained standing, but indicated he was in a listening mood by unfolding his hands from his belly and refolding them judiciously behind his back.

"Well now that the gathering's here," said Godderer, "the party can really start." He bustled around distributing drinks.

Sheila and Spout asked for Cokes, and Henry Rule said he wanted Fresca. He explained their choices benevolently. "We're not being caritical of you," he said. "It's just a question of a different life-style."

"Well," said Ottilie Sinclair, "enough of this sparring. We want to know about you and the CIA, Burgess. What truth's in the story?"

"Yes," said Pritchard, "the time has come. Who are you, John Burgess?"

Silence descended in the room. The pre-trial examination had ended; my jury, my peers, were assembled and waiting. Out of the darkness beyond the light shed by the lamp, I heard a stage whisper: "We begin." It was the ineffable Godderer, speaking, I think, to Lawton.

Once again I thought of getting up and leaving. But I found I didn't want to. Spout was there in front of me almost thumping his tail in his excitement, and I was as interested in what was going to happen as the next man.

18

I turned on the genial smile that all who know me love. "Well," I said, "what was it you wanted to know?"

"We want to know the truth," Pritchard said. "Only that."

"Only that?" I said. "A small thing. I suppose you mean, am I a member of the CIA?"

"Precisely."

"If I were a member of the CIA, I'd deny it, wouldn't I?"

"Now John," said Lawton. I was John to him. We were co-conspirators in a good cause. "There's nothing simpler than just telling us you're innocent and giving us the evidence."

"I'm to prove a negative, is that it?"

"I have alaways held the conavickshyun," Henry Rule said, "that facts speak for themselves."

I was pondering this piece of wisdom when Godderer appeared out of the darkness. "There's a telephone call for you," he said, sounding puzzled. "Someone named Vogel." He led the way to a telephone in the bedroom.

"Mr. Burgess," Otto's voice came over the phone a bit scratchily, "I would have called you at home, but I couldn't reach you. Are you all right?"

"Of course I'm all right."

"Sheila Sanders told me she was going to see you tonight."

"Oh, do you know her?"

"What there is to know. Are you sure you're all right? I mean, like, it's a dirty trick getting you there with that crowd."

"I'm doing fine."

"You know that boy? The soldier in the sanctuary?" Otto's voice was strained. "He turned himself in to the Army today. He said he didn't know what to do any more."

"Oh. How did you hear about it?"

"I heard about it. What difference does it make?" Otto was on edge. "Like, what can anybody do about it? What can anybody do about anything?"

"We could talk about it tomorrow."

"I don't want to talk about it." His voice moved up an octave, and I thought for a moment he was going to lose control, but he settled down. "Mr. Burgess, I'm coming to Professor Godderer's house. I've got hold of a car. I'm on my way."

"Otto, you're not invited, are you?"

"I don't need to be. They didn't tell you why you were invited, did they? I'm coming. I don't like the idea of you there alone."

I was puzzled by Otto's desire to join me. I suppose it was because it was one of the few uncluttered human impulses I'd run into since coming back. "Otto," I said, "I've lived in strange countries, I've been in a war, I've been kidnapped and come through it alive more or less. I think I can take care of myself."

"I know that. How stupid do you think I am? I'm not on a rescue mission. It's all that solidarity there. You're in a sanctuary there. It bugs me. Give me a break. Say you'll be glad to see me."

"Well, hang on a moment." I went off and found Godderer in the kitchen. He was piling cheese on a tray.

"Godderer," I started, but he interrupted me to insert a piece of cheese in my mouth. "Godderer," I repeated, trying to work my teeth loose, "there's this student of mine, Otto Vogel, who wants to come over."

He pressed down on my chin and inserted another piece of cheese in my mouth.

I turned back and went to the telephone. "Come on over, Otto," I said. "I'll be very glad to see you."

"R-right," Otto said, and hung up. I could almost hear him running to the car. I went back into the living room, got myself a new drink, and descended into the conversation pit. My admirers were waiting for me, just where I'd left them.

"Now where were we?" I said. "Oh yes, Mr. Lawton had just said that all you wanted was evidence of my innocence. That rather reverses the usual order of things, doesn't it?"

"John," said Lawton, "we can approach this in a spirit of argument or in a spirit of frankness and mutual understanding."

"Well, in that spirit of frankness and mutual understanding," I said, "can you tell me what prompts your interest? Surely not an interest in a foolish young woman's hallucinations? Surely not an interest in me?"

"Call it caution about you, natural caution." That was old Ottilie, bringing comfort to one and all.

"Why not an interest in you?" said Pritchard. "Your life, your experience in Uruguay, your recent behavior among us, we can't help but wonder what makes you tick."

"The mystery of a soul," said Father Cantwell. His eyes were a gravedigger's, but there was the slightest movement around his mouth.

That was when Sheila Sanders spoke up and introduced a note of poetry into the proceedings. "Oh, they make it sound so awful, Mr. Burgess," she said. "Your soul and all that. But they're really just dying of curiosity, like me. You're a romantic figure, don't you know that? I mean, you've been kidnapped and wounded, and then this story about your being a secret agent, and you keep your silence. It's like, well, you're enigmatic."

Spout might have been a happier dog if he'd had a companion like Sheila. I hoped young Waterman knew that he had the girl he needed. I smiled at her like a tired man of the world, and said, "Well, I have lived a bit, I admit that." I took a reflective sip of Scotch, and looked off into the middle distance at all that living I'd done.

"And would all that living a bit include the CIA?" It was Spout, trying to be a police dog.

"To the best of my knowledge," I said wearily, "I've never had contact with the CIA." I looked around at the silent group. "I'm sorry," I said, "I wish there were more to tell you. It would make your Saturday evening more interesting. But there isn't."

"Not at all?" said Sheila. She was disappointed.

"Not so far as I know."

"You keep saying 'As far as you know' and 'To the best of your knowledge,'" barked Spout. "Aren't you sure?" The poor boy was pushing himself to be brave, and miserably wishing he could stop pushing.

"Well, of course, no one can be sure," I said. "If you're talking to a CIA man he won't tell you. In fact, anybody here could be in the CIA."

Sheila giggled. Spout grew indignant. "It's nothing to laugh about, Sheila. Mr. Burgess is just trying to make the whole thing seem ridiculous, but it isn't." He fixed his police-dog look on me, but his ears were drooping like a beagle's. "If you're trying to turn the suspicion away from yourself by spreading it around to everybody, well, that's . . ." he paused, looked for the word, found it, pushed it back as too strong, and then decided to use it, "that's fascistic."

"Not in the calassic form, of course," Henry Rule said diplomatically, "but it is fascisatic in tenadency."

"Sorry," I said, "that's one thing I don't want to be, fascistic. But consider my problem; consider yours. As I said before, if I were a member of the CIA, what would I say? That I wasn't. And so if I say that I'm not, what does that prove? If I deny, I affirm. Isn't that why you enjoy hearing accusations of this sort? They fill a room with ghosts, ghosts one can't get rid of, and that brings excitement into our dull lives."

Father Cantwell spoke. His voice was impersonal. "I think you understand the situation better than you admit, Mr. Burgess. These young people, all of us, young and old, have been lied to rather steadily for years and years. And so if we're suspicious to the point of paranoia, if we feel blocked in our want to trust or know one another, there's a reason. If I may use the old expression, we've all the need to confess to ourselves, to confess to one another, to hear one another confess, so that the air around us will be clean again."

I knew what he meant, more or less, but some games aren't for me. "I've told the simple truth, Father, uninteresting as it is," I said, "and that, so far as I'm concerned, is the end of the matter. When it comes to confession, I'm not very good at it. I particularly don't like public confessions. They don't clean the air, they pollute it still more."

"Time was," said Father Cantwell, "when confession could

be a secret thing. But can it be any longer? Don't we all have to come to terms with one another again?"

In that room, at that moment, I didn't hear the general principle he was asserting—I wouldn't have agreed with it if I had—but I heard the specific challenge. "All right," I said, the Scotch running in my veins and the blood running to my head, "I'll give you my confession. I'm a solitary, more or less. I don't like involvement in organizations or activities that confuse the mind or corrupt the soul. That certainly includes the CIA. And government, churches, anti-churches, the Republican Party, the Democratic Party, the Communist Party. I'm beginning to think it includes universities. It certainly includes faculty meetings, demonstrations, the Culture, the Counter-Culture, and styles, by all means styles, in hair, clothes, or ideas. They're all prisons of the soul. I want to be my own keeper. And I'd appreciate it if you'd let me be."

"Mr. Burgess," Cantwell said, his mouth moving out to the trenches and back again, "you have all the makings of a monk."

"No, they live in groups. I've told you, I'm a non-joiner, an isolate. Not even the CIA."

"You have cut yourself off," Pritchard sang, "from the human race."

"Have I? I'm merely confessing. You're getting what you wanted, a full confession."

"Don't talk about confession, Mr. Burgess," a high piping voice out of the shadows said. "No one's interested in confession, not really." It was Otto. He was standing at the edge of the group, his hair wild, a moth-eaten sweater, a couple of sizes too large for him, falling off his shoulders.

"Confession, you say, Father?" he said, turning to Cantwell. "That's fantastic, that really blows my mind. We beat our gums together, talking about honesty and sincerity and communicating, and it's a fraud. Like, for instance, the CIA, you say you're indignant about it. That's for laughs. It lines people up on one side or the other and won't leave them alone. It does what you do or would like to do. You all make me sick; I make myself sick. People take a boy and put him in the Army and beat on him till he runs away, and then other people take him and put him in a sanctuary and beat on him till he runs away. It's a game, that's what it is, a word game, like scrabble. Confess, Father, it's a game."

"Who let this apparition in?" Ottilie Sinclair rumbled.

"Apparitions let themselves in," Otto said. "We penetrate walls, we come through the floors."

"Otto," said Sheila Sanders severely, "who said you could come here?"

"Hello, Sheila," he said. "Nobody told me. Nobody needs permission to do anything."

"Young man," said Pritchard, his tenor pipes sounding as though there was an obstruction in them, "you have come in here and produced a considerable interruption."

"That's me," said Otto, "I'm an interruption." Now that he'd spoken he'd turned cold calm. "I'm Otto Vogel," he said to the group. "I'm probably crazy."

Lawton coughed. "Godderer, I think everybody needs a fresh drink. We've pushed this business with John about as far as we should, I think."

"No, go right ahead," said Otto. "I'll watch. What's the next move? Thumb screws? I'd better warn you, Mr. Burgess, you won't be able to prove your innocence except by a full confession of guilt."

"What does that mean?" Ottilie Sinclair rasped.

"I was just quoting, I don't know, Torquemada or somebody," Otto said. "You can look it up. That's Casey Stengel." He turned to go. "Well, toodle-oo," he said. "Good-bye, Mr. Burgess."

I pushed myself up from my chair. "I'll go with you, Otto," I said.

There was some minor commotion after that. Godderer took me aside and pleaded with me not to go, it would be unfortunate after all the emotion, as he put it, and Sheila Sanders led Otto to a corner and began to talk to him. I could see him arguing back, but after a moment he subsided and she did the talking. We stayed two or three minutes, trying, without much success, to make things look as though nothing had happened, and then we made for the door as undramatically as we could. As we stepped out into the air, the door opened behind us and Cantwell came out. "I need a ride," he said. "Do you mind if I join you?"

It had stopped raining, and the air was moist and cool. The car Otto had borrowed was a convertible. He started it, swung it around, and we poured out into the road. None of us said anything for a while, but then Otto slowed the car down and spoke.

"I meant what I said about confessions, Father," he said. "At least I think I did." At some moments in the evening he'd sounded elated, at other moments on the edge of cracking. Now he sounded tired and withdrawn. "I'm not even sure there is such a thing as confession. In fact, I think it's an impossibility."

"It is difficult," Father Cantwell agreed.

"No, I mean more than that," Otto said. "I mean it's a metaphysical impossibility. You know Saint Augustine, how in his *Confessions* he says time is a human illusion, that in God's eyes the past and the future are present here and now? But that means that in God's mind, in reality, since there's no such thing as time, nothing ever really happens. And so what's a man got to confess to? He never does anything."

"He confesses to just that, precisely," Father Cantwell said.

"To his nothingness. To his illusion of somethingness." The moon had come out and in its light I saw Father Cantwell's face. It was more melancholy than ever.

"So there's nothing to do about anything," said Otto. "Is that it?"

"I wish I could be sure," Cantwell said. "You're asking how the Word becomes flesh, and that's a mystery."

"Words and flesh, they're two different things," said Otto.

"Yes," said Cantwell, "and yet sometimes not just words but the Word, the truth or part of it, becomes flesh. We think that should be magical and exalting, but it needn't be. It can seem unreal, embarrassing, obscene. Like much of what happened back there at that house before you came in, if I may say so. There's so much difference between the Word and the flesh that the Word comes through warped, even comic. But perhaps it's there. You noticed, I am sure, that we were just at a religious meeting."

"Good God," I said, "was that what it was?"

"Why not? An evening in the presence of the Second Coming."

Otto, at the wheel, turned to look at Cantwell, and then drove to the side of the road and stopped the car. "I can't drive while you talk that way," he said. "Excuse me, but I think like maybe you're crazy too, like me."

Cantwell's mouth gave its aborted smile. "No, I'm a different kind of crazy," he said. "What I think we've just seen is Mystery, one more example of it. Something's erupted into the world, broken into the natural scene. It may be diabolical, I wake in the morning thinking it is, but I go to sleep persuaded I'm wrong."

"Good God, are you trying to say," said Otto, his voice turning shrill, "that what we've just seen is the greening of America?"

Cantwell's mouth twitched to the sides again and went back. "Rest easy," he said, "I belong to the old school. Until recently anyway we were very careful in the Church, downright stingy as a matter of fact, about announcing miracles, apocalypses, greenings, a new breed of men washed clean. We left that sort of thing to Holy Rollers and professors of education. I don't say the Second Coming's here. But perhaps something's happening that's happened before—a freshening of religious feeling. It goes with talk about a Second Coming."

"Good God," said Otto, "it may be religion, but are you saying it's good?"

"Not at all, if you mean do I like it. As I've said, I'm of the old school, and from my point of view it's a nightmare. It's puritanism at its worst—the drawing of hard lines, the moralizing of every issue, the search for simplicity in everything, even sex, the overheated sense of guilt, the censoriousness. Every man a watchdog of the Lord's. I like my religion with more ambiguities, more pity and irony. But that's my taste, my background, and something may be taking place, just the same, that's not so easily dismissed or easily judged. After all, it's not a local occurrence, it's worldwide. A kind of mood has come into the world that's come into it before, and left it changed. I don't say that God's Truth has come back, but perhaps people are rediscovering that God's Truth isn't here. The creature has begun again to resist his natural condition. Maybe the worm's turning, the worm in man that knows it must be meant for something more than the ordure it sees."

"The worm's turning pretty clumsily, Father," I said.

"What do you expect?" he asked.

Otto let out a little smothered growl, something between impatience and despair, and started the car again. We drove into town in silence. At a corner near the outskirts, Father Cantwell asked Otto to stop. "I get off here," he said. "My house is just down the street." He'd been sitting between Otto and me, and I fumbled my way out of the car, he got out, and I got back in.

"Do you mean what you said?" asked Otto.

Cantwell shrugged. "I don't know, I'm not sure. I've been talking about Mystery, about the way the world turns." His face was stony. "Sometimes I think it's the best of all possible worlds. I mean that everything in it is evil but necessary. If you'll permit me, you both say 'Good God' too much. I'm more careful about putting subjective descriptions before His name." He shook our hands. "Thanks for the ride."

He walked off down the street, and we pulled away from the curb in silence. Half a mile farther into town, at a red light, Otto said pensively, "For a man like you, you know too many odd balls." The light changed and we started off again. "Boy," said Otto, "that priest's way out. I was impressed when he was talking to me, but now that he's gone and I think of that Mrs. Sinclair . . . Do you see her as an instrument of religious awakening?"

"She might be, Otto. That's what Cantwell meant, I think. That's the awful part of it."

He looked at me quizzically. "Professor Burgess, I think all of this is getting to be too much for you. You're losing your cookies." I'd never seen him in quite that mood. For a moment he seemed almost serene.

I thought back to the evening. Something like serenity, to my surprise, was creeping over me too. "Otto," I said, "I think I ought to pin your ears back. For what you did back there at Mr. Godderer's. You shouldn't pick on people older than you."

"Was that what I was doing?"

"I think so. Anyway, you turned the evening around."

As we drove by the campus, we saw a red glow in the sky.

"The rain's over," said Otto. "The children are out building a bonfire."

When he dropped me at LaRosa's the clock in the hall said it was midnight. I looked around at the empty house, started to take off my jacket, and felt a weight in my pocket. It was the book I'd been given to study, *Bodies in Revolt*. I looked around at the empty house again and walked out. Irene lived in an apartment house four blocks away, and I got there without noticing that I had a leg that didn't work. In the vestibule there was a row of buzzers, and I pressed the one next to Irene's name. There wasn't any answer and I pressed it a couple of more times. I was about to press it again when her voice, sleepy, a little anxious, came over the speaker.

"Yes?"

"There's a man down here," I said, "with a problem."

"Who is this?"

"John. John Burgess. May I come up?"

"What time is it?"

"What a question."

"Is there something the matter?"

"Of course there's something the matter. I hope."

"Oh." There was silence for a moment, and then the buzzer rang and the door clicked open.

I took the elevator and got out at her floor. She was at the door waiting for me. She'd put some sort of wrapper on. Her eyes were half-closed, and her cheeks were pink from sleep.

I pulled the book out of my pocket. There was a bookmark in it marking the page. "Irene," I said, "I think I may be on the edge of learning something important. Let me read it to you: 'If one's conditioning is in the traditional kind of perception and behavior typical of the Western fear-aggression approach of constrictive conscious control, then an attempt to cultivate the somatic experience of accommodative, sensual behavior . . .'"

"Come in and explain it to me," she said.

19

Sunday evening, along around five or six, I opened the door at the LaRosas' and found they were already there. They had suitcases all over the living room.

"Hello, John," Joe said. "As you see, we're back, but we're going again."

My mind was moving along pleasant paths of its own, and for a moment I didn't focus. "Say that again," I said.

"What we went away about," said Joe, "we've decided." He wasn't being exactly lucid, and I said so. Joe stopped collecting the papers on his desk, and said, "I didn't tell you why we went off, did I?"

"No."

"I've had it, John. I'm leaving here. Ruth and I discussed it. We're leaving."

"Say that again."

"I'm quitting, getting out. I can't stand the smell."

"But where are you going?"

"The Fraser Institute has had a standing offer to me for years: Come there and write my books. No students; better yet, no faculty meetings. I called them this afternoon and said I was on my way."

I'd had a weekend during which I'd found some reasons for being where I was. I suppose I looked shocked. "You're thinking it's the middle of the term, are you, John, and it's not right to leave?" Joe asked.

It was just one of the thoughts in my mind, but it had occurred to me. "Yes," I said, "something like that."

"We thought about that. I called Elliot Wright this morning to tell him I'd be leaving at the end of the term. He told me that as of yesterday he'd resigned as dean. He was going on leave of absence immediately. I doubt that he'll ever come back."

"He's resigning?"

"Yes. Nevis thinks he hasn't done all he should for those students who were arrested. Elliot told him to get another boy. He also said that he doubted there'd be classes this week, that there'd be pickets all over the campus. That settled it for me. If the university can't guarantee me the elementary conditions necessary to do my work, I don't think I owe it anything. No more masquerade. I can't teach under these conditions."

He didn't seem angry, only relieved. The weariness that had been in his voice all fall was gone. Ruth, too, was more relaxed than I'd seen her.

"And so you're pulling out right away?"

"For a week or so, to get away from the people who'll be trying to argue me out of it. Then we'll slip back quietly, wrap things up, and leave."

I sat down. "Any other news?" I said.

Joe sat down too. "Well," he said, "a question. Not a suggestion, just a question: what are your plans?"

"Plans?" Lots of plans had been working themselves into my mind that day. "I'd been beginning to think that I was glad I'd come back. I wasn't making any plans, except to stay."

It was Joe's turn to look surprised. "The telephone calls?" he said.

I shrugged. "I don't have to answer the phone."

"You think this is no time to get out, do you, John? I ought to stay and fight? Hold the barricades? The issues are too important? That sort of thing?"

"I haven't begun to think that far," I said.

"I've thought about what my leaving means, I've talked about it with Ruth, God knows how many times. Maybe I'm wrong; I don't know. I do know that I feel better now that I've decided to do something simple and unmistakable—cutting myself free. I can't save the university, but I can save my own sanity and do my own work. Universities aren't universities any more, John. They're political playpens. A bunch of shoemakers would have done a better job defending the conditions of honest labor than we professors have done. I'm tired of playing house with a lot of children, including the infants my age who've joined in the game."

There wasn't much to say except that it was going to be a different place without him, different in particular for me, and I said that.

"Well, come along with me," he said. "Not that I'm making any suggestion. Do you know the disillusionment that's been the deepest, John? It's been the discovery that so many of the people here, men I've admired, don't really believe in what they're doing. They don't think there's any reality in the classroom, anything important. They talk about 'new educational values,' but what they mean is, they're sick of astronomy, sick of poetry, sick and tired and ashamed, and they want their students to forgive them. Why shouldn't students want to find some people, somewhere in the world, who are doing their jobs and aren't apologetic about it? But what the students have found here is that we're nothing but a society of the super-fluous. We think so, and so they think so. Let's admit it's hap-pened: universities are relics of another age. I suppose our society will need places to keep people who feel themselves superfluous, and let them act out their visions of life. What we now call a 'university' will do, and men like Nevis are perfect as head keepers. It's a pretty humane arrangement on the whole, if you don't think about the drugs, the cheap ideas, or the way the inmates claw at each other. But if you want some-thing more dignified, if you want educated people, maybe something else will have to be created. The research center may be the nucleus. Think of me that way: I'm going off to work for a better future." He smiled and went over and mixed a couple of drinks. "Will you have a drink with me, John?" he said.

So that was that. We had the drink, a couple of hours later he and Ruth set out again, telling me to hold on to the key until they returned, and I called Irene and went back to her apartment, feeling more subdued than I had when I'd left.

Monday morning was picketing weather, and the pickets were out. I had ten different leaflets given to me between the main gate and Rollins. Four of them cancelled one another out: different factions among the strikers were arguing with one another. The rest pretty much covered the waterfront: an end to police repression, university shelter for the welfare people, stop the war, open admission to the university for all who wanted to come, academic credit for strike activities, and no more courses that term, just strike activities to bring an end to fascism and imperialism.

At Rollins the picketers were thick. About half of them, I'd say, were dressed as Indians, with headbands around their hair; the other half were dressed as cowboys, rough riders, and other spokesmen for the free intellectual life. Around the fringes half a dozen minstrels were sprawled on the grass, strumming guitars. Somebody on the second floor of Rollins had a bull-horn, and was calling strike slogans through it. There weren't going to be any classes that day, that was plain. But I made my way through the crowd, and nobody stopped me when I entered the building.

Donald Rhodes was in the corridor, smiling.

"What's happened?" I asked. "Anything new?"

"No," he said. "Not really. There's talk about a march downtown this afternoon."

"Who's marching? The dope pushers?"

"The students."

"Any special reason? Or just the same old reasons?"

"I'm not sure anyone any longer knows," Rhodes said. "By the way, you're in the paper." He held out a copy of *The Badger*. The story wasn't on the first page: that was given over to the strike. It wasn't on the second page either: that was given over to an editorial, plus a brief story about Elliot Wright's resignation and a long interview with Nevis about the future of the university. As I turned to page three I caught the last sentence with the corner of my eye: "Communication, above all communication: that is the heart of the matter." No question about it: the interview was with Nevis.

On page three Spout Waterman had written a little piece. He didn't describe the stage setting in any great detail, but he said that I'd left little doubt that I really wasn't in the CIA. On the other hand, I'd gone a little too far perhaps. I'd actually described myself as an "isolate." Wasn't I making a fetish of irrelevance? I walked on down to my office, and somebody had scrawled a slogan on the door: "Isolation Ward," it said. Above my head I could hear the fellow with the bull-horn rasping away.

I settled down and read the rest of *The Badger*. It alluded to the possibility of a demonstration in the middle of town, had a column of interviews with various faculty members about the events on the campus—Singer, Sinclair, Inkelmann, they were all in favor, but I wasn't sure of what—and a fairly long story about life in the dormitory wing where the welfare people were. Also, the football team had lost a game; not all the players had turned up.

The editorial was on radicalism. The message was that all the alternatives to radicalism were essentially for the people who didn't really care about what was happening. Emotional isolates, it said. That was Spout all right. The only exception the editorial made was for genuine conservatives, like the Young Americans for Freedom. For these it expressed respect; it simply disagreed. No doubt about it, the editorial was Spout's. It expressed his *Weltanschauung:* Growl, and maybe nobody will know you're scared. I wondered where Otto was, what he was doing. It suddenly came over me how scared he was too.

Donald Rhodes opened the door, and Godderer was behind him. "All recovered, John?" Godderer asked. He was a bit tentative.

"Nothing to recover from," I said. "Thanks for the party." I seemed to have developed a new amiability, a kindliness toward the world. Perhaps I went too far. Anything can cause anything, as I now think, and these genial words may have led to the fact that I spent the next two days living with those characters, locked up with them, to be exact.

Because, a moment after I thanked Godderer for the party, a rumbling noise arose, there were shouts down the corridor, and I heard people running through the halls. Godderer and

Rhodes turned and looked behind them, and I went to the door. A throng of students was inside the main entrance. We went down the hall toward it—cowboys, cowgirls, Indians, and Indian maidens running past us—and gaped as a couple of young characters, their faces red, eyes bulging, pushed the doors shut, ran a chain around the handles, and put a padlock on them. And there, overseeing the operation, yes, right there, was Dorothy Bell.

"Just a moment," sputtered Godderer, "what are you doing?"

There was laughter in the hall.

"What *are* you doing?" Godderer said.

"We are closing the doors," Dorothy Bell said. "We are liberating the building."

"But *we're* here," Godderer remonstrated. The observation didn't seem to surprise anybody.

"But we're *here*. You're locking us in," said Godderer.

"You are repeating yourself," said Dorothy Bell.

"You have no right to do this," said Godderer. More laughter.

"We've the power," said Dorothy Bell. "No one should have been in this building. There were pickets outside. Now you're in, you stay in."

Above our heads, on the second floor, the man with the bullhorn had started again. "Rollins is being held by the people," he called. "Join us."

"We're letting people in," said Dorothy, matter-of-factly. "But nobody goes out. Your being here gives us some protection, you know."

I walked back down to my office, closed the door and locked it. Character is destiny, I thought, and what was it about my character that had led to my destiny? Here I was again, kidnapped. A hostage of the revolution. The roulette ball, back in double-O. The damned thing was getting monotonous. I never really liked *The Perils of Pauline*.

Then there was a knock on the door, and it was Godderer

and Rhodes, and I didn't feel like laughing any more. Rhodes was pale, and a tic had shown up over Godderer's left eye.

"My God, what do we do?" Godderer asked. I made him sit down, and looked out the window. There was a ledge running around the building, just under the window line, and students were standing or sitting on it every twenty feet or so. Beneath them there was a line of pickets. Beyond them was a crowd—from the signs they were holding, a supportive crowd. One sign said: "Leave our minds alone." There was no escape through the windows, that was plain.

"Do the phones work?" asked Rhodes.

"Not mine," I said. "It was disconnected last week. I'll try yours. While I'm gone lock the door."

I went to Rhodes's office, entered, and locked the door behind me. I dialed the central campus switchboard, and asked how people were reaching the president of the university these days. She told me. It was a different number from Friday's which had been different from Thursday's. It rather fit my picture of Nevis: a new idea every day, why not a new phone number? I dialed the new number, and Irene answered.

"Hello," I said. "It's me."

"Where are you?" she asked.

"In Rollins."

"Did you call for a reason? Or did you just call, which would be nice?"

"Well, as a matter of fact, Irene, and don't laugh, I called for help. Students have just occupied Rollins, and padlocked the doors from the inside."

"And you're inside?"

"I'm inside. They're holding me. And Godderer and Rhodes too."

Irene became very angry, and it was all I could do to keep her from coming to Rollins alone to break the blockade. Then she talked about calling the police, and finally she agreed to get Nevis on the phone. He came on, and right from the start he sounded a little abstracted.

"Burgess? So you're in Rollins, you say?"

"Yes."

"How did you happen to be there?"

"How did I happen to be there? I work there."

"But there were pickets around the building, weren't there?"

"I must have been thinking of something. I never noticed."

"Your being in the building complicates things. You realize that, don't you?"

"Well, uncomplicate them. Get us out."

He sighed. "Sometimes," he said, "events are just too much." He was, I gathered, feeling sorry for himself that morning.

"What do you propose to do?" I asked.

"I'll think of something," he said. "I'll try to." That was very encouraging.

"And what do we do in the meantime? I'm not asking for myself, I'm an old hand at this sort of thing, I'm asking for my colleagues."

"Oh," he said, "just hold the fort." A weak gurgle came over the phone. The old affirmative Nevis was trying to reassert itself. "And Burgess," he said, "Try not to make things worse. I mean, be as understanding as you can about the situation."

"Of course," I said. "Love thy captors." I hung up and went back to my office and knocked on the door.

Rhodes opened it a crack, peeked out, and let me in.

"I called Nevis," I said.

"What's he going to do?" Godderer groaned.

"He said he'd think of something. He'd try to, anyway."

"Good God," said Godderer, "we're captives. This is real. What are we going to do?"

"Maybe Dorothy Bell will teach us knitting," I said.

20

We set ourselves up in Rhodes's office as best we could. It was bigger than mine, had more chairs, and the telephone worked. About an hour after my conversation with Nevis, Irene called. She had her voice under control, but she sounded so angry all the same that I thought the line would melt.

"Nevis," she said, skipping the prefatory honorifics, "has been in touch with the leaders of the group in Rollins. They're adamant. They want an agreement from him that police will stay off the campus for good. He more or less agreed, but they're not satisfied. They want a promise from the chief of police and the mayor."

"That's jolly."

"Nevis thinks he could win over most of the students in the building if he could talk to them. He has the feeling the leaders are shutting them off from what's going on."

"He could come over here and speak to them."

"They won't let him in. And there's a great crowd in front of the building. He can't get close."

"He could use a bull-horn."

"The administration, the chattering, incompetent fools, have distributed every bull-horn on the campus to student groups. They forgot to keep one for themselves."

"It's all right. We're comfortable enough here. Lots of books to read. I'm deep in Frantz Fanon."

"But what are you going to do?"

"Call you every hour on the hour."

"I wish you'd sound angrier."

"I can't. I'm talking to you."

"Oh John," she said, a helpless note in her voice, and I began to get angry at the people who were doing this to her. Before the feeling could grow worse, I put an end to the conversation and hung up.

Around one o'clock there was a rap on the door, and my old friend, the Amazon who'd picketed my classroom door, brought in some hamburgers and fried potatoes. She collected a dollar fifty from each of us for the food, which proves, I suppose, that even in revolutions somebody has to make ends meet, and on the way out she told us that we didn't have to keep the door locked, we were safe, the members of the commune didn't believe in violence."

"Are we in a commune now?" I asked.

"Of course," she said. "It's just been organized. During the last hour." History certainly didn't let any grass grow under its feet. Not in Rollins, not in my university.

After she left, Godderer, despite her injunction, got up and locked the door. He looked at the hamburgers and said they looked sickening, and I had to agree with him. Rhodes ate alone. When he finished I could see him begin to practice his smile, like a man taking a few tentative swings with a golf club after a long layoff.

"I think," said Rhodes, "that if we don't hold ourselves aloof, if we make them aware that we're not really against them, perhaps they'll see that this is really quite an inconvenience to us, and, er, well, soften their position." He worked a little harder at his smile, but the muscles were still stiff.

"What do you propose to do?" said Godderer. He was beginning to be irritable.

"We could begin by unlocking the door," said Rhodes.

"If you insist," Godderer said.

"I'm not insisting. I merely made a suggestion."

"Well, it sounded like more than a suggestion," said Godderer sullenly. "But go ahead and open it if it makes you feel any better."

Rhodes no longer seemed sure what he should do, so I got up and opened the door and wandered out into the corridor. The air was getting a bit close in the room anyway, I felt. Down the corridor, in the large central hall leading to the main door, something that looked like a council of war was going on. Perhaps thirty students were sitting in a circle on the floor. White students formed half the circle; black students formed the other half. Standing behind the circle were seventy or eighty other students, also in two groups, black and white. They didn't look very friendly, but they didn't look angry either. Neutral is about the way to put it. One of the blacks was speaking in a low voice.

"All right," he was saying, "we'll take the second and third floors. You keep this and the fourth." The people on the floor stood up, the groups separated, and the blacks trooped upstairs. The Amazon was coming down the corridor toward me.

"More recruits?" I asked.

"They came in half an hour ago. We've divided the building."

I rejoined Godderer and Rhodes. "The plot thickens," I said. "Black students are occupying the second and third floors. Our commune governs the first and fourth."

"When are they going to let us out?" Godderer asked.

Down the hall somebody turned a record-player on, loud. I recognized the sound. Sanctuary music. I closed the door. Upstairs, from the second floor, I heard other music. It wasn't going to be so easy to be locked in the building after all. I called Irene.

"Probably nothing to report that you don't already know," I said, "except that they're playing music now. Can you hear me?"

"Pretty well," she said. "But things are heating up. A couple of hundred of our students paraded downtown during the lunch hour, some of the bystanders threw things, or maybe the kids did, the police got into the act, and some of the students have run wild. They've broken a lot of store windows, and some automobiles are on fire. I'm afraid Nevis has stopped thinking about you."

"Well, go home. I'll call you there."

"And what about you?"

"I think I'm in about the safest place there is," I said. "That is, if the police don't come."

They kept the music going, and it was a long afternoon. Around five or six, as it was beginning to get dark, Godderer began to fidget. Finally he got up and went off. When he came back, his eyes looked a little clearer.

"Godderer," I said, "not to press too hard, three men in a lifeboat and all that, but you wouldn't have just had a drink in your office, would you?" The son of a bitch looked guilty, and I felt the anger mount in me. "Godderer, dear colleague," I said, "where is your office, and where is the bottle?" I turned around and led the way. "Coming, Rhodes?" I asked.

It was bourbon, but it would do if we rationed it. Godderer even had paper cups. Rhodes and I each had a drink, and I went out looking for my friend the Amazon. I found her tinkering with a spare padlock.

"Does the commune starve its prisoners?" I said, taking the offensive.

"What does that mean?" she wanted to know.

"What you brought us for lunch was putrid, and don't think we won't tell the world. Bring us something better this evening. As a matter of fact, bring it right away, and I'll tell you what we want: fried chicken, beer, fresh fruit, cheese. Professor Godderer likes cheese. And by the way, the commune pays for it. We're its guests."

She put the padlock in a pocket of her slacks, and stood up. "You'd better wait here," she said. She went off, and five minutes later, when I was beginning to think that maybe I'd overdone it and I'd never see her again, she came back with Dorothy Bell. Dorothy had been knitting, and she still had the needles and wool in her hands.

"What is it you want?" she said. It was hard for her to sound as clipped and businesslike as she wanted because the music was going full blast, and she couldn't make herself understood in an ordinary conversational tone.

"Nothing much," I said. "Just humane treatment. Humane revolutionary treatment. You're starving us."

"We brought you something for lunch." she said.

"Something inedible. And you overcharged us." I took the same line with her that I had with the Amazon. I was getting hungry, which had something to do with it, but I think I was also getting worked up about the principle of the thing. Anyway, she didn't argue; she sent the Amazon out to get what I'd ordered. That's what I liked about that commune: somebody was in charge. Miss Bell even accepted the principle that we shouldn't have to pay for prison food—well, not the principle, but the fact that we weren't going to. Not that she was nice about it, of course. The scorn dripped from her eyes. That was the difference between her and Pritchard. The Bell girl dripped scorn; Pritchard shot it at you.

The fried chicken was passable, and the beer was cold. When we'd finished eating, I went out and found the Amazon again.

"Tomorrow," I said, "if we're still here, we want real napkins. None of this paper napkin stuff. And you'd better get a line on a good wine merchant: we may want champagne." Her chin dropped six inches, and I went back into the office feeling greatly refreshed. Even Godderer and Rhodes looked better to me. Besides, the music had stopped. The devil can go only so far with his tortures, and then even he needs a chance to breathe.

I felt so good, in fact, that I made Godderer lead us all into his office, and we got out the bourbon. I'd send the Amazon out for Scotch in the morning, I decided. With paper cups in our hands, we looked over the book shelves in our three of-fices, found books, and sat down to read. Rhodes called his home and I called Irene, and we spent a decent enough even-ing, all things considered. We were beginning to think about retiring to our separate offices to try to sleep, when I heard an uncomfortably familiar sound down the corridor.

It was the sound of a human voice being used as an organ, a church organ. I went to the door, looked down the hall, and it was as I feared. Pritchard was there.

It was quite a scene. In the central hall a great circle had been formed, and at its center stood a boy and girl. The boy was dressed in a white blouse, striped bell-bottoms, and sandals. He had a flower in his hair. The girl was dressed in a psychedelic smock that came down to her ankles, and bare feet. And between the boy and the girl stood Pritchard, holding their hands, and beaming on one and all. The smell of marijuana was in the air.

"Dearly beloved," Pritchard was saying, "and all are dearly beloved in this assembly, in this commune, we meet in this moment of our spiritual renewal to participate in the union of William and Wanda. The joy of our Movement joins us together, joins us to them. Through us they are united. Through them we are united." He made a curious sound in his throat, and I could have sworn I heard fountains spraying.

I looked over the assembled worshipers. They weren't as unadulteratedly young as they'd been during the afternoon. Ottilie Sinclair was there, wearing a kind of floated look on her face which I suppose was euphoria. Her husband was there too, wearing a red armband, and nodding in time to Pritchard's music. The fountains stopped spraying, and Pritchard went back to words.

"We do not ask," he chanted, "whether this marriage is legal. It is holy. We do not ask if it meets with the approval of the State. It is human. It needs no approval from bureaucracies, organizations, officials, the dark powers of this world. It is opposed to all such powers. In its light these powers are seen to be all the darker. In its strength these powers dissolve. This marriage, this union of two bodies and two souls, needs only the permission, the approval, of the people. Do the people give their consent?"

A hushed murmer started at the point where Dorothy Bell was standing, moved around the circle, and came back to her. The people consented.

"William, Wanda," Pritchard organed, "you have heard." He

stepped back, and put the girl's hand in the boy's. "In the love of this company, I declare you man and wife, man and wife not in a selfish, exclusive relationship, but man and wife in the great body of the people." Pritchard stepped back another measured pace, leaving William and Wanda standing alone in the middle of the circle. They were holding hands, but in a kind of absent-minded way. Their attention was on the great body of the people.

At this point, there being no set ritual for this particular kind of ceremony, there was an uncertain pause. William and Wanda didn't seem to know if they should keep on holding hands, or rush back and rejoin the audience, or what. Pritchard stepped forward and murmured something to them. You could hear it as it echoed back from the ceiling. "Perhaps you would wish to say something," he said.

William dropped Wanda's hand, took a couple of steps to the side to put some distance between himself and his bride, and said in an apologetic tone: "Mr. Pritchard, fellow Movement members, er, well, the fact is, like, I'm not really sure I believe in what's just happened. I don't mean I'm opposed to marriage, just the institution. I mean it stands for the idea of private possession, private property. I've given that part of it lots of thought, and it's bothered me. Wanda too." I looked at Wanda Too to see how she was taking the news. She had a fixed, dazed smile on her face. William continued: "But you know, Wanda and I have been into something special. So we decided to marry. But like we're still part of the commune, you know? I mean it's not an exclusive relationship, it's not just for each other, we're not forgetting the Movement. I don't have the words, but you know. We don't like belong to each other, we belong like to everyone."

Wanda was too overwhelmed, or, like, you know, to say a word, so the populace then took over. The boys and girls rushed forward, embraced the pair, there was considerable milling around during which I lost sight of the happy couple, and then, above the crowd, Wanda emerged, horizontal, on the shoulders of two boys and the Amazon. Behind her, sitting on a friend's shoulders, was William. They carried Wanda across the threshold of a classroom, and William was deposited there with her. Then the crowd reemerged, and the Amazon shut the door of the room solemnly. I thought it broke the spirit of the occasion, this reassertion of privacy, but I was greatly relieved just the same.

In the commotion the crowd had spread out, and I found myself standing near Pritchard and Dorothy Bell. He smiled at me companionably, not at all surprised to see me, and said to *la belle* Bell: "A beautiful ceremony."

I made my way back to Rhodes's office. Rhodes and Godderer were sitting in their chairs snoring. I went into Godderer's office and helped myself to his bourbon. No need to ration the stuff, God would provide. Nature's resources were infinite, her powers of renewal perpetual. I took another drink, felt my way carefully to my office, took off my jacket, tie, shirt, and shoes, and stretched out on the floor. I found I needed something to pillow my head, and got up and went looking. In the departmental office I found a mail sack full of departmental brochures describing our graduate offerings. I dragged it back to my office, put it on the floor, and laid myself down again. The sack was what I'd been looking for.

Outside I heard the murmur of voices, an occasional laugh, the scampering of feet. The spontaneity of youth. The freshness of a world being born.

21

Tuesday dawned bright and cheerful. Around six I heard Rhodes's telephone ringing, and he came down to my office, looking very rumpled. "A call for you," he said.

It was Irene. "Are you all right?"

"Great. I was at a wedding last night."

"Oh do be quiet and listen." I'd irritated her. "We've got deep trouble now, I think. Crowds of students were downtown last night breaking and burning, people from the town have formed groups and are out hunting down the kids, the cops have been uncontrollable. The National Guard's been called out. They'll take over the town, we're told, around noon."

"Are they coming to the campus?"

"No, Nevis is fighting to keep them off. He's downtown now,

with the mayor. And I may not be able to call you again. The police want to know why the telephones in Rollins and the other occupied buildings haven't been cut off. They want to cut off all access to the buildings too: let people out, but don't let anybody in. The police chief called last night and asked, 'What are you people playing games for?' "

"It's a good question."

"He said that they're having a revolution on the cheap, they talk about learning from social action, okay really let them learn."

"He's been doing a lot of reading."

Irene's irritation returned. "John, will you stop talking as though you were a hundred miles away?" she said. "You're right in the middle of things, and they're very likely to be dangerous. The police chief can't control his men, he's got to deal with them just as Nevis has to deal with the students, they're miffed because the National Guard has been called in, and a lot of them want to come on the campus and take charge. Nevis is trying to keep them away."

"For once he's probably right."

"But John, if they come it's likely to be terrible, and if they don't come, then what? Is there any way you can get out of there?"

"Not that I can see."

"Can't you talk to some of the people holding the building?"

"Not likely," I said. "Dorothy Bell's in charge."

"But John, what can we do? Are you just going to sit there?"

I didn't like the sound of her voice at all. She'd been up a good part of the night, obviously. She was worried, and she was ready to burst from not being able to do anything.

"Irene," I said, "I can stay out of the way. I don't have any alternative but just to sit here. There isn't anything else to do. But if trouble starts I can close the door and lock it, and I will,

I swear. I won't come out till it's over. It's really much better here than you think. Imagining is always worse than the reality. Really."

She quieted down. I suppose the same thought may have flitted through her mind that had just flitted through mine: somebody could set a fire, even throw a bomb; those were rules of the game, too, now. But she kept her counsel and merely said, "Well, I'll try to keep the lines open. If they're cut, you'll see me out front. Look for me."

Rhodes and Godderer had been listening, and they'd got the main idea. I filled them in on the details, and I will say for both of them that they took the news pretty well. They paled, but Rhodes ventured a smile, a real, honest-to-goodness smile, lugubrious, self-deprecatory, half-amused. And Godderer said, "Well, I wasn't in the war, and I've always wondered whether I missed something valuable." Their captivity was a fact, an inexorable fact; maybe that was what gave the new edge to their minds.

We opened the door and walked out together into the hall. Our captors were just beginning to wake up, emerging from classrooms where they'd been sleeping, coming out of offices down the hall, sitting with their backs against the wall, the girls combing their hair, the men putting on their shoes. The smell of freshly lit tobacco and marijuana was in the air. Somewhere, behind a closed door, somebody began to strum a guitar.

The Amazon approached. "You're not going to get much breakfast this morning," she said. "Coffee and rolls, that's all we can manage. We found a coffee-maker in one of the offices."

"Nobody's going out for breakfast?" I asked.

"Some are, not many. We have too much to do."

We went to the washrooms, cleaned up as best we could,

and went back to Rhodes's office. In a little while, our keeper brought the coffee and rolls. There was a kind of sullenness in the air that hadn't been there the day before. The crowds outside the window were thinner, quieter. We were waiting for something, and we all pretty well knew what.

In the main entrance hall, a meeting began. I went out to listen, but didn't catch everything that was said. There was another meeting going on upstairs, on the second floor, and so there was a lot of static in the air. But I heard enough to know I wasn't missing much; I'd heard all the speeches before, at Godfrey, at faculty meetings, in front of the administration building. Dorothy Bell was up front, knitting, but she spoke for only a minute or so, quietly, to the group as a whole. She did most of her talking to the speakers, before they spoke and after.

It was hard not be be restless, but I more or less managed, and Godderer and Rhodes made noble tries to sit still. We read, I suggested a drink, Godderer said no, I accepted his decision, Rhodes asked me what I knew about LaRosa's decision to quit, I said there wasn't much to know, he was just fed up, and then I suggested a drink to Godderer again. He said, No, not until lunchtime, and he said it firmly. It was time to call Irene. I dialed, and the phone was dead. I tried the phone in Godderer's office, and it was dead too. The police were scoring some points. I looked out the window at the crowd around the building, and I saw a woman waving—Irene maybe, but I couldn't be sure.

I walked back in to Rhodes's office and told my friends there wasn't anything to do about it but be useful, so I thought I'd go to work. I went down to my own office, pulled my typewriter out, and began to work on my article. After the first two or three minutes, as it turned out, I picked up steam, and it was probably an hour or so later when a noise at the door made me look up. Otto was there, a strip of plaster over an eyebrow.

"It was hell getting in," he said. "Dorothy Bell wouldn't let me."

"How'd you do it?"

"I kept coming back. She kept saying no, she knew me, I'd only make trouble, and anyway I was a friend of yours. Then I came back with this bandage over my eye, and they let me in. It still took a lot of arguing, but the bandage did it."

"Otto, you're a manipulative type. How'd you explain the bandage, and what difference did it make?"

"I didn't have to say anything about it. There are kids all over the campus with bandages. All hell's broken loose, last night, this morning. The cops have split a lot of heads, and they've got some split heads themselves. So I put on a bandage, and they let me in."

He walked into the office and sat down. He looked exhausted. His shoulders, their whiteness showing where the big sweater fell away from them, were twitching spasmodically. But he smiled.

"I don't feel so well," he said, and shivered. I felt his brow. It was hot. I got up, went to the departmental office, found some aspirin in the secretary's desk, and came back and gave them to Otto. He took them placidly enough, and smiled again.

"I feel awful," he said. "Not the fever, not the body. Something else. It's like a feeling all around me, I'm in a tight sack or something. I didn't sleep all night. I wanted to kill Dorothy Bell. Then some of the kids came back, bloodied up, and I was mad at the cops and mad at the kids. I don't want to kill anybody, you know, I just don't know what to do. It's like a haunted house."

I told him to stretch out on the floor, and I put the sack of mail under his head and covered him with my jacket. He was terribly wound up and he kept talking. "When we get out of here, Mr. Burgess," he said, "I'm going away. It's crazy staying here. Only is there an away? Is there? I mean a solid place? Maybe I should come to grips with myself. Like I'm crazy, I know that. But it's not incurable, is it? Only it's not getting cured here, I know that. It's not working out here for me, except maybe a little with you maybe."

I told him it was going to be a long day and we'd talk later. After a little while, he dozed off. I adjusted my jacket over him, and then turned and looked out the window. The crowd was moving, running. Beneath my window a boy came by, running hard; there was a policeman behind him. Around the corner two more policemen came. The boy stopped running and held up his hand in the V-salute. The cop behind him hit him hard across the back of the knees and he fell. The other two picked him up, and as he came up he tried to jab the V of his fingers in their eyes. One of the cops clubbed him in the pit of the stomach and he fell again. It was all as though it had been rehearsed.

Two more students came running around the corner. They saw the boy on the ground and ran to him. The cops grabbed them, the boys twisted, they got the back-of-the-knees treatment. I lifted the window and called out: "For God's sake, stop!"

One of the policemen looked up. "Well, well, well," he said, "it's a professor." He pulled back his club and threw it at the window. The pane smashed and glass fell over me. A sliver caught my hand, and I felt the blood in my palm. The policeman who'd thrown the club vaulted to the ledge and pulled himself through the window. The others followed. They pushed past me, ripped the door open, and ran out into the corridor.

I put my handkerchief in my hand to stop the blood and followed them out. Police were coming in at the other end of the building. More glass smashed, and they came in from offices and classrooms. Somehow, I expected screams. But there weren't any. Except for the sound of breaking glass, and the policemen's steps in the hall, there were no sounds at all. The police were deadly silent. And there, clustered together in a tight circle in the middle of the entrance hall, was the commune, deadly silent. I don't know where the people on the second, third, and fourth floors were: still there, I suppose. They had their own scripts to follow.

Two girls in the front row suddenly stepped forward.

"Pigs," one of them said. "Fucking pigs." The two of them let down their slacks. They had nothing on underneath.

A cop stepped forward, waggling his club joyously. "You little whores," he said. "You goddam little cunts." He seized one of the girls by the hair, pulled her to the floor, turned her over, and beat her hard on the buttocks with his club. The other girl made no effort to stop him. "Pigs," she screamed. "Fucking pigs." The rest of the students were silent; the other cops were silent. The man who'd been beating the girl stopped and stood up, breathing hard. Then he took the other girl, threw her down, and began again.

I pulled myself forward as best I could, and I got to the cop. I put down my hand and took his shoulder—it was curious, I noticed that the blood from my hand was staining his shirt, and I had the momentary impluse to pull back—and said: "Stop, please. That's enough, really." I shook him gently and repeated what I'd said.

He turned around and looked up at me, surprised, and then he stood up. Tears were in his eyes. He suddenly looked very puzzled. He didn't look more than a couple of years older than the students.

"Who the hell are you?" one of the cops behind him said to me.

"I just happen to be here," I said. "They've been . . . I was here when the building was occupied."

"One of the hostages?" the cop said. "You don't act like it."

"Officer," I began, but I never finished. I heard a voice behind me. It was Dorothy Bell's.

"We don't need your help," she said.

I turned to look at her.

"We don't need your help," she repeated. "Get out of the way."

"Why don't you take good advice?" the policeman who'd been doing the talking said. "Just get out of the way."

"We're not going to," somebody said. It was Otto, standing next to me. "We just happen to be in the way." We were, there wasn't any doubt about it. The students were backed against the entrance door, which was locked. The cops had come through the two wings, and were massed together facing them, thirty feet away. And there, between them, were Otto and me. It was the first moment that I realized what I'd contrived to do. I was facing the cops and Otto was facing the students.

I heard something, an oath, a snarl, behind me, and felt Otto move suddenly, and put his back to mine. I felt a cushioned blow, and felt him slide to the floor. When I turned around, he was on his hands and knees, his forehead on the floor. There was a brick lying beside him.

Dorothy Bell came forward.

"Get up," she said, "get up. You're not hurt."

Otto was breathing very hard. A kind of whistling sound came from his throat.

"Get up," Dorothy Bell said, and reached down and pulled him up. The shriek came from his mouth, the animal cry, it was no longer his voice. She dropped him and he fell all the way to the floor, one knee curled under him. A slow shudder began at his shoulders, and then another. Under his mouth, where it touched the floor, the blood formed, a puddle, and then a rivulet, and flowed slowly across the floor.

The cops moved pretty well after that. Some of them came forward and held the kids back, gently enough, and others looked at Otto. One of them finally stood up and said to me, "He's got a rib in the heart sack."

When we got him to the hospital, he was dead. I don't know, no one knows, if the worst part happened when Dorothy Bell tried to move him. Maybe the damage had already been done. Probably it had. He was on the way to being completely unhinged, and he knew it. He thought people really got hurt in this world and real blood flowed. He didn't belong to the telephone age. He lived on more than words.

22

Irene and I went down to Philadelphia together for the funeral. Godderer and Rhodes made the journey too, on another train, and Nevis was there as well. Before the ceremony, he did most of the talking to Otto's parents. There wasn't much he could say, he kept saying.

After the burial, Otto's parents asked Irene and me to come home with them. It was a miserable time.

"Otto wrote us about you," his mother said to me. "He loved you."

"He may have saved my life," I said.

"I wonder if he knew what he was doing?" she asked.

"I don't know," I said.

A little later his mother picked up again. "He was such a tortured boy," she said. "Did he need to be?"

His father asked me, "Did he have talent, do you think?"

I told them, yes, he had great talent, and said we would have to go. Irene and I didn't say very much until we'd changed trains in New York and started back to the university.

"Perhaps he was a tortured boy," I said, "but he didn't come through to me that way, not really. He was full of joy."

Irene nodded and looked out the window. Later on, it seemed hours and miles later, she turned back to me. "I'm leaving the university tomorrow, John," she said. "I've already told Nevis."

It wasn't really a surprise, but I couldn't think of what to say. "I think things at the university will probably be quieter now, Irene," I said weakly.

"Maybe and maybe not. People have short memories. And too much about them has been revealed now. There's a kind of indecency about it. It's not for me."

I asked her where she was going. She thought she'd go to New York, maybe go abroad, she hadn't thought much about it. I said I'd quit too, and go with her.

"No, John," she said, "I'm going off alone for a while. I've got to get the taste out of my mouth. Not the taste of you, John." She took my hand. "But I'd rather be alone."

We rode along in silence, both of us feeling wretched. "I think it's the people on a campus," Irene said. "I find it hard to believe in them, that they're real, that they're there. I'm not sure they believe in their own reality. It's as though they thought they lived in a world in which causes don't have effects. Maybe it's because when you teach or write you can never be sure just what the consequences are. You live so far away from them. And so you come to think that nothing you do really has consequences. It's all just gestures, postures, symbols, nothing more."

She was right of course. That was what was the matter with

them, with Nevis, Pritchard, the Sinclairs, the lot. Their bodies
were one place and their souls another. They had homes, and
jobs, and people to teach, and books to write, but all that was
secondary, accidental, almost illusory. Not even the politics
that they talked about so much was really politics. It didn't
have anything to do with the here and now. It was the politics
of eternity. When they asked, Who am I?, they didn't mean
anything as simple as, What's my name and address, and what
can I do with the time and powers that have been given me?
What they meant was, What is the essence of me, the sum and
substance of me in God's eye, the picture of me on the
stained-glass window? Am I the soul of love, of flexibility, of
truth, of eternal youthfulness? Am I an act of God, a proof of
his plan?

The things that moved them, the war, the poor, the blacks,
were only coincidental. What they wanted was to see the pure
image of themselves reflected in the world. What they couldn't
stand was a world so ill-made that their essence didn't shine
through, that they couldn't speak perfectly and be heard perfectly and have their way entirely and be loved entirely. They
couldn't stand being mortal, they were crying out against it,
and they were asking for an answering cry from the universe.

And it wasn't only the people like Pritchard or the Sinclairs
—the people who, trying to define themselves, made carica-
tures of themselves. Izard and Cantwell, with their realism,
their talk of Evolution and Mystery, were they very different?
Theories, explanations, words, Otto had said, he'd had his fill.
When the bite came, when people had to decide and act here
and now, Izard and Cantwell were someplace else, betting on
the future, dwelling on the blackness of existence, but they
weren't here.

The conversation Otto had had with Cantwell came back to
me. If time isn't real, Otto had said, if nothing ever really hap-

pens, then nobody ever does anything, and nobody ever does anything wrong. Get up, Dorothy Bell had said to Otto, get up, you're not really hurt. Nobody is really hurt, not if the consequences flow out into eternity, not if you have nothing to do with the world and the flesh. In the beginning was the Word. For the people at the university the beginning and end was the Word. They'd built themselves a city behind the wall of their words and it was a magician's, an illusionist's city, where matter was annihilated, where you could do anything, try anything, an idea, a new sensation, a make-believe revolution, and it was all for free, it was all without a price.

"I want to go away with you, Irene," I said. "I want to marry you."

"I suppose I'd like it," she said. "I don't know. It's the wrong time."

"A month from now?"

"I don't know. I'm not sure. You know that you drink too much, John, but you're quite something. You're tough, you say no with relish, you say it as well as any man I've known. Better than any man I've known. And that's not a small thing. But perhaps no isn't enough. Not that I know what you should say yes to. You have to find that out for yourself."

I'd said no, but wasn't that what the others had been saying in their way? They blew the smoke of their pipe dreams around themselves to shut off the perversity of the universe. How different had I been? I'd clutched my leg and hoped it would let me off. I'd kept myself drunk so that I wouldn't feel the pain of a world so crawling with phantoms that it didn't let me know whether I was drunk or sober. I'd had my own hallucination, that I could go it alone, that I could keep my own private territory clear. I'd enjoyed the empty space around me, enjoyed my solitary state.

"I'd like to begin saying yes," I said to Irene. "I'm saying yes to you. Not so that I can quit or go away, but so that I can get out of my hermitage, get connected with the world again. No, that's too general. I want to connect with you, connect so there's no backing out, and start a life from there. Yes, Irene?"

"Maybe yes, maybe no," she said. "I wish I could do better at the moment, but I can't. That's the way the world is these days."

It's two months later and I've got this story out of my system. The letters I've sent she's answered. It's still maybe yes, maybe no.